Illyrian Spirits

A CROATIAN TALE

FRANK BUCHAR

Illyrian Spirits
A Croatian Tale

Copyright © 2022 by Frank Buchar

ISBN 978-1-7782251-0-9 (print)

Dedicated to the indomitable Croatian spirit,
past, present, and future

CONTENTS

Only part of us is sane: only part of us loves
pleasure and the longer day of happiness, wants to
live to our nineties and die in peace, in a house that
we built, that shall shelter those who come after us.

The other half of us is nearly mad. It prefers the
disagreeable to the agreeable, loves pain and its darker
night despair, and wants to die in a catastrophe
that will set back life to its beginnings and leave
nothing of our house save its blackened foundations.

- Black Lamb and Grey Falcon, Rebecca West

Pula Beginnings

PART ONE

OFF AND AWAY. AT LAST. From my window seat I watched the jet gather speed, its engines working hard to break the pull of gravity, a kind of manic drive at play which I always find exciting. So here I was en route to Croatia, to Pula to be exact, to write, I hoped, a travel article or two, but also to see something of the land my ancestors came from. A two-pronged purpose I guess. I didn't know quite what to expect. But I knew it felt good to be leaving a dead in the water marriage, to be leaving Gloria. My ships were burning behind me. This was my mid-life adventure, and that entails some degree of risk. There's risk even in this comfortable night flight, I thought, as I sipped reasonably good French wine flying high at thirty-five thousand feet, the dark, cold Atlantic far below me.

The flight was a blur, landing in Munich with a quick transfer to Pula and a bus ride to the city, and then a short taxi ride to the apartment. I was jet-lagged, but I needed to be out and about. The Airbnb accommodation met my expectations and for once the website photos were accurate. Bright, clean, and functional. It lacked the essential coffee maker, but I had come prepared with my trusty coffee filter apparatus, and so I was all set for the day ahead. After a quick shower and three cups of coffee in rapid succession, I set off with a song in my heart and Euros in my pocket, soon to be changed for Kunas. Within an hour I was sitting in an outdoor café overlooking the ancient Roman Coliseum and enjoying a cold draught beer. The late afternoon May light was casting blue shadows about me. I was excited and elated with the anticipation of exploring this old Roman city in the days to come. I had time. I felt content knowing I had an eight-month sabbatical, beginning in September, and a chance to be the travel writer I dreamt of being.

I slept late into the next morning, and over the next few days I made a personal tour of Pula, making notes on the fly and trying to find the right hook for an article or two. About history and about food, or something along those lines, something to catch a reader's interest, and whether the medium was print or digital it didn't matter to me. But first I needed to get the feel of the place by walking about and observing people. Every day I could see groups of tourists ambling about, oftentimes with a tour leader holding a small colored flag on a selfie stick. They were enjoying the sunshine and the spirit of the place.

I tried to think like a travel writer, deliberately and descriptively. Pula was surprising in its Roman past. The main Roman sites seemed to stand aloof and apart as if later history, post Roman, were a travesty against the architectural brilliance and solidity of Rome. I played with the concept and hoped I could use it in my articles. I scribbled down a few notes in my moleskin notebook with my favorite pen. I didn't want to forget anything I'd seen. I was standing in the small square fronting the Temple of Augustus and using my imagination to erase the non-Roman elements and then rebuilding, in my mind's eye, the modest commercial and residential parts that would have been there in Roman times so I could get a better feel for the place as it might have been.

Even the light rain couldn't dampen my enthusiasm for the architectural wonder of the place. The Temple, surprisingly small and compact, a single room really, stood fixed in its silence of stone. The broad stones of the forum lay at its feet like a supplicant. I felt excited to be there, peering into history, seeing the modest sweep of the forum that belied the power behind it, the power that demanded subservience and unquestioned obedience or crucifixion.

Obviously, Rome meant to stay. The architectural gems prove that. But more than that. The street grid is clearly Roman. The spread of the city itself across and over rolling hills is comfortable and spacious, fitting for an imperial power. The echoes of Empire linger and the odd juxtaposition of buildings from later conquests such as the Habsburgs isn't a stretch. Imperial powers shoulder each other. The Roman theatre nestles gently beside the Habsburg castle fortress and two separate histories celebrate their existences under the Pula sun. It took me quite some time to find the theater tucked away below the castle and on a hill above the flower market on one of the main streets. Just when I was about to give up in my search for it, a tiny sign on a wall adjacent to the flower stalls gave me the clue to its whereabouts. Tourist maps aren't very helpful in finding many of the attractions here. The ancient hills keep their secrets well. Scattered about in the ruins of the small theatre were brilliant red poppies and small golden dandelions gracing the landscape with their vivid color in contrast to the ancient, broken gray stones. I was beginning to think like a writer I thought.

Each day I focused on something grand and monumental, at least at first. The great masterpiece of the Coliseum, the Arena, is the jewel in the Roman crown. The Arena surprised me with its heavy, implacable magnificence. Imposing, yes. Overwhelming, no. I stood transfixed by it, but I couldn't figure out how to communicate that in an article. How could I pass along the way history lies embodied in the stones and in the sand?

I tried to imagine a fixed point pitched high above the very center of the Arena, a fixed point three hundred feet above in the Roman sky. From there I could see the small Roman theatre and the Temple of Augustus, and nearby, the Twin Gates and the Gate of Hercules, and the home where Agrippa lived, and the Roman mosaic. From that fixed point, I could see all of these and more, spread across the low hills of Pula. I was enjoying the rampant speculation and glad that I had come. I could write here I thought.

Later that day in my apartment, I lay back on my couch and thought about my life. Despite the excitement of seeing a new place I would get incredibly lonely every now and then. I would check my e-mail several times a day, but there was nothing there but junk mail. An eight-month sabbatical can be an incredibly long time if you have no one to share it with. But there was no one in my condo back home. Gloria wasn't there. She was probably checking out the latest dating app. Neither was my son. He had his own life now and I was happy for him. Before I came to Croatia I envisioned it as the answer to all my lost dreams. A new life in the ancestral home beckoned. New friends perhaps. New opportunities.

Maybe I was just being impatient for things to happen. Rome wasn't built in a day. Neither was Pula. On that note I rose from the couch and went to the fridge where I pulled out a cold Croatian beer, a Karlovačko to while away the hour.

On a miserably rainy day I ducked into the Temple of Augustus to get out of the rain. A few couples stood under the portico of the Temple on one side of the ancient forum. I paid for a ticket and looked about. There wasn't much to see in the one room of the Temple, a few pieces of Roman sculpture, some postcards, and little else. The ticket seller received a call on her cell phone and had trouble hearing what was said so she hurried out to the portico where the reception was better. I shook the rain from my poncho raincoat and read the print exhibits detailing the history of the Temple. Just as I moved to get a closer look at one of the sculpted Roman torsos, I slipped backwards and fell heavily on the wet stone floor knocking the back of my head hard, and for a moment I was dazed and semi-conscious and just lay there, alone in a stupor. It couldn't have been more than a moment or two. I struggled to my feet cursing the worn tread on my favorite sneakers. I felt the back of my head and there was a small tender bump there, but no blood. I walked out to the portico and stood beside the ticket seller who was talking animatedly on her cell phone. She was obviously very angry about something. Everyone else on the small portico had left as the rain had stopped. I stood there for a moment and then crossed the small square, the ancient forum, and returned to my apartment.

Nearing dusk, it seems to me that Pula has another life. Perhaps then, as the evening descends, even the stones can breathe. History envelops everything here. Or maybe pre-history because Pula has the atmosphere of a place that has been lived in for millennia. The Roman presence of two thousand or more years ago is simply one of the latest. Echoes linger in the air. The blood lust of the Romans lies centered in the Arena as I approach it once again. I can't seem to get enough of the site. I use my imagination to probe it. The blood memory of ancient gladiatorial combat circles the place and invests it with latent menace and dread, even today so many centuries after the events took place. Bread and circuses, the stuff of empires.

Sometimes, in the periphery of my vision, I fancied that shadows leapt and blurred backwards in time so that I could feel the place come alive in a different way. I hoped I could touch on that in my articles, the way the past can intrude on the present and inform it. At least that's what I felt intuitively.

◆ ◆ ◆

I soon began to frequent the many cafes, and one in particular. Once again I found myself at the small café overlooking the Coliseum. There were a few couples enjoying drinks and light snacks at the café tables around me. At the nearest table a middle-aged man in his early forties, thin, with long gray hair, was holding the palm of a young woman and speaking softly to her in hushed tones. The woman was attractive with brilliant purple hair that had a sheen to it. She was listening closely, her head bent downwards, clearly surprised by some revelation the palmist had given her. She nodded rapidly in agreement, mumbled something to herself, and then hastily withdrew a fifty Kuna note from her handbag, murmured her thanks and departed in haste anxious to be somewhere else to reflect on the revelations she had received. Her strawberry pastry was untouched.

At the far end of the café, very close to the stairs leading down to the Coliseum, I noticed a stunning couple. An older man, possibly in his mid to late fifties with handsome, rugged features and a full head of gray hair sat close to a younger woman in her thirties, of striking beauty. They were speaking quietly to each other and seemed to be commenting on the passing scene around them, alert and curious.

Suddenly, the palmist, engaging and friendly, is standing by my table. He asks politely in excellent English if I would care to have my palm read. I'm taken aback by his graciousness and courteous manner, and I wonder how he could tell I was a tourist. I gesture for him to have a seat. In a moment he is sitting and looking intently at the palm of my right hand that he had gently taken into his. He studies it very carefully and turns it slightly using both of his hands in his quiet, gentle examination. I glance away for a moment and catch sight of the handsome couple looking directly my way and smiling. I nod in polite response to their attention. They nod back. The palmist draws his fingers across the side, fleshy part of my hand apparently surprised by what he sees there. His eyes are gentle and amused.

"You carry so many memories!" he says with an edge of excitement in his voice.

"What do you mean?" I ask, confused by the remark.

"Here, on the bottom side portion of your palm, are the memories of your ancestors. The slight pink flush indicates that you are in your ancestral lands. Is your background Croatian? Are you one of us?"

"Well, yes, my parents were born here but emigrated to Canada as small children. You can see that in my hand?"

"I see only the impacted memories that signify Croatian and early Illyrian times and back, back even long before them when the only records of times past were songs and dances around a celebratory fire. You are blessed with great intuition. Welcome brother!"

"I don't know how you knew that about my being of Croatian heritage, but I am impressed. I know we haven't met before. We couldn't have. What gave me away? Does my face look Croatian?"

With a slight, short wave of his arm he dismissed my question good-naturedly. We talked about other things as the long day waned, and I was impressed with his intuition. It was quite remarkable. He seemed to know things about me that he couldn't have known, and that baffled me. He hinted at a difficult marriage, at a career as a college teacher that I didn't enjoy, at a son in the military. He touched lightly and deftly on these things and then, abruptly, he said he must go to another appointment. I asked him how much I owed him. He smiled and said whatever I wished. I gave him a hundred Kuna note and then he nodded graciously and walked away, stopping to say hello to the attractive couple at the far end of the café whom he obviously knew. They chatted happily for a few moments.

◆ ◆ ◆

I settled my bill and walked back to my apartment. I was feeling pleasantly tired and enjoyed the sights and sounds of Pula spread across the rolling hills. Soon I was under the bedcovers and beneath my eyelids images of home danced erratically about me like a butterfly's flight. My wife Gloria. Gloria Mundi I had called her in happier times, times gone forever now. Gloria Mundi standing by the kitchen microwave making popcorn, saying that our marriage was getting stale, saying that we should see other people, saying that our son Peter was a young man now and living his own life, saying things without looking at me as the popcorn popped. And I, feeling gut-shot and alone, leaning against the refrigerator, listening. I knew things hadn't gone well for a long time, but it was still a surprise, like an emotional sucker punch when all was said and done.

Flash frame image of my son Peter, a head and shoulders photo of him in an armored tank somewhere in Afghanistan. An image melded with anxiety and pride and some consternation. Another image. My college English class: a student asleep at his desk and drooling on his arm as I lecture. Images blurring into each other. And now this new experience. Maybe Pula was a way of distancing myself from all of that. Sleep.

❖ ❖ ❖

I returned to my favourite café the very next day hoping to see the attractive couple I had seen the day before. Perhaps I could meet them. After all, I knew no one in the city and I needed to be more proactive in meeting people. Gloria always said I was too shy and needed to extend my comfort zone, to be proactive. That was the word she used, proactive, a term she probably learned at a management networking seminar. I saw them at once. They were speaking intently to two large gentlemen. They were not obese. They were just very huge youths, tall and muscular, and dressed in blue, fashionably so. Long sleeved blue shirts, blue jeans, and trendy boots, polished and well worn. I chose a table close to them, but not too close. As soon as I did, the two men left, smiling and obviously pleased with the encounter.

The woman nodded at me, recognizing me from the day before. The man smiled. I was just about to pull out my Pula guidebook from my backpack when the woman asked if I would like to join them. I couldn't have been happier. She was without a doubt one of the most beautiful women I had ever seen. Short auburn hair, high cheek bones, a full sensual mouth.

"I am Zora Sekulić and this is my friend Davor Dukovac."

"Glad to meet you," I replied. "I am Christopher Radelja."

"Ah, a Croatian name! You are visiting?" Zora asked smiling, her blue eyes sparkling above dimpled cheeks.

"Yes, for a time. I am Canadian of Croatian heritage. I'm on sabbatical from teaching and am hoping to write a few articles." I stopped for a moment to order an espresso when the waiter came to our table. He shooed away a brindled cat sitting on a nearby metal chair.

"You are alone?" Davor asked.

"Yes, my wife is back in Canada. She could not come. Work obligations."

"Well then," Davor said, "you must regard us as your new found friends. Pula is a beautiful city with many sights to see."

We chatted for a half hour on the city and the places to visit around it. Rovinj, Brijuni, Poreč and others. They suggested a few restaurants, and I jotted them down in my notebook.

Suddenly, Davor leaned forward conspiratorily with a broad smile on his lips. "And yesterday, the fortune teller you met with here, was he good?"

I was surprised he remembered. "Well yes, he told me things about myself that he couldn't have known. He was amazing really. Quite astounding."

"Yes," Davor said. "Petar is very intuitive. He can read people and is kind."

"What do you mean by kind?" I asked.

"You can divine things about people, about their circumstances, about their future, and still be cruel in the telling of it. To have knowledge of a person's fate is a powerful thing and some diviners can be insensitive to that responsibility. Fortune telling can be a parlor game, an entertainment. It can also be a life changing event with great risk involved."

I was enthralled by his comments and the deep conviction with which he spoke. His voice was low and gravelly. I took a sip of my coffee and found it was cold. I had barely touched it. The time had passed so quickly.

◆ ◆ ◆

For several days after our first meeting I would return to the Coliseum café hoping to see them. If they were there, they would always wave me over to their table. They were very popular. I was always amazed by the number of people who would stop to talk with them, people of all stripes from what I could see. I would sit quietly at their side. Mind you, I spoke Croatian but not well. It had been years since I used it to converse. I could not understand the nuances of conversations, but it was plain to see that both Davor and Zora loved the interactions and would often laugh uproariously at something said. I would sit there smiling, feeling slightly uncomfortable in not understanding everything, but it was enough just to be there and in good, congenial company.

I listened hard and was remembering the basics of the language. I would jot down words and simple phrases in the small moleskin notebook I carried with me. Later, when I was alone in my apartment, I started thinking about the language, about Croatian. It was far different from English, more immediate somehow, more visceral. Words with endings freighted with meaning that revealed so much, endings that informed you about gender, case, and number. I remembered my parents, grandparents, and relatives speaking to me in Croatian, and I had spoken it as a boy. But now, a new world and a host culture was contained in the structure of the language. I was starting to listen and be attentive to the nuances and syntax of Croatian, the language of my ancestors, the language of Davor and Zora. It felt good to have the words in my mouth, rolling with my tongue slowly and surely. Little wonder the Croatians had fought so hard to keep their language and with that their customs and culture. I was one of them, different in that I was Canadian too, but still the rich heritage was there, and I meant to explore it. I was determined more than ever before to relearn the language.

Their friendship meant a lot to me. They would speak of modern Croatia, its problems, its potential, and they would ask me about Canada, about the cost of things and about the culture. They introduced me to some fine restaurants where the grilled fish and seafood was absolutely divine. Zora said to me that the fish in Istria swim three times, once in the sea, once in olive oil, and once in wine. I quickly jotted down the anecdote to use in one of my travel essays. She laughed then and said her remark wasn't original. It was a saying that waiters told to tourists all the time. That didn't matter to me. It was still useful. And I learned too that the cost of meals was a third cheaper than in Canada. I was beginning to feel very comfortable.

Davor possessed a great love of literature and told me that he would keep only one book in his apartment at a time. That way he said he could give himself to the experience fully without the distraction of other books. I thought that strange but interesting. I thought about my apartment back home where I had floor to ceiling bookshelves that were crammed with books of all kinds. He told me that he found Rebecca West's book Black Lamb and Grey Falcon, on the old Yugoslavia, very insightful, but with very difficult prose and clearly racist in parts. But he loved what George Bernard Shaw said about Croatia, that on the last day of Creation God wanted to crown his work and so fashioned the Croatian coastline out of tears, stars, and breath. The image stayed with me and throughout my travels later on, along the coast, it proved to be spot on.

Zora told me she had been married once. No children. Just an abusive husband who drank too much and worked as an engineer in the Pula shipyards. One day he came home to their tiny apartment and in a drunken fit of rage he began to beat her. She waited until he passed out and then she took the heaviest cast iron frying pan she could find and let him have it as he slept. He would carry the traces of her revenge for the rest of his life. An ambulance came. The police came and went, shrugging their shoulders at still another scene of domestic violence as common to the country as cabbage she said. Her husband took her to court. The judge exonerated her, and she found herself a free woman without a drunken partner. She said it was the happiest day of her life and she and a girlfriend of hers celebrated by spending the long weekend in the resort town of Makarska on the Dalmatian coast. Life became rich and juicy for her, once again like a ripe tomato. That's exactly how she put it. "Like paradajz Kristof, like a tomato."

It soon dawned on me that Davor and Zora were not a couple. They were close friends. Why that fact delighted me so greatly was a surprise to me. They asked if I was enjoying Croatia and why I had come. Without revealing too much of my past and the emotional baggage that I carried I told them that I was recently separated from my wife and left it at that. I also told them of my plans to write a few travel articles and to explore my Croatian roots. They were quite supportive of that and gave me the names of some good restaurants in town. And then Zora turned her wonderful blue eyes on me and began speaking.

"Kristof, what was it like to grow up in Canada with Croatian parents?"

"Not so different from many other ethnic groups I would think. The culture was strong in Mississauga, near Toronto where I lived. At the Croatian Hall there were concerts and dances and weddings that were quite special. And the food, the barbequed lamb, was so special. It was a real treat. I look forward to having it here."

"So why didn't you marry a Croatian girl then, a Croatian Canadian girl?"

I was surprised by her boldness, but I have to confess that I enjoyed it. She took an interest in me, and it had been a long time, a very long time since an attractive woman had done that.

"I don't know. I didn't meet the right Croatian girl I guess. And when I thought I did meet the right girl, when I met Gloria who wasn't Croatian-Canadian, I was wrong. Unlucky in love I guess."

"You're not too old yet. You have a second chance." I wondered what she was seeing. A forty year old academic of middle height and weight and not particularly good looking. Zora looked intently at me for a moment, and I was struck again by her beauty. She had a model's face. We talked about various things in our past, and it was all very comfortable and easy. Another hour passed, and then she left walking towards the Coliseum, brisk and businesslike. She had wonderful legs.

◆ ◆ ◆

It started off innocuously enough as these things go. Harmless talk. Curious talk. Over the course of several meetings at cafes and bars, more and more talk of spirits and ghosts. It seemed to me that Davor repeated himself a lot. He took great pains to make the distinction between spirits and ghosts. Ghosts were silly malingerers haunting old homes and familiar places they didn't want to leave. Davor said they needed to be identified, found out, exposed, so they could start on the long journey to the afterlife. They offered spirit guides good exercise. Once you found one, you grasped them by the neck, literally, and then they ran off, disappearing into the nether world. Dogs and cats were helpful in identifying ghosts because they had no smell. Spirits, on the other hand, were altogether different. The vast majority of spirits were content in the afterlife, but there were a few who desired to return to the living state. For something unfinished or left undone somehow. A desire to rectify a situation. A drive to change an outcome. Davor spoke of new breakthroughs in the spirit world, developments altogether unexpected. He said the word Brijuni in a soft, reverential tone. And he said I would be a part of it all, a new venture into the history of mankind.

Days passed, and I considered myself lucky indeed when I chanced to see Zora sitting alone in the café by the Coliseum. She was helping me with my Croatian which was improving rapidly because I was immersed in the culture and the language was all around me, but invariably she would often ask me about Gloria, and what our life together had been like. Where we had met. What we enjoyed doing together. When I had last been with my son.

She was very frank and direct, sometimes alarmingly so. One day, out of the blue, she said to me something that surprised me with its insight.

"Kristof, I must say that I think you have been a victim, like me, only differently. Something in you is broken. I was beaten physically in my relationship with Vilko, but you, I think, were brutalized in a different way. You were attacked emotionally and psychologically. I sometimes think your politeness is a kind of defense mechanism. You are like a puppy dog wanting approval and love from everyone."

I felt myself blushing suddenly at her remark. I winced as if I had been struck. But then I saw compassion in her expression, and knew that she had not meant to sting me. She was so blunt and truthful, and perhaps that was part of my attraction to her. She didn't play games. What she said was what she believed.

"I am sorry. I do not mean to hurt you. Really, I don't. But you are my friend now, and friends share the truth, even when it is painful. Do you understand what I am saying."

"Yes, Zora, I do. You just caught me off guard, that's all."

She smiled then, and I felt my heart soar for an instant, altogether unexpected. She had called me her friend. She cared. For a moment neither one of us spoke as if something precious had been uncovered, something rare and vulnerable. I was suffused with a new emotion. I looked up and way into the clear blue Pula sky and felt more at home than I had for a long, long time. She reached across the heavy glass table, and placed her hand gently on my forearm. It was warm.

◆ ◆ ◆

Davor and I were sitting on a bench in a small park that we often frequented between the Coliseum and the waterfront. He was looking pensive, and I could tell he was about to embark on some topic that had been percolating in his mind for some time. I had begun to anticipate his intellectual forays by watching for certain facial expressions of his. I rolled up my pant legs to catch a bit of sun on my calves. Then, I raised my face and felt the Istrian sun warm it. Turning slightly towards Davor, I began.

"What a great spot this is, isn't it Davor?'

"Of course, the place is as much ours as we are its."

"I was talking about the park being nice. That's all. I don't know what you mean about we being its."

"My dear Kristof, I was talking about the spirit of the place, about all of Croatia, not just this park. For well over a thousand years the Croats have lived here, in this particular place on the earth. We are it, and it is us."

"OK. What do you mean by the spirit of the place? How can that be real?"

"Istria is part of the Croatian homeland, just as the American West is part of the United States of America, and the Nile River, of Egypt. Different places on the face of the earth exude specific forces that polarize a people in a particular place. Maybe the stars and constellations have something to do with that polarity making it different from anywhere else in the world. But it's a reality. Just as a river runs through a landscape and creates something special and unique to the land, say the Thames or the Danube, just so the spirit of place is an indelible element that is part of the mix."

Davor's eyes were closed as he spoke. He too held his face to the sun, and he was smiling. He stopped for a moment reflecting on his subject, and then continued.

"I cannot imagine Croatians, either living here or away in the Croatian diaspora, say in Chile or Argentina or Australia, without this land, this place, this Croatia, as part of their rooted identity. They say the early Croatians came here originally from Iran and later from Poland, but here is where they came and stayed, where the spirit of the place infused them and became a part of them and their character. It was as if exhalations from the ground, from the earth, breathed robust life into their spirit. There were others here before them of course, the Illyrians and others, and they were absorbed by the Croatians and became a vital part of them."

"Well Davor, it all sounds very romantic in a way, very poetic, the way you put it. It's certainly something that can't be measured."

"No, perhaps not, but you can feel it when the national anthem is sung, or when the country is besieged by its enemies. Then it is very real and not to be dismissed."

"So," I asked, "are you referring to their military traditions, and prowess?"

"Croatians have never been imperialists. They defend what is theirs to their last breath, and do not covet what does not belong to them. Our great sculptor, Meštrović, recognized that. For well over a millennium they have struggled to defend and keep what is theirs. It is in their spirit and never to be dismissed, never. Their spirit and the land are one and the same. But this is such serious talk and the day is early, so now let us have a drink."

♦ ♦ ♦

The day was brisk and bright as we took our usual seats in the café by the Coliseum. It was three in the afternoon with only a few people sitting and drinking coffee. Davor's face in repose showed an ineffable sadness. It almost pained me to see it. He was drinking a double brandy and looked rather content in his sadness. Suddenly he noticed me observing him, and a brilliant smile bobbed up through the fog of sadness.

"This was all very different once. Pula, I mean. In Roman and Illyrian times Kristof. We are here now but back then there was a majestic sweep to the city, a glorious magnificence that made you savour the very air that you breathed. The Roman monuments were vital then, imposing, eternal.

Imagine all of these modern buildings gone, with here and there only a warren of smaller dwellings and markets along the famous routes. The Roman imprint was here and you could walk from the Coliseum to the gates or to the Amphitheater and be a living part of it all. These modern times can't compare with it, with the way it was. But I'm forgetting your comfort. Would you like another glass of wine?"

"The same red would be wonderful."

He ordered for me, and then turned to me with his huge, wonderful smile. I could never get over how perfect his teeth were. There was a tiny gap between his front teeth that was part of his charm. Later, when the waiter left the bill under an ashtray, Davor pushed it towards me, smiling and mumbling something about being out of pocket.

I enjoyed walking around Pula with Davor. He loved the bustle of the city, the flower market, the stream of tourists wandering about, the ebb and flow of the streets on a cool, shining day. He would comment on the passing scene before us, the quality of the fruit displayed by a vendor in his small kiosk, or the tasty crepes that we ate on the main street. But there was something else that I grew to love about him. He could remark on the daily reality about us, and then suddenly shift gears and move into entirely different areas, embellishing his opinions with a quote or an anecdote.

"I will continue to call you Kristof as Zora does. It is easier. Everywhere Kristof, but particularly in places like Pula that have hosted different peoples throughout millennia, throughout ancient and pre-ancient times, there have always been spirits. And there have always been ghosts as well. Resident ghosts, visual echoes that remained after their time had lapsed."

He stopped to light a cigarette, and then began to smoke and talk as we walked. I continued to be surprised at how many people smoked in the city. He inhaled and then exhaled deeply as if to emphasize what he was about to say. A cloud of blue smoke rose above him. He pointed to a small bench overlooking the street and we sat.

"I want to tell you something important now. About spirits and ghosts. It may sound odd at first, but stay with me. It takes a full two hundred years for a spirit to return, not necessarily consecutive years, to remedy something, perhaps to take revenge, or maybe to correct some tragedy that befell them.

However, there is a distinction between spirits and ghosts. I'm not talking about spirits now. There are also what can be called thin ghosts that linger. They're harmless enough, these ghosts. Who hasn't stayed at a party too long"? And with that remark Davor shrugged and gave his enigmatic, sad smile.

"How is one to tell the difference between spirits and ghosts?" I asked.

"Oh you will know my friend, soon enough. In a few days, if you agree, I want you to visit Brijuni. It's a national park with a history both ancient and modern. I want you to see things there. Exciting things are about to happen."

I nodded as we rose from the bench and continued our walk. I got the feeling that Davor wanted me to learn things on my own. He didn't simply want to tell me things. He wanted me to experience the spirit world, whatever that entailed. He asked me if I would mind meeting a friend of his, an eye doctor, and undergo some tests related to the spirit world. I laughed and told him that it would be no problem. He looked at me out of the corner of his eye and chuckled. I think I amused him.

We parted after a few moments, Davor to do some grocery shopping, and I to continue walking on a beautiful day, the brilliance of the sun taking precedence in my mind over the talk of spirits and ghosts.

◆ ◆ ◆

I walked down Giardini Street in Pula, somewhat perplexed and disheartened. I had come hoping to write a few travel articles. Fat chance of that now. Since I had met Davor and Zora even my sense of what was real and what wasn't was challenged. All this talk of ghosts and spirits and redemption was so odd. And how was I to tell the difference between a ghost and a spirit? Were they all mad? Was I losing it? I looked at the faces in the crowds of tourists as I walked. If I were to believe Davor, some of these people were not people at all, but ghosts, shades from the past. Davor had told me a few days earlier that a ghost could not cast a shadow. But around me, passers-by were moving so quickly that I could not tell if they had shadows or not. It was late afternoon, and I tried my best to find a tourist without a shadow, but to no avail. Many tourists were sitting at cafes under sun umbrellas and shadows of any kind were not to be seen. Davor had also said that most ghosts would not hold my gaze, would not look directly at me, but to me that seemed to be just plain politeness from a stranger. In Canada we don't stare at strangers. But who was to know if a stranger was a shy Canadian tourist or a ghost?

I reflected on what I knew to date regarding spirits. Davor suggested that my role was to work with some of them, with spirits, and help them somehow to find peace. And he told me to be mindful that there were great dangers involved, dangers regarding evil guardian spirits. Nothing made sense to me as I walked. It was all so crazy, but when I was with Davor and Zora it seemed real and my old sense of reality was out of synch. I didn't know what to do. Should I forget my plans and return home? Or should I embrace this new reality before me and live as I had never lived before with daring and verve. I needed to decide on a course of action and I needed to do it soon.

◆ ◆ ◆

I had arranged to meet Davor the next day near the Arch of the Sergians in downtown Pula, and I hoped Zora would be with him. She was the most beautiful woman I had ever seen and just to be near her was like a tonic for my soul. I hardly thought of Gloria anymore. Davor was sitting outside a small corner café. Zora hadn't come, and I was disappointed. It was mid-afternoon and there was a cool breeze blowing, refreshing, not chill. He was enjoying a double brandy while I sipped at an American coffee, an Americano. It had become my drink of choice. For one thing the cup was much bigger and you could get a decent amount of coffee in it. From where we sat we could see across Sergijevaca Street to the sitting James Joyce statue and the nearby Arch of the Sergians. Invariably, people would stop by at our table to say hello to Davor and thank him for favours he had done. What those favors were I hadn't a clue.

◆ ◆ ◆

One day as I wandered about I caught sight of a tall, lean man, handsome with curly blonde hair leading an entourage of sorts. I thought of him as the head man, someone who had the presence and charisma of a celebrity,

19

someone famous. The posse around him, about twelve individuals in all, was stylish and quite extraordinary looking, dressed in fashionable clothes that accentuated their good looks. One of them in particular caught my attention, walking just behind and to the right of the head man himself. A compact little man, a dwarf I assumed, attired in a parody of the American flag. His satin pants were the red and white stripes of the flag while his satin jacket was based on the white stars of the flag against a blue background. He walked with a heavy limp, his face contorted with his efforts to keep up. I could see he was saying things to the head man, trying, without any apparent luck to get his attention. As they walked, passers by gave way before them and let the group pass freely.

I noticed that the head man moved with a panther-like gait, staring straight ahead. As he strode by I caught sight of the purple satin lining of his bespoke jacket. A flash of purple like the edge of night, the edge of darkness. When they reached the Temple fronting the Forum, a point man entered the Temple first, striding quickly up the stairs and seconds later a custodian inside the Temple hurriedly left with the point man slowly following behind her. I took him for a bodyguard. The head man then signaled the group to wait, and he strode ahead into the structure, alone. It was as if he really was some sort of celebrity. I waited several minutes thinking he would come out of the small one-room Temple but he did not, and so I left to explore other parts of Pula.

◆ ◆ ◆

A few days later I was sitting in a small park across from the Coliseum when the dwarf I had seen in the entourage by the Temple of Augustus walked by, limping. He was wearing the same blue satin jacket and upon it the stars of the American flag. His jeans were a stylish patchwork of different colors, faded and worn in that very expensive way that you see in GQ magazine.

Three boys, around nine or ten years old, came up to him and simply stared, blocking his passage through the park. They just stood in front of him and stared, mouths agape and seemingly stunned at the sight of him. I shooed them away and watched as they ran towards the waterfront, laughing and crying out to each other. The dwarf smiled warmly at me and approached me.

"It's OK sir. They just haven't seen anyone like me before. I don't take offense. If you happen to be a dwarf, you've got to have a thick skin. Otherwise you'd be a recluse."

"Have a seat if you've got some time. It's a beautiful spot. I'm Christopher."

"My name is Sam, Sam Stark. Pleased to meet you Christopher."

We shook hands and chatted about the city, sights we'd seen, and places nearby that we wanted to go. I learned he was from Bennington, Vermont, and we talked about Robert Frost and the small museum behind the church there, and the wonderful monument to revolutionary soldiers, all within a stones-throw of each other. His New England accent was delightful to my ears. His family had become wealthy through the manufacture of luxury pontoon boats. And then I asked him about the group I had seen him with that day when they walked towards the Temple of Augustus.

"Oh yes. I remember that time. Malek, our leader, wanted to see the Temple of Augustus, and we waited for him by the Forum. Oh I wish you could have heard him speak later that day. I hung on to every word. The man is an emissary of light. He makes you feel what can be done in this world to stamp out darkness and the rampant, diseased materialism that fouls this earth. He says that one day the light from the stars and the sun will spread and illuminate the universe and all the true believers, the elect, will hear the celestial music of the stars. The darkness will be defeated for once and for all. There will be no viruses that kill the pure of heart. The selfishness of man will be at an end and the heavens will open up to the restored brilliance of light."

I didn't know quite what to make of him. He was so enthusiastic over this man Malek. He continued for some time talking in a kind of rapture about the light of the world and how men and women must confront the darkness about them until the heavens light up in a celebration of reason and truth. It seemed to me, as he spoke, that this man Malek and his followers were a cult of some kind, and this little man before me was completely under its influence.

"Oh, if you heard him speak you would realize how special he is. He is a remarkable man. I have been on his yacht, the Light Sabre, and he has shared such wonderful insights, talking with us through the night until the sun came up at the very time he spoke of the light of the world infusing and illuminating the darkness. And he has told us to be on guard for what is to happen. He said we must be ready to attack the darkness and ignorance of the world and free the particles of light that have been imprisoned there. We must be ruthless in destroying the hard matter of the world that robs us of our virtue and goodness. The Messiah, the light of the world, was slain by darkness and lies imprisoned in the hateful ground of being. Malek will show us the way to free the light of heaven, and we must not be timid of spirit. The Apocalypse is near and strange things are afoot. You must come to one of his lectures at the central library here."

I was intrigued over how totally smitten Sam was over this man Malek. His eyes took on a surreal cast as he spoke about the man. He talked on and on, happy to be in Pula and in an extended family of believers. His New England family had donated a considerable sum to Malek's foundation. It seemed to me he had given up any kind of critical thinking about Malek's ideas and accepted everything the man said as truth. I wondered over that.

"But Sam, what if you find out that it's not true, that Malek's ideas are not true. What do you do then?"

He was a bit taken aback by my question, went quiet for a bit, a moment of doubt crossing his mind, and then he recovered.

"It's not whether or not a thing is true. It's if you believe it to be true that matters."

Then, as if my remark had stung him, he nodded at me, smiled awkwardly and left.

◆ ◆ ◆

I was to encounter the man called Malek a few days later at a popular restaurant near the Coliseum. That his presence commanded the space around him was an understatement. I watched him closely as he entered accompanied by two gorgeous women, and chose a table where he could sit with his back to the wall. His eyes, the colour of a robin's egg, scanned the large space about him weighing everything, estimating, judging. He had a strange unsettling smile on his lips. There was a small, curling scar on his left cheek. It could have been an old dueling scar I thought. Imagine that, a dueling scar in the age of Facebook and Instagram.

Dressed in fine, custom-tailored clothes that accentuated his handsomeness, there was an unmistakable threat in his bearing and movement, a resident anger. There was a coiled power about the man. But my eyes couldn't help but settle on his beautiful companions, two of the most beautiful women I had ever seen. Almost as beautiful as Zora, but not quite. One, a statuesque blonde in a wonderfully form-fitting dark blue dress and the other, a petite brunette, darkly exotic and attired in beige leather pants and jacket. I was surprised that neither of them wore jewellery of any kind, not rings, necklaces, or bracelets. But they were of such beauty that adornments of any kind were not needed. They lit up like Christmas when Malek leaned closer to them to say something, to which they laughed uproariously. I tried not to stare, attempting to look about nonchalantly, a pose that I have never fully mastered.

The café was quite busy with the evening tourist trade. One table of five young Italian men was particularly noisy. They wore A.S. Roma football jerseys. As I glanced about I could see Malek's brow wrinkle in distaste. His two attentive companions followed suit and glowered at the loud group. One of the Italians caught sight of them, waving at them and laughing, raising his beer glass in tribute. I could see Malek stiffen and extend his chest, an unconscious movement that captured the essence of his proud bearing.

One of the Italians was finishing his spaghetti dinner. To my surprise and disgust he removed his denture and with his tongue sucked the remaining tomato sauce from the piece amid the unbridled laughter of his companions. Malek continued staring and when one of his beauties began to speak he silenced her with a brusque wave of his arm. She stopped immediately, feeling his roused menace. The Italian, oblivious to them, inserted his denture ceremoniously for the benefit of his friends, excused himself and walked unsteadily to the WC. Malek then stood and followed the man calmly and without haste.

I was somewhat surprised at how gracefully he moved for such a tall, powerful-looking man, lean and hard. It was like watching a big cat striding insouciantly across the open space of the café. My eyes, of course, went back to the companions at his table. They didn't speak to each other. It was as if they turned themselves off the moment he left. And then, quite abruptly, the blonde beauty turned her head towards her companion and softly placed her hand over the arm of the brunette, as if waiting for something to happen. There was an expectancy hovering in the air that I felt was almost palpable. Seconds passed, perhaps no more than a moment or two, when suddenly a horrendously sharp cry from the direction of the WC shattered the relative quiet normalcy of the place. It seemed to rend the café air in a transforming way. The Italian burst from the WC corridor with both of his hands covering his bloody mouth, his eyes wide with terror and shock. Malek was nowhere to be seen. Two waiters rushed to the man's aid trying to help him in whatever way they could. All of the man's teeth were gone, denture and all. His Italian companions were shouting loudly, presumably asking what had happened. The victim pointed frantically to the WC. A waiter and two of the Italians proceeded warily to the WC and returned almost immediately. There was no one there. The diffident waiter held the pulverized denture in his hand like an offering. Another waiter called the police. The two women hurriedly left the café leaving some currency on the table. The whole episode was bizarre. I didn't know what to make of it, and it was quickly forgotten. Regardless, the days passed contentedly for me.

I don't know how or why but I began to feel things I had never felt before. Call it premonition or some kind of prescient awareness. It was as if someone was stalking me. I remember walking to my apartment late at night after some heavy drinking with Davor and suddenly feeling that I was being watched and followed. There were few light standards as I made my way up the hill to my apartment. Suddenly I felt goose bumps on my forearms and turned quickly to look behind me. Was there someone lurking in the shadows? I thought I saw a tiny flash of movement barely discernible but there, yes there, in a darkened doorway, a deeper shadow against the night. I turned away and quickened my pace. Behind me the sound of running footsteps and then nothing. I was almost home. I fumbled in my pocket for my key as I ran to the entrance. And then as I opened the door I felt a rush of movement below me at my feet, brushing against my pant leg. I cried out just as I saw the familiar housecat leaping up the stairs and then to the corridor in front of me. The light above my apartment door was on, and I felt a wave of blessed relief move through me. I was home and fell at once upon my bed tired and drunk.

◆ ◆ ◆

One afternoon Davor took me to see his friend Dr. Antun Spehar, an opthamologist. The reception area in his office had a few artifacts from the Roman and Ottoman eras that were neatly labeled as such. It was like a very small museum of sorts, but uncluttered, without that feeling you get in museums that are overwhelming, that make you want to leave quickly. We followed him into a clinical office that was modern and bright and replete with what looked to be the latest in optical technology. He was a plump little man, completely bald, with a trim beard and extremely bushy eyebrows. Beneath his white medical cloak he was dressed in a three-piece tweed suit and was constantly smiling even when he was speaking. I liked him from the start.

"Davor has told me about you. You are Croatian Canadian I understand and may help us in our work, yes?" he said, with his eyebrows rising significantly at the end of each statement.

"Yes, I am considering it," I replied, looking at Davor who sat cross-legged across from me in a comfortable leather club chair. As always he looked amused and sad simultaneously.

Dr. Spehar took a few samples of my blood and spittle, and then with various pieces of equipment examined my eyes, making notes as he proceeded. I thought it strange that the blood and saliva specimens were needed but he said it provided a more complete profile.

As we left the examination room, Davor stopped for a moment and began to examine an artifact on one of the shelves in the front office. He raised a glass partition and picked up a silver coin from the display unit and handed it to me. "This is Roman, from the time the legions marched on Karlovac. Am I correct, Doctor?"

25

Dr. Spehar smiled with obvious satisfaction at his interest and stopped. He picked up a small magnifying glass from a glass tabletop and examined the coin.

"Yes Davor. You have a good eye. The Romans under Octavian were marching to Metulum, an Illyrian stronghold near Karlovac when this coin was struck. It was the year 32 BC. The campaign against the Iapodes, an Illyrian tribe, was particularly brutal, but Octavian triumphed, putting the torch to the settlement and enslaving those he didn't kill. The Roman way. Simple and expedient. The coin commemorates his victories and his status. But how did you know?"

Davor chuckled, and for a fleeting moment the stamp of sadness on his features departed. It was a treat to see him enjoying himself.

"I'm recalling what you told me a few months ago. The coin is exactly in the same place where it rested the last time I visited with you."

Dr. Spehar laughed, wagging a finger at Davor, and then he returned the coin very carefully to its position on the shelf.

"The stones and karst caves of Lika hold many treasures from Roman times and beyond that, treasures that remain to be discovered. Who knows what we may yet find?"

♦ ♦ ♦

Call it coincidence, chance, or just the toss of a random encounter, I observed Malek a few days later walking under the Arch of the Sergians, stopping for an instant to lay his hand on one of the great plinths supporting the structure. He looked up briefly and then continued, turning left and walking by the flower market and the busy, noisy street. He didn't make any effort to move to the side as people passed. It was for them to get out of his way. I followed, curious as to where he was going. I had never seen him alone before. I was struck that he walked so gracefully for such a tall man. He seemed to glide along the street, easy and assured in his movement. I don't know why I was so fascinated with him. There was something cold and brutally arrogant about him, the kind of man I imagine many people felt it was best to be on the good side of. He stopped at a small park just off the street and sat on a bench, his back to me. I walked past, confident that he hadn't seen me, and then I turned to look at him. As it was, I didn't think he would recognize me, for the only time he could have seen me was the evening where he had disappeared after the denture man had been assaulted in the bathroom of the café. But then he held up his left arm, and without turning at all, appeared to summon me, his two fingers wagging me forth. I was stunned. I looked about. There was no one behind me. How could he know I was there? But I knew I was the only person he could be signaling in such a manner.

I hesitated. Here he was with two fingers wagging me forth from across the street, and not even looking in my direction. Why should I even bother with that, with crossing the street, with somehow acknowledging that I had tailed him by the very act of responding to his two fingers. He didn't know me. It was embarrassing enough to be caught in the act, of watching and following him. Did I need to be further humiliated by answering his two-fingered call and speaking with him and explaining somehow that he intrigued me. How weak was that? No, I could simply turn away and walk towards the Coliseum, away from all that. But within the shell of my hesitation was the kernel of curiosity and so I ventured forth, minding the traffic and crossing the street.

I threaded my way through a group of tourists and answered the call. I approached him from his right side and stood facing him, his fingers still airborne. He slowly lowered them and sat smiling, the small scar on his cheek pale against his handsome tan. "Please, have a seat," he said, and he patted the park bench beside him. I felt contrite, like a schoolboy caught in a spot of trouble, but I sat down, looking straight ahead. He turned to me, smiling broadly, and held out his hand.

"I am Malek. I do not believe we have met." I shook his hand and felt a cold chill move through me.

"Christopher Radelja," I said. "Is Malek your first or last name?" I asked.

"Both," he said, not bothering to explain further. A subtle smile spread across his handsome face.

"My little friend has been telling me about you. Do you remember Sam?"

"Well yes", I said, "we had an interesting conversation in this same park a few days ago. He was very impressed with you, and your teachings."

"Ah yes, my teachings. I am always a little disconcerted when people focus on me. I am but an instrument, nothing more: an instrument of light. Have you heard of us? We belong to the Academy of Light, a foundation supported by believers and contributors from around the world. We are non-denominational and non political. I often lecture at the main library here. Have you been?"

"No, but I will. I'm very curious about your group."

"I am happy to hear that," he said. I watched him closely as his face tightened. His tiny scar grew paler against his tan. He looked intently at me for a full moment before he spoke.

"We simply desire that the evil materialism of our times be subjugated to the forces of what I call illuminated goodness. We are creatures of the light and we have lost our way. Perhaps it sounds so very abstract, but abstractions are necessary in my work."

"I would certainly like to know more about the Academy of Light."

"Come to my lectures then. We discuss life and death issues. There is no fear once you know that death can be defeated, but that takes some doing, confronting death."

"How do you do that?"

"By actively pursuing and destroying the dark forces around us, the death in life. Confronting death is like looking at the sun. You quickly need to look away. But then you continue looking again and again until you vanquish death. Each of us has a point of light within us that we must free and let run rampant in the world. That's how the dark forces of materialism are defeated."

"That's pretty intense for me to follow."

"Of course. It takes time to understand things." He leaned forward, his elbows on his knees, and then turned and looked at me. "By the way, have you heard anything about some sort of spiritual meeting on Brijuni?

I was taken aback by his remark. Davor hadn't told me to keep secret his invitation to me about joining him on Brijuni, but instinctively I knew that I must keep it confidential.

"No, what's it about?" I replied.

"Oh, something to do with returned spirits. Spiritual matters of some sort."

"No, nothing at all."

"Ah. But now I must go. It was a pleasure to meet you. I am sure we will see each other again. Bye." He stood and walked away, melding into the crowded street, a full head taller than any of the tourists heading to the nearby Coliseum. I continued sitting in the park, confused by our conversation, and oddly perplexed by his comment on something happening on Brijuni.

♦ ♦ ♦

I didn't know what to expect as I made my way to Dr. Spehar's office located on the third floor in an office building very close to the Arch of the Sergians. Davor had given me the address earlier. It was near the end of the working day. I had made my decision to act as a spirit guardian, and had agreed, with some trepidation, to a number of tests. He said the tests measured visual acuity whatever that meant. Dr. Spehar was also very curious about my memory capacity. I remembered telling Davor that I had a memory that could recollect images with unusual vividness and detail, and he must have discussed that with the Doctor I presumed.

Doctors' offices have always had a certain effect on me, a combination of fearing the worst, of dread, and of curiosity. A comely young receptionist politely bid me to sit and wait as the Doctor was running behind schedule. She informed me that he was busy with his last appointment of the day. She said proudly that he worked as often as he could in order to purchase archaeological objects of interest to him. I walked over to a small glass cabinet and studied a bronze amulet with strange circular markings on the face of it.

Twenty minutes later I was ushered into the Doctor's examination area where I waited several more minutes. Suddenly Dr. Spehar entered in a rush of activity and sat next to me, opening a document on his laptop with my name on it. Beneath his white cloak he was wearing a dark three-piece suit and a gray silk tie. His eyebrows needed some serious trimming.

"So, Mr. Radelja you have decided to join us in our work," he said with clear delight.

"Please, call me Christopher, or Kristof, as Davor does."

"Thank you. Our preliminary tests reveal you to be a healthy, middle-aged man. Your DNA by the way shows your ancestry to be Croatian with traceable elements from Istria, Dalmatia, and Croatia proper. That was why we required a saliva sample. We thought you would be interested. " He printed a map from the document showing several crimson circles where my ancestors originated and handed it to me.

Suddenly I felt an imperative need to ask a question. "Does it matter," I asked, "whether I'm Croatian or not, for the spirit work I'll be doing? I mean I'm very proud of my heritage, of being Croatian, but how does that affect the work?"

Dr. Spehar hummed quietly for a few seconds, and then in a tone of reassurance continued. "We have the help of many different people from the Croatian diaspora who are spirit guides. In that respect we are truly international in scope. It is your innate ability, your intuitive capacity, that we want to harness. Your Croatian background may make it easier in some respects, in an understanding of our culture, but not necessarily so. Intuition, compassion, and empathy are the keys in our work, along with memory capacity of course."

I nodded my agreement to his words. He excused himself for a few moments and then came back to the small examination room with a stainless steel tray upon which there were three artifacts similar to the ones I had seen in the reception area. All three of them looked to be metal and fashioned out of bronze. He then turned down the lighting and spent a good half hour conducting a progressive relaxation exercise to make me feel as comfortable as possible. He said it was a kind of clinical hypnosis and that I would find it interesting. He asked me to fix my sight upon a point on the ceiling and then he asked me to count backwards from 100, and as I did so, he said that my eyelids would close whenever I wanted them to. And then I listened to the sound of his voice offering me deep relaxation and great comfort if, as he put it, I so chose.

I have to admit that I was completely relaxed within a very short time. He began by asking me to relax the muscles in my feet, and then my legs, and gradually, very gradually, my whole body became relaxed, and finally my shoulders, neck, and head. His voice carried me along until I felt an out of body experience just attending to his voice alone. But he made it very clear throughout it all, the choice was mine to relax more and more deeply or to come back to alert consciousness once again.

I followed his voice to a point where it asked me to visualize an image from the distant past, from Roman times, from when Pula was a young city. The voice suggested a pleasant market scene near the Arch of the Sergians. The voice would utter simple words at random such as apple, cabbage, grapes, and I would find that the image of a market beneath my eyelids began to build until I felt I could reach out and grasp a bunch of purple grapes, or a greenish-white cabbage, or a red apple glistening in the sun. The voice asked me to describe what was happening around me if I wished to. I seemed to be bodiless but that didn't prevent me from seeing the sights around me. I began by looking to my right and in a slow, heavy voice I described a wooden meat stall where an incredible number of flies buzzed around three legs of pork hung by metal hooks from the ceiling of the crude wooden stall. When I looked to my left I saw and described a small pyramid of green lemons sitting atop a wine colored blanket. A young woman with braided blonde hair smiled and said something that I could not quite make out. I was about to reach for the topmost lemon of the pyramid when I heard the voice that had brought me here.

"Christopher, I am going to place a bracelet in the palm of your hand. It will not disturb your comfort. If you wish to hold it, your palm will open to receive it. It may be the palm of your left hand, or it may be the palm of your right hand. Only you can decide which of your hands it will be."

I felt a mild irritation at having to open the palm of my hand because of the comfortable state I was in, but after several moments I felt the palm of my right hand open to receive the bracelet. It didn't open all at once, but rather in short stepwise movements. There was hardly any weight to the bracelet. The voice continued to guide me but I felt free to continue or to stop whenever I wished. But the voice seemed to me to be the voice of a close friend, and so I went with it. The odd thing was that as I held the bracelet the vividness of the market scene was incredibly realistic. It was as if I was actually there in the ancient Roman market. I told this to Dr. Spehar, and he simply hummed and nodded before he spoke.

"The bracelet was found during the excavation for a parking lot. It was found on the site of the Pula market. It dates back to Roman times. It is extremely valuable though I consider it priceless. Now, may I conduct a few visual acuity tests?" Dr. Spehar asked.

"Sure," I said slowly, "please do whatever you wish." I watched him as he went about his work. He was very focused and intent and, as always, humming quietly to himself. He seemed to me to be very efficient and totally absorbed in his examination. He held what he called a retina scanning device in his hand as he examined my eyes. He positioned the scanner directly in front of my eyes and held it there for a few moments. I noticed that the device was linked to a small projector to one side of the stool he sat on. It was very compact and looked heavy and expensive. It was marked Tesla Retina Scanner in bold letters along the side of the device. It was wireless. Behind me there was a white screen against the wall. He asked me to think of something, of anything that came to mind. Just then I experienced strong flashes of light that were quite startling in their intensity. I blinked repeatedly. Immediately, I thought of Zora. I don't know why. I just did. I saw a subtle smile cross Dr. Spehar's face.

"What's so funny?" I asked.

"It's your retinal image. It's so very, very clear," the Doctor replied.

"What is it?"

"It's of a woman, a very attractive woman I might add. I know her."

"Who do you see?" I asked.

"Zora," the Doctor said. "Zora Sekulić."

I was totally amazed and could feel myself blushing. I had no idea he could tell what I was thinking.

"But how?" I said. "How did you know?"

It is the Scanner that does it. You have a thought or an image and the Scanner captures it. It projects it onto the screen. Now I will continue."

His examination was thorough, and he was very courteous throughout. The entire procedure took about two hours. The Doctor thanked me profusely, clearly excited about the device and its accuracy. Afterwards I left to meet Davor, as we had prearranged, for drinks at a bar nearby.

◆ ◆ ◆

Davor was excited to hear of my meeting with Dr. Spehar. He looks at me with a bit of a twinkle in his eye, a twinkle that contains elements of compassion and grace. He says something in Croatian that I couldn't quite hear. I ask him to repeat it.

"Everything lives," he says enigmatically.

I look at him puzzled for a moment and then I shrug.

"Sure," I say, "except for everything that is dead, or stone, or changed by the hard hand of man or the universe." I smile and tease him, trying to tear a tiny rent in the tight fabric of his equanimity. He continues to look at me, lifting his chin slightly, and I look away first. He knows what I'm thinking. How can a stone live? How can the ashes of my ancestors live? How can a pot or a pan or a wooden spoon live? How can a dessicated piece of leather live ? How can a bronze bracelet or a Roman breastplate live?

The thoughts petered away and I just looked at people walking by. Some of them stopped for selfies with the sitting Joyce sculpture outside the bar. I don't know why they are so enamoured. From the little I read of him, Joyce didn't really like Pula and left for Trieste when he could.

Suddenly Davor leans towards me earnestly and places his hand on my forearm. He speaks softly to me as if confiding a secret.

"So, once again, you must remember the essential distinction between ghosts and spirits. Ghosts are lingerers, slight shadows that haunt a particular place they loved in life, or that somehow was very meaningful to them. Think of them as you would of people who just can't leave. Now spirits are different. They have returned to life to seek redemption, or to settle a score, or whatever. These spirits need our help. They are the heavyweights so to speak." Then he once again gave me things to look for in order to distinguish between ghosts and spirits. I noticed that he often repeated himself. Ghosts were a dime a dozen he said, but actual spirits were very rare. He said that was about to change and I would be a part of it if I wished. At Brijuni.

We didn't stay long at the cafe. As always Davor left me with the bill, and I noticed he had quaffed two double brandies before I had joined him. Par for the course I thought. Soon, I settled the bill, and left for the walk to my apartment. I needed time to think, to try to make sense of it all. I needed to figure things out. Had I been concussed from my fall in the Temple of

Augustus and, as a result, dreaming all of this? Was all this talk of spirits and ghosts just a temporary thing, a temporary aberration, a result of an accidental head injury? Was it something that would resolve itself with time, like the effects of a bad hangover dissipating itself? Or had I stumbled and fallen onto ancient truths? I didn't know. Soon I was in my apartment and decided to identify the things I knew for sure or thought I knew about spirits. I took a pen and scrap of paper from my carry-on bag and jotted down the one thing I'd experienced on my own regarding spirits, that I'd seen with my own eyes in Pula. I wrote it down: three sets of spirits walking through each other, simultaneously, inhabiting the same space but in different realities, different times, oblivious to each other. That was the only thing I knew for sure. There was nothing else that came up, so I decided to take a nap and sleep on it.

◆ ◆ ◆

Davor and I were standing outside the Coliseum, looking up and admiring the structure. The day was overcast with the threat of rain. There were few tourists about. A black dog tethered to a bicycle rack was barking loudly a few meters away. I was beginning to know when Davor was about to speak. He turned away from the Coliseum and looked at me intently, his brow wrinkled in thought, his blue eyes shining.

"Last year I visited Prague. Such a wonderful city. A city of church spires and deep convoluted mysteries. The city of Kafka. But I learned something there of great value, something I knew but didn't know I knew until I saw it plainly before me. It was in a small museum crypt beneath the Church of Saints Cyril and Methodius. It was the place where a group of Czech paratroopers, men who had assassinated Heydrich, died fighting off Nazi attackers in the church and in the burial crypt. With their last bit of ammunition they committed suicide rather than face certain torture and death. They were brave men and bold courageous fighters. But the artifacts there, the objects used by the paratroopers, were referred to as silent witnesses. That was the term used: silent witnesses. It got me thinking about our own silent witnesses, like this Coliseum or like the artifacts you've seen and handled in Dr. Spehar's office. Everything lives."

I pondered over what Davor was saying. It was intriguing but certainly not actually true. It couldn't be. How could a homemade bomb or a pocketknife or a photograph of a Czech freedom fighter, be a silent witness, be alive?

"OK Davor, you don't mean that literally. You can't mean it to be true, that these objects actually live. That doesn't make sense. After all they're material objects, inanimate things. It's not logical."

Davor swung about facing me and grabbing me roughly by the shoulders. "But I know it to be true," he said emphatically. "These things live. They're silent witnesses to history. Kristof, for Christ's sake, use your intuition. Do you remember the tests given you by Dr. Spehar?"

I straightened my jacket, making a show of setting it right, and moved away from him, putting some distance between us. I remembered the objects I had held in my hand in Dr. Spehar's office, but they were no more than useful aids, props that helped in conjuring images. I shrugged it off.

"It's too much of a stretch for me to accept that. Surely you can't believe that. Where's your proof?"

"The proof is right there in the objects themselves," he said, looking at me askance.

I felt a few raindrops falling. I knew we needed to change the topic. "Let's grab a coffee at the cafe on the corner," I said. Davor smiled and nodded. A young man was untying the black dog from the bicycle stand as the dog licked his hand repeatedly, its tail wagging in canine greeting. Just as we were crossing the street a white cargo van drove by at high speed coming a little too close to us for comfort.

◆ ◆ ◆

The next day was like so many others I had experienced in Pula. Davor and I were sitting on a park bench close to the twin gates. A young mother nearby was nursing her infant, covering her breast with a light blue shawl. The pleasant sound of children's voices wafted through the air. When I recounted to Davor what I had seen of the man Malek and his entourage, a tight grimace spread across his features. His eyes glanced down and to the left of him as if he were accessing some remembered information. I could tell it was painful for him to dredge up these memories.

"Malek is a strange creature with many followers. Bold and cunning and yes, brave too. A man who prefers cruelty to kindness. If you decide to assist us he and his minions will be waiting at the gates, or within the dark passages that you pass through on your journey. But more of that later. You must be careful."

Then Davor smiled wanly, shaking off his untoward thoughts, warming to the beautiful day surrounding us. He raised his face to the Istrian sun, as he did so often, feeling its warmth pervade his being, and then continued.

"Chaos is a choice as much as order," he said, his eyelids flickering for an instant. "Never forget that. Never forget that your choices are anathema to Malek. He thrives on hate and will welcome your challenge. Of that you can be sure."

Soon I retreated back to the security of my apartment. All of what Davor was saying struck me as totally weird and other worldly. Some sort of convoluted, dark mystery. Whatever kind of man this Malek was, it seemed to me that the wisest course was just to avoid him. Keep out of his way. Keep vigilant. I needed to keep my head clear. Here I was, a middle-aged Canadian of Croatian heritage, and I was being asked to help in strange and utterly alien ways. It was good being needed, but were these people just plain crazy? Were they all nuts? Davor with his grim warnings. Zora with her curiously warm attention to me. After all, she was out of my league. A stunning beauty beyond my reach. All of those stories of ancient Illyrian spirits and cruel enemies. A kind of mystic poetry. Had I somehow stepped into a parallel universe where things like this could happen? One part of me was fearful while the other was bold and curious. On the one side was the boring sameness, the tedious sameness of my life, and on the other, high adventure spliced with danger and fortune.

I must admit that being with Davor had helped me to become more attentive and more observant to the world around me. Before meeting him I suppose I just ignored things, paying attention to what concerned me at the moment, and even in conversation, I was hardly listening, spending more time planning what to say and little else. I find most people are like that. The world is filled with big and little egos like the stars of the sky.

Davor encouraged me to think for myself and not to accept the status quo as something that could not be changed. Anything can be changed. Anything.

From what Davor had told me, certain spirits take a long time to reappear after death. Not all spirits mind you. The vast majority are content with the afterlife and the peace that it offers. But others aren't. They want a return ticket to the big show to complete something, and that takes time. In most cases, about two gradually cumulative centuries even though they may have been dead for a millennium or so. There is a kind of incredibly long gestation period for them to go through. Most didn't make it, simply falling back into the dark oblivion with all of their efforts cancelled. Of course, the spirits need help and assistance from living beings. I don't know what brave new technology or magic they needed, but I knew in my heart that it would happen at Brijuni.

But the ghosts linger for a while, maybe in the house they lived in, or the fields they loved, and then with some prodding they simply drift away into the vast halls that death kept open for them. They are inconsequential, meandering ghosts.

But spirits persist. Some are determined to return to the living state and make different choices. They and whatever issues they held when they were alive stay, and so they persevere waiting for an opportunity and I guess you could say they seek some sort of redemption ultimately before returning to the death state. And it was up to human guardians like Davor to provide the linkage with people like myself to assist spirits in seeking the fulfillment they didn't receive in the living state.

Sure, I was learning, but not fast enough. Who'd think that something as invasive and curious as grabbing someone by the throat would prove a test, that of whether a suspected ghost was indeed a ghost or human. Davor didn't seem to think it was any big thing, lunging at ghosts and taking them down. Back home in Canada it would be considered an assault unless you were a Prime Minister or something and treated as such, but here it wasn't or at least that's what Davor suggested. But then the police kept a low profile in tourist-ridden Pula. Davor had given me a test. I was to be on my own later that evening, and I was to have a go at it as he put it. I was to seek out a likely ghost, approach it, and go for its throat. He said it was only by doing it that I could progress. I would learn things about ghosts that need to be experienced, not talked about. So I did the thing I always did before I had to do something unpleasant, something that made me nervous in the anticipation of it. I went for an afternoon nap that lasted longer than it should have. It was dusk when I awoke. I washed my face and reluctantly made my way to the café near the Coliseum. I sat at a table next to a young couple in their early twenties enjoying coffee and speaking softly to each other. Love was in the air.

I ordered a double brandy and waited. Everything seemed so normal. The café was nearly full to capacity. There was that happy hum in the air of people enjoying themselves.

I spotted one, or what I thought was one. The ghost was fidgeting about in his chair. There was a pint of beer, untouched, on the table in front of him. He was looking about, but clearly avoided looking my way. The café was deserted except for him. A middle-aged man, in his early forties, balding, and wearing a striped blue and white t-shirt, mariner style. I took a seat at the table next to his, and when the waiter approached me I pointed to the beer and gestured that I wanted one of the same. The waiter nodded and left. The man was squirming madly in his chair trying desperately to look nonchalant but appearing anything but. The waiter returned with my beer and then went inside the cafe. The beer was very chilled and there were beads of condensation on the outside of the glass. I hoisted it, nodded to the man writhing about at his table and toasted him. Then, seeing no one was about, I hurried over to him and throttled him by the neck. And then the strangest thing happened.

His body seemed to shimmer under the patio lighting. And his face became contorted in a very unnatural manner. His face and body appeared tight and then in the next instant, loose and oddly different. It was as if there was a great struggle within his physical frame and then suddenly he was much younger, in his teens, and then in his twenties. Before my very eyes he was transforming into a younger version of the middle-aged man I was looking at, but all within a few seconds. The entire incident couldn't have lasted more than five seconds. It was alarming and supernatural and yet it was happening right there in front of me, the waiter having gone inside the café. And then the same man, the middle-aged man whom I had seen sitting at the table next to mine before the transition stood up with panic and fear in his eyes. He upset his beer and ran out of the café whimpering like a beaten refugee from some fateful encounter. My eyes followed him as he ran down the darkened road away from me and the café lights. I had found and outed my first ghost.

I was so elated that I decided to go ghost hunting at another bar. Within twenty minutes I was sitting in a bar near the Forum. A few tables away from where I sat three men in their fifties were having an animated conversation. They were drinking bottled beer and the way they gesticulated and emphasized their points in grand manner told me they had already consumed several beer. One of the men looked about and when our eyes met, he looked away immediately. So, I thought, here was the first indication that the man was a ghost, at least according to Davor's training. A warm reddish glow suffused the space around the night-lit Forum adjacent to the café. The tables began to fill. A young man at the table next to mine leaned over and kissed his companion on the cheek. She smiled shyly, and when she did, I was struck by how beautiful she was. A dimpled beauty with shoulder length chestnut hair and marvelous teeth. The stout man who had avoided my eyes stood up and made for the washroom. Now or never, I thought, and I hastened to follow him. I stood at the urinal next to his and waited. He finished and went to the sink to wash his hands. My heart was pounding and my stomach felt suddenly queasy. He did not look at me. He looked only at the mirror above the sink. There was a heavy scent of sprayed lavender pervading the air. When he turned to leave I lunged at his throat with my right hand, shaping my hand into a V. I had him. He cried out. Nothing happened. He was not a ghost. I ran through the café toppling one of the outside tables over in my mad dash to get away. His screams filled the air. I raced past him to run away. Soon I was a block away and in a residential area. The lights along the street lit the darkness. I took the long way home to my apartment, eager to be away from the café and the Forum and my failure and perhaps the police. I had trouble falling asleep that night and looked forward to meeting Davor at his apartment.

◆ ◆ ◆

Davor did a curious thing that I have puzzled over for some time. Just before we left for the Roman theater, he took a pencil, a sheet of paper, and a ruler, and told me to split the page in half with the pencil. I grabbed a pencil, placed the ruler vertically in the middle of the sheet and marked a line down the length of it. He smiled. Then he placed his hand against the ruler and ripped the sheet in half, and held it up for me to see, not only splitting the page, but creating a new plane with the half ripped sheet. There were now two planes, one vertical and one horizontal, where before there had been only one. Then, he crumpled up both pieces of paper and stood, thereby signaling it was time for us to leave.

We walked for several minutes to the small Roman theater situated on a hill just below the star shaped Habsburg castle and above the flower market. We sat quietly on the crumbling stone where centuries before audiences had watched Roman dramas and listened to the entertainers of that far day. Davor plucked a dandelion from the ground before him, twirled the stem between his thumb and finger, and then rubbed the flower head across the base of his thumb. He turned towards me, raising his hand for me to see.

"Look at the color it leaves on skin," Davor said, showing me his palm. "Yellow, almost golden, like a benediction."

Suddenly I grew frustrated with his poetic speak. "Let's cut to the chase Davor. Why should I help you? I mean you have to admit it's pretty strange. Returned spirits of the dead and all that. Even if I took a leap of faith to help you, what's in it for me? I haven't been able to write the travel articles I was planning on because I've been spending so much of my time with you. Not that I mind, but it's changed my trip. And I want to be honest with you. I need to get something out of all this. I'm forty-four years old coming out of a failed marriage with no great prospects in sight. What's in it for me?" I was being honest, but petty. I was still unnerved from my experience at the Forum café the night before.

Davor smiled wryly, amused I guess at my predicament and my earnestness. But I really did need to know. I also needed the incentive, the motivation.

"All right," he said, leaning forward on the stone bench. "We need you and people like you. Your heart beats to the same rhythms as the spirits that you will serve. But more than that, your intuition and your special memory capacity is extraordinary, and we want to use it in our spirit work. You will be amply rewarded."

If I continued my relationship with Davor, I would be going down a rabbit hole and I wasn't sure what I would find there, or if I would be safe. But the prospect of payment sparked my resolve and I wanted to learn more.

◆ ◆ ◆

We were back in Davor's apartment once again. The living room was sparsely furnished, like a monk's cell. The only book on the glass shelving was a novel, **Heart of Darkness**.

"Let me tell you something about fear," Davor began, abruptly and strangely. "It is something you give to your enemy as a gift. To feel fear initially is a natural thing, and to be readily acknowledged, but to persist with it, to hold it, and to let it infect your will and ability is scornful, and more than that, shameful. Imagine that, giving your enemy a precious gift, the gift of your courage and having him trample it into the ground. Death would be better. Fear erodes the will. Fear incapacitates you and makes a mockery of courage. Each of us has a still, hard point within from which issues our courage. Fear is a soft, formless thing that given time and space, takes away the man, and leaves nothing but a residue, a hot stink, to be shunted aside like an empty husk, and forgotten. Courage is the most precious quality we have and within it is just the tiniest particle of fear. It must be felt and then dismissed to allow courage to take the field."

Davor went silent then, rose, and walked to the window where he lifted the sash abruptly and let the cool, night air of Pula enter the room.

He stood by the window for a long moment, leaning forward on the window sill, as if meditating, and then he started speaking again, jumping from topic to topic and expecting me to keep up with his eclectic ramblings.

"Boundaries are elastic or in flux. Everything changes, nothing remains the same. Look at you, our resident Croatian Canadian. You've already changed from the man who had his fortune read that first afternoon I saw you. And now you're about to experience boundaries between life and death, a no man's land of the soul. Spirit boundaries. You'll meet all kinds

41

coming and going, eager to have your aid in accomplishing their belated missions. But, you must be careful."

Davor walked over to where I sat on the couch and patted me on the shoulder affectionately.

"Look, you can help many spirits find peace, find rest, and we can offer you wealth, but nothing is without its attendant risk. You can stop now, here and now, and play the tourist writer. You can write a few articles and go home, losing nothing, and gaining nothing of consequence. This will have been an interesting minor episode in the life of Kristof Radelja, a few curious anecdotes to tell your friends back home. But if you continue and take on this daring adventure your life will never be the same again. You will be something other than who you are now, and far richer than you can imagine. If you pick up a stick, you pick up the other end too. Remember, you are dealing with the dead and the accumulations they have brought with them from their day. There are, however, malignant spirits who thrive on terror, chaos, and hate. You will encounter them soon enough should you remain here with us. I want you to know that the attendant risk is your death. This curious game can end very badly for you Kristof. You must realize that. My influence is limited. Whatever I can do to help you I will, but I and others are not invincible in the face of the powers of destruction."

"Your soul is at play here. The soul is most content when it meets a kindred spirit. You must realize that. It's as if a distant part of the soul is restored when it encounters its own kind. Join us if you will. I'd like you to meet some distant parts of yourself. Better by far than scribbling on paper or keyboarding on a laptop. Remember even the best articles you can write are used to wrap fish up when all is said and done."

Davor smiled his enigmatic, slightly sad smile, his eyes alight and shining as the evening fell slowly upon us. "You always ask why. Let me try to explain things to you, but there doesn't have to be an explanation. There doesn't have to be anything at all. The spirits have stories. But many stories are lost on the wind. Stories of loss and regret. Stories of heartache and bitter desperation and hunger. Stories strong enough to engender spirits that have challenged the abyss. The mere passage of days and the accumulation of time couldn't dislodge them. Some, to be sure, will want revenge, but many more simply want to make a different choice than the one they did, so they can find a belated peace. You have been chosen to help them. I don't know why. In some curious way you are one of them."

"How could I be one of them? After all, they're spirits, and I'm alive. I don't know what you mean by stories."

Davor glanced away from me and shrugged. "Stories are something different than you suppose. Stories are life and death to us, whether to the living or to the dead. Spirits carry their stories from life into death, and sometimes back again. Each of us has their little stories, most of them quite insignificant. But sometimes a little forgotten story can be like a seed swept by chance into a tiny crevice between huge stones. In time, the forgotten seed can flower and split the stones apart and take down a temple or a palace or a fortress, and then the insignificant becomes significant."

Davor stood by the window, paused and looked at the sliver of a moon above. The trace of a smile was on his lips.

"Nothing is quite as simple as it appears. Spirits, like blood beings, like people, want help in getting past unresolved issues in their past. Otherwise, they face an eternity of quiet desperation. Some seek atonement or redemption. Some want a second chance, or a last opportunity to be brave. Others as I have told you want revenge and the opportunity to revisit an occasion where they or their loved ones were brutalized. These spirits want peace. They want to rest in the huge expansive chamber that is the afterlife. It takes about two hundred years for these spirits to reconstitute themselves into life again, into existence. And when they are ready to act, they need someone like you, the living host to serve as the vital bridging instrument, the change agent if you will. So, I want you to join us at Brijuni, and if you can put aside your doubt, your fear, and your misgivings, you will be shown such things that even Emperors and Kings could not dream of."

"But why me?"

"Why not you? Why not? Sometimes the gods enjoy a good joke."

I felt a surge of righteous anger course through my veins. "Look, I'm a Canadian of Croatian heritage. My first allegiance is to Canada. I'd be less of a Croatian if I didn't honor the country of my birth, and less of a Canadian if I wasn't fiercely proud of the country of my ancestors."

"Well said Kristof. Bravo, well said."

Davor turned suddenly and looked deeply at me. He held my eyes for the longest time with his gaze. Almost, but not quite uncomfortable for me. I looked away. I didn't know if he was measuring or assessing in some silent way the depth of my soul. Perhaps it was the necessary preliminary to what he then said to me in a voice that was almost a whisper.

"Places of great beauty attract violence. And already you can see and feel the piercing beauty of this place. This very ground where the tourists take their selfies is rich with the blood passage of many. The passage from life to death."

Suddenly Davor went silent for a moment and then continued.

"What is pain but a different form of experience for sentient beings. The counterpoint to pleasure. Pain can be excessive, but so can pleasure. Why we should covet pleasure exclusively confounds me. Pleasure and pain are sustained by the same common root. Best to take the middle way and then neither can fail you. Balance, balance, always balance. The gymnastics of the human soul. Many of the spirits you will encounter are focused on ancient pain memories and they need a counterpoint to that."

◆ ◆ ◆

I remembered the moment when I made my decision to become a spirit guide. It was early afternoon and grey clouds were scudding across the sky. It looked a bit like rain was coming. I was walking up the hill behind the Coliseum towards my apartment on Pazinska Street. I stopped, turned around by the cafe to take a look at the Coliseum, took a deep breath, and it was done. Not much fanfare in that, but I reckon momentous decisions are made just like that. Besides, I was different now from whomever I was when I first arrived in Pula. I smiled happily as I trudged along, thinking about it. I'd throttled a local ghost and had a go at strangling an Italian tourist whom I mistakenly thought was a ghost, and I had used my intuition to see and interact with spirits from the past. I'd crossed a line, and I knew nothing would ever be the same again. The impossible had become a reality. Life turns on pivots. So it goes.

Back in my apartment I lay on the bed and read a few pages of Kurt Vonnegut's **Slaughterhouse Five**, intrigued by Billy Pilgrim's time and space travel. I put the novel aside and just lay there thinking about what was happening in my life, every bit as fantastic as Billy Pilgrim's. Propped up on the pillows with my hands interlinked behind my head, I let the images in my mind fly. Images of leaving Canada and Gloria. Images of meeting Davor and Zora. Images of spirits from the past in the café by the marketplace. All of these images floated about in my mind's eye until I felt myself falling asleep in fits and starts. I buried my face in the pillows and let go of my waking consciousness. When I awoke it was evening, and I could hear rain pattering against my bedroom window. I was refreshed but hungry.

I made myself a ham and cheese sandwich on rye bread with plenty of mustard. I enjoyed it as I drank a cold bottle of Karlovačko lager. It felt good to be here. Suddenly I heard my iPhone sound and checked my e-mail. It was a note from Gloria.

Christopher. I hope you are well and enjoying your well-deserved sabbatical. I have thought a lot about our situation. I know now I was hasty and wrong in some of the things I said to you about us and about our relationship. But I want to try again. I want us to try and save our marriage. Do you feel the same way? Could you feel the same way? How would you feel about my joining you in Croatia? Let me know.

Gloria Mundi

She wanted me back. She wanted us to try again. I didn't know what to think after all that had happened lately. Was it even possible to begin again? Did I even want it? Did I want to go back to a marriage that ran hot and cold? I remembered that the year before last she had us renew our vows as if that could shore up a crumbling marriage. That charade didn't last long before she left for a long weekend in Bimini with one of her workmates from her insurance office. Some feelings still lingered of course, and I knew that, but to have her here in Pula with me? Now? I didn't know about that.

♦ ♦ ♦

Around me the bustle of Pula, modern Pula, carried on oblivious of the images I was seeing and the magic of my intuition. Tourists sauntered by enjoying ice cream or sausages and commenting on the passing day in different languages. Waiters in black vests over white shirts stood outside their restaurants urging passersby to look at picture menus of their specialties, inviting them to dine within. A well-dressed middle-aged woman sat at a café table under a sun umbrella feeding her small spotted dog bits of čevapčići that he ate very carefully from her fingers. An elderly British couple, sunburnt from too much sun, talked incessantly about the Brexit supply chain impact, as they fingered seashell souvenirs and haggled for senior discounts. It amused me that I could see things that other people could not. I loved seeing into the past if I so chose, while around me, on the perimeter, everyday life continued on, not stopping for an instant.

♦ ♦ ♦

The next morning Davor and I carried on our conversation in the Roman theater.

Davor looked away from me and towards the center of the theater. We were standing amid the second row of stone bench seats. Some brilliant red poppies grew between the ancient, crumbling stones alongside some of the ubiquitous dandelions, golden in the late morning sunshine.

"So, our returned spirits, after two hundred years, not necessarily consecutive years, have accumulated enough living particles, enough of the right stuff, to re-enter life and for a limited time, at best a few months, change or alter what happened to them. That's where you come in. They need you to help them, through your intuition, through your memory, to guide the process along to the right moment, to ease them in and then to ease them

46

out. I'm just a manager of souls, a spiritual administrator, but you, you're on the front line. Do you understand what I'm trying to tell you?"

"But why two hundred years? And then why just for a limited time? And why me?"

Davor looked up at the sky in frustration and then smiled. "Kristof, you have to remember that the science of today is based on the imagination of yesterday. Or as someone put it, any technology that's sufficiently advanced enough is indistinguishable from magic. Some things you just have to accept. You don't have to know the exact processes behind your autonomic nervous system to be able to breathe and have your heart supply your brain with blood, but it happens. Accept that reality. Live with it. Some things don't have a ready explanation. Trust your intuition, after all, that's what brought you here. At that, Davor stopped speaking and sighed heavily."

"I need to know exactly what you want me to do with them." I was growing frustrated with so much ambiguity and, in turn, Davor was tiring of my incessant questioning.

"Don't worry. Our friend, Dr. Spehar, will explain your role," he said sharply, ending the conversation.

◆ ◆ ◆

I met Dr. Spehar in the bar of the Coliseum Hotel. It was seven in the evening and I waved him over as soon as I saw him. Few people were at the bar as it was still early in the Pula night. As always, he was well dressed in a three-piece suit, pinstripe brown, and well tailored to his portly figure. He smiled cheerfully and sat across from me. After we ordered drinks, he rubbed his hands together vigorously and began to speak in an excited, amiable manner.

"Kristof, I am quite impressed with your test results. Quite remarkable. Your memory capacity, the ability to see and hold images for a prolonged period of time is without a doubt the finest visual acuity I have seen. Coupled with your intuition, the way you can conjure up images from a past event and move into it, well, it is masterful."

The waiter served our drinks, a glass of Istrian red for the Doctor and a cognac for me.

"Doctor, I was astounded that your apparatus could project an image of my thought as I was thinking it. It blew me away. How in the world could you have done that? That's the closest thing to magic that I've ever experienced."

Dr. Spehar chuckled, twirled the wine in his glass, and took a long sip, savouring it. Then he hummed for a moment before continuing. His enthusiasm was infectious.

"Not so remarkable, when you remember that what is now proved, the invention you saw, was once only imagined. The machine that projected the retinal image in your eye was once only a concept, an idea in the mind of our greatest inventor, Tesla."

"I'm afraid I don't understand. I don't know much about this man Tesla, but I know he's famous and worked with Edison at one time. What do you mean? What's the process involved?"

Dr. Spehar placed his thumb and forefinger on the stem of the wine glass and made tiny circular motions with the base of the wine glass on the glass countertop. He was the kind of man who thought carefully before he spoke and measured his words. I admired him for that trait.

"Tesla believed he would be able to photograph thoughts, through what he called a thought camera. He said that a definite image formed when thinking, must by a kind of reflex action produce a corresponding image on the retina. He thought that with the right kind of apparatus or machine, the retinal image could be projected on a screen. That's what we did in my office. We were able to project the image you were thinking about, the image of the woman, of Zora, onto the screen."

"So," I said. "These thought cameras exist? They're real?"

"There are three in existence, and I have one of them, the one we used in my office."

"But what is really exciting for me is you and your photographic memory. You, my dear Kristof, are the only person I have met who doesn't need a camera or a screen to see the image on the subject's retina, the very image created by the subject's thinking. You can do it on your own, and with your intuition, your compassion, your memory, and the use of facilitative objects from the past, you can manipulate images, memory images, and transform thought. You can change reality, my friend, and that is an incredible advantage in our work. You as I've heard them say in America, are the man. Kristof, I raise my glass to you. Živio!"

We chatted amiably for some time, enjoying a second drink, but I was growing somewhat anxious because he had not mentioned anything about my compensation for providing assistance. I've always hated bringing up the subject of money, but it's necessary.

"Dr. Spehar, how will I be paid?" I said it flatly, a little too loudly, and perhaps I could have brought the matter up with more elegance and subtlety, but there you have it. I watched a broad smile infuse his features before he spoke.

"Yes, indeed. Compensation. Not to be forgotten. Kristof. We will transfer sixty thousand to a local account here in Pula. Davor will help you with the details. Sixty thousand now, and eighty thousand in a few months, after the work is successfully completed. Future contracts, should you be interested, will be compensated at the same rate, in addition to term insurance. Indeed, I wish I could be compensated in the same manner, but the work is my reward. I just wish my wife felt the same way. But there is one other key item I need to mention. We will also cover all operating expenses. Is that OK?" He signalled the waiter to bring the bill, and hummed silently to himself.

"That's fine, but is the money in Kuna or in Euros?"

Dr. Spehar chuckled under his breath. "Now I am convinced that you are of Croatian heritage. Euros, of course. OK?"

"Yes." I felt awkward and offered to pay our bar bill, but he simply waved me off courteously, shook my hand, and then left. I almost stood up and danced with joy at my good fortune, but ordered a third drink instead. The money was far more than any I could have earned from writing a few travel articles.

Brijuni and Thereafter

Part Two

YOU WILL FIND IT UTTERLY fascinating Kristof. Of that you can be sure." Davor made the remark with a nod and a wink, whatever that meant. I had yet to understand all of the nuances of Davor's enigmatic expressions. At any rate, he was clearly excited.

Davor was speaking of Brijuni, the biggest island among an archipelago off the Istrian coast. I was to make my way there, taking a bus to Fažana and then an excursion boat across the sea for three and a half kilometers to Veli Brijun. I would spend the day there, sightseeing, and then meeting him later that evening near a large Mediterranean garden. He said he would look after my transport back to Pula. It was a great way to explore the region around Pula I thought, though I wished Davor could join me for the day. He said that I needed some time alone to gather impressions without the filter of someone like himself making comments and thus destroying the natural contact between myself and the spirit of the place. It made sense to me and so on a bright, brisk morning I set off.

Davor had given me a special excursion ticket for Brijuni. The ticket was encased in clear plastic on a cord that I wore around my neck. Beside my name in bold black lettering was a small red-and-white checkered Croatian shield, the proud symbol of Croatian sovereignty. He said it was for a private party, beginning mid afternoon after the last tourist boat had left. He had organized the event and advised me that security would be tight, but not to worry with the ticket invitation. Wealthy friends from the Croatian diaspora, he explained had provided the funds to rent the island for part of the weekend and only those with an invitation were welcome.

As I approached Brijuni I noticed three sleek speedboats cruising about. They approached the excursion boat where I was standing on deck and I saw our captain wave cheerfully to the pilots. They waved back and then careened away at high speed.

It proved a delightful day. Brijuni was a national park that had once been the private residence of Tito and there was an interesting photo exhibit of his life on the island. One photo that I found particularly curious was of Tito with a drink in hand and a rifle in his lap sitting with a dead antelope below him with a caption that read "on Brijuni Tito was constantly taking care of the animals."

It was odd to me, taking a tourist train through a safari park and viewing a small number of exotic animals like zebras and an elephant spread in zoo enclosures across the low hills. There were plenty of schoolchildren running and shouting with happy excitement and loads of German tourists taking selfies and wandering about. It would have made for an interesting article, but I had made my choice. I spent a few hours hiking about and wished I could have had access to the ruins of the Roman country residence from the first century A.D., but it was not permitted. Nevertheless, the sight of it in the Bay of Verige was wonderful.

I was finished sightseeing in about three hours. I grabbed a ham sandwich and mineral water at a small kiosk near the church and found a place to sit by the Mediterranean garden. It was pleasant and touristy. Nothing extraordinary. I wondered why Davor had thought I would find it "utterly fascinating," as he put it. I guess he didn't know me as well as I thought he did. The two of us were in that curious zone between being friends and being close friends. Friendship, like good wine, takes time.

Later that afternoon, after the excursion boats had returned to Fažana, I looked about for a spot where I could take a nap and wait for Davor to show up. I had taken more than a few drinks with Davor the night before and a restorative nap was in order. Only invitees were now allowed on the island. Near the garden, there was an ancient, gnarled olive tree from the fourth century A.D., a low fence surrounding it. It was quite remarkable and magnificent and I wanted to be close to it. No one was wandering about to stop me. Very gingerly I stepped over the fence and found the right place by the trunk of the tree. I folded my jacket for a pillow and lay beneath the ancient branches of the olive tree. In front of me was a vast field covered in grass. In the center of it was a huge mound of dead wood, branches and the trunks of trees, cut and piled high for a bonfire. Soon I drifted off into a contented, dreamless sleep.

I awoke to the sound of men and women talking to each other in the far field. The sound of happy voices filled the air, expectant and excited. It was dusk and the night was fast approaching. I decided to stay where I was and make my way later to the nearby Mediterranean garden where I would meet Davor. I finished what was left of my ham sandwich and waited and watched as half a dozen people inserted kindling in and around the large pile of wood. Soon a light darkness enveloped the field. I put on my jacket against the evening chill and observed a man and woman with lit torches setting the kindling ablaze.

Within a few moments there was a bright blaze of light illuminating the field. It was so mesmerising. A wonderful bonfire with flames shooting high up into the night sky, its sparks alive, curling upwards, and then falling dead. Thousands and thousands of sparks piercing the night sky, rising erratically and then falling away. I watched and watched, almost forgetting I was to meet Davor in the garden.

I left my spot under the ancient olive tree and seemed to glide through the night air, the mystical chill night air, and looked about me. One of the men moved away from the bonfire and walked deep into the darkness where he took a pee by the trunk of an old pine tree. An old woman dressed entirely in black with a black head kerchief stabbed at the flame embers with a stick and laughed happily. Her face was flushed and ruddy from being near the fire.

And then the oddest thing. I thought perhaps I was hallucinating the image. It was several yards to one side of the bonfire, away from me. A huge figure eight, vertical and massive in two connected loops, was somehow suspended about five feet above the ground, but I could see there was nothing to hold the figure where it was. Nothing at all. It didn't make any sense at all. There was no supporting structure. The outline of the figure eight was ten feet high and ten feet across, or thereabouts, the number clearly illuminated and distinct against the darkness. Perhaps it was a rent or a gap in time. Two curious loops suspended in the air, open-ended on both sides, the lower one bathed in strange ethereal light and the inside of the top loop a dark entity apart from the outline. The number eight. It was puzzling and utterly fascinating.

Soon there was a sound, very low and deep and sonorous coming from the bottom part of the figure eight. The five or six people that had tended the fire stood back, not afraid, but rather in eager anticipation of something. They were clearly waiting. I fell away into the darkness beyond the circle of fire and stood among a corridor of pines, their darkness a deeper darkness against the black of night. There was no moonlight. There was just the bonfire, still blazing and brilliant, and the curious, impossible figure eight.

Suddenly I noticed the small number of the fire tenders gathering near the bottom part of the figure eight. They were standing and ready for something that was about to happen. Then, a naked man descended from the bottom open circle, spectral in the firelight despite the illumination of the number 8. He was followed by a woman, also naked, and then another man, and another, and still another. They hopped easily to the ground and moved to one side, and as the group grew larger and larger they linked hands and spread apart gradually circling the bonfire, still blazing and bright with sparks flying high into the air. Dozens more issued in silent succession from the bottom part of the figure eight and joined the circle around the fire until at least 70 or 80 souls made it complete. They were men and women in their prime, possibly in their early twenties. They looked strong and fit and their bodies appeared to be covered with a light oil or ointment of some kind. They formed a pale chain with their linked hands and began moving in a silent, slow dance around the fire. They were moving in a counter clockwise direction, and whenever any one of them wavered or almost tripped or lost step, they were steadied by someone from among those who had started and maintained the fire. The paleness of the dancers dissipated gradually, slowly, and then they came to a stop for a moment. In the stillness of that moment something changed, the pivotal moment held in abeyance for a period of time, and then turned. A great transformation was happening before my very eyes. They began to move in a purposeful clockwise direction with cross-linked arms, and as they did so, a rosy glow emanated from their naked bodies. Their physical condition was splendid.

They were of all body types and sizes. It was a pleasure to see them. They seemed to glisten with strength and health. Their flesh was tight to the bone. I saw them looking at each other and smiling. Everything was so silent and strange to me. I didn't know what to make of it. The circle dance continued for some time, developing a certain rhythm, and I was struck by the beauty and magnificence of the sight with the dancers glowing with robust health, and moving around the bonfire. The strange thing was that I could hear no music but they obviously did.

I heard steps behind me and turned to find Davor smiling excitedly and lifting his hand to shake mine. I didn't know what to say and simply waved my arm at the bizarre scene in front of us.

"I wanted you to see how it all begins. This is the first event of its kind. I wanted you to know what you are getting into. It is a strange new world before you, unlike anything you've seen. What do you think Kristof?"

"It can't be happening. All of this. Is it real? Am I in a strange, waking dream?"

"No. What you see before you is happening now, here in this place, right in front of you. These are souls from the past become living again for a time. As I've told you before, they have waited through at least two hundred years of incubation to come again and deal with something they left unfinished or unresolved somehow. You will help them fulfill their destiny, their truest desire."

Davor turned his head and watched as the naked figures gradually left the circle and walked towards a large tent by the Mediterranean garden. They formed a line at the entrance and slowly moved in. In a few moments all of them had entered the tent.

"They will dress and then we will depart the island. Zora and others are there to help them. We have a ferry waiting, and from Fažana, buses will take us to accommodation on the outskirts of Pula. From there we move throughout Croatia, both spirits and spirit guides with them. There are about eight other spirit guides like you. Oh, before we leave there is a gentleman I want you to meet."

Davor took me by the arm and led me to a spot just outside the tent. There I saw a compact little man who stood smiling, with his hands in his pockets, obviously pleased with the activities around him. Several people stood near to him and behind him as if part of his entourage. Davor strode up to him and then stopped, hoping to get his attention. The little man smiled broadly when he recognized Davor. He was very thin and short with a strong aquiline nose and large ears.

"Davor, my friend, what a splendid night this is for everyone."

"Mr. Šubić, it certainly is. I wanted to introduce you to one of our spirit guides, Kristof Radelja, from Canada." I was somewhat surprised at the deference in Davor's voice as he spoke to the man. Davor obviously respected and admired him very much.

"Ah, it is a pleasure," he said, taking my hand in his and shaking it firmly. "We have excellent representation from our diaspora. We have spirit guides from Chile, Argentina, Australia, New Zealand, and the United States. Others too, from Europe. Without you, we could not be successful. That is a given. Thank you and welcome."

Everyone surrounding him was a full head taller and much heavier, but they waited on every word he said. He spoke with quiet authority and commanded a presence I have encountered with only two other people I have met in my lifetime. A tall, lanky man next to him whispered something in his ear, and he excused himself graciously, and then entered the tent to a great roar of approval. The canvas flap of the tent opening fell closed behind him.

Davor beamed delightedly and said that we must be off. Together we made our way to the small harbour. I was speechless still trying to make sense of what I'd seen. Davor placed his arm around my shoulder, and then tousled my hair with his hand and chuckled softly. I barely knew I was walking, my mind was so disordered with what I had seen.

Later that same night Davor came to my apartment in Pula. He was excited and obviously moved by what had happened.

"Kristof, now is your time. You and the other spirit guides will be assisting the spirits you saw this evening. We have only several weeks before these spirits must return, so our time is precious. Two hundred years to get here. A week or so to do their business, spread over a few months, and then they're gone forever. So, are you ready my friend?"

I was still totally confused and not a little frightened, but I nodded to him and then grew quiet. What I had seen on Brijuni was fantastical, beyond anything I had ever witnessed before. These were not thin ghosts hovering about haunting old houses. Neither were they zombies lurching about seeking blood victims. These were returned spirits seeking redemption and peace, the peace that passes understanding. How could I help them I wondered? I knew I had come this far, and I wanted to go all the way.

Davor patiently outlined what would happen. I would be given what he called client spirits to work with. Tentative schedules had been drawn up, and locations selected across Croatia where I would meet with individual spirits, establish a rapport, and guide them through the necessary memory images until the requisite changes were facilitated. Zora would organize the events. He spent a considerable amount of time warning me of dangers from Malek and others. He didn't explain why. He said it came with the territory, the no-man's land between life and death that had suddenly opened up with the arrival of these spirits from the past. He spoke of the breakthrough that had been accomplished between life and death, and how we were in the vanguard of a new era in human experience. There were tears in his eyes as he spoke, and I noticed he was trembling. Finally, Davor wished me a good night, embraced me warmly, and then left.

Early the next morning I sat on the couch in my apartment and thought about the night before and the countless nights and days before that. History is nothing more than an accumulation of personal, private events that become shared public knowledge and, in time, are taken for granted as truth. It's an old story. The party that wins writes the history. But you can't consider it to be the final truth. Truth is as evanescent, as mercurial, and changing as a swallow in flight. I remembered the Rebecca West book that I had thumbed through once in Davor's apartment. There was a passage that said sometimes it is very hard to tell the difference between history and the smell of skunk.

The only truth is personal experience, and there are as many aspects to it as there are blades of grass in a verdant meadow. Each spirit is a blade of grass with perhaps an unfinished story to tell. That's why many linger here, the ghosts, between life and peace, and then other more focused spirits waiting for release at the very gates of mystery and potent darkness. Davor had helped me out a lot, but I was beginning to figure things out for myself.

History leaves behind a sticky mess. Some spirits, can't let go of life entirely because of some incompletion. Perhaps that's what I was seeing there in that enchanted kolo dance on Brijuni, certain spiritual residues become living for a time, become particles of flesh once again to make amends or to pursue something that they'd left unfinished, or whatever. I wasn't afraid. I was intensely curious. I was connected. And for the first time in a long time, I was content.

♦ ♦ ♦

The next few days were a blur. I wandered through the streets of Pula for hours, amazed at what I had seen on Brijuni. Twice, I accidentally bumped into people, my mind in overdrive. Nothing in my life before that day had prepared me for it. Nothing. The figure eight gateway that had opened life's door to the long dead. The deep mysteries of it. Returned spirits kolo dancing back into life with vigor and youth and purpose. The wonder of it. And now I was a part of it all, a spirit guide, and I felt surcharged with new energy. I slept well that night.

The next day while I was shopping for vegetables at the downtown market I chanced to see Sam Stark standing alone and staring into space, quite oblivious that I was a pace or two away. He seemed stunned for a moment and then recovered his composure. He supported himself on crutches and there was a cast on his left leg. He gave me a warm greeting and then abruptly said that he needed to talk to me urgently, and did I have time to talk with him right then. I asked him what had happened to his leg. He dismissed my comment with a shake of his head and said he had witnessed something terrible. I don't know why he felt he could confide in me. Perhaps because I had related to him as a man when we had first met in the park. I suppose many people saw only a dwarf when they looked at him. An oddity, something strange and bizarre somehow, a curious anomaly. But I saw a human being, an American named Sam Stark, an inch under three feet, who needed to free his conscience and share what he had witnessed. I wish in retrospect he hadn't chosen me, but he did. When we went for coffee at a nearby backstreet café near the Temple of Augustus I could see the torment in his face and the cast on his broken leg. He leaned his crutches against an empty chair and ordered a double brandy, and began by talking, rather nervously, about football, American football, and the New England Patriots. He was an ardent fan and he raved about the team. I think it gave him solace somehow, to talk about players and quote stats, details that took him away from the hard reality of his recent experience. But then he suddenly looked away from me, his eyes downcast, as if culling up sharp memories. Suddenly, he started talking about Malek and his yacht, Light Sabre, where three days earlier they had been cruising several nautical kilometers west of Brijuni.

"Malek was at the wheel on the bridge. He snapped his fingers and bid me come to him. I didn't know what he wanted me to do at first. He told me to fetch night vision goggles for us. I saw him nod curtly to Lars and then gesture with his arms as if holding a rifle. Lars left immediately knowing what he wanted and hurried off. I was puzzled. Malek smiled oddly at me and winked."

I noticed that Sam was writhing in his seat as he spoke, viscerally upset with the images that he was dredging up. It was as if he was reliving moments of intense discomfort and shock.

"It was about three in the morning and we had been drinking French cognac all night. I watched him set up his high-powered rifle and adjust his night vision scope. I didn't have a clue as to what he was going to shoot. He instructed me to put on the night vision goggles I had brought forward and to report on what he referred to as his target accuracy. I thought he might be shooting at buoys in the water or something like that. But, when I had the goggles on and looked through the green telescopic lenses, I couldn't believe my eyes. There were about two or three dozen people, men and women and children all huddled together in a large rubber dinghy. But migrants had never come so far north. After all, we were in the Adriatic Sea. I looked again and confirmed that it was so. I was stunned and confused. What was Malek going to do? Several moments passed before I heard the sharp reports of the first shots. I watched dumbstruck as bodies fell into the sea, again and again, large bodies and small bodies. There was no sound coming from them. We were too far away from them to hear any cries. I saw the bodies on the boat scrambling to take cover, pushing each other to find a place to hide, but there was nowhere to go. Malek shouted that he wanted me to give him a rough count of targets hit. That's how he put it. Targets hit. As if this was sport, a game. I remember how he cursed them and called them soft, pathetic invaders, dark interlopers. The man was so calm and poised. It was incredible to me, beyond belief. I just reacted instinctively. I ripped off the goggles and ran to Malek to get him to stop. I grabbed at his pant leg and saw him take the butt of his rifle and smash it against my head. That was the last I remember before I fell to the floor unconscious. When I came to I was in a galley pantry with pots and pans all around me, pressing into my flesh. I couldn't move. I cried out but no one came to help me. Later, when I could feel the yacht engine slowing and getting ready to dock, the pantry door swung open and Lars grabbed me by the neck and hauled me out to the top deck. It was just before sunrise and there was no one about in the harbor. I was crying out for Lars to let me go. Malek ordered Lars to toss me onto the concrete dock, two stories below the deck on which I stood. I couldn't believe Lars was doing this to me. He was my friend. He threw me away like I was a bag of garbage. I broke my leg when I landed but I scrambled like an animal as best I could to get away. Malek was crazy and I feared for my life. I haven't gone to the police because I know what the man is capable of. I guess I'm a coward. I'm leaving town tonight, but I had to tell somebody. Maybe you can do something. Maybe you can tell my story to the police. Please help me Christopher. Please!"

I tried my best to calm him down, but he was distraught and troubled. I asked him if he wanted another drink, but he just laughed, grabbed his tiny crutches, nodded a hasty farewell, and hobbled away. I was confused. What was I to do? Did it actually happen? Should I go to the police?

On the way back to my apartment I saw a group of people huddled around a newspaper kiosk and talking very loudly in Croatian. I could hear the tone of horror and surprise in their voices. It was unmistakable. I approached a young man who was shaking his head in disbelief and I asked him what had happened. He spoke in rapid fire Croatian telling me a boatload of migrants had been shot at leaving only three survivors from a group of thirty. He said that it was very unusual for migrants to be found so far north and at sea near Rovinj. Apparently, the survivors had told the authorities that they had been shot at in the middle of the night. Even those who had jumped overboard were picked off. They had hoped to reach Germany. The group was mainly Syrian and Afghani but there were a few sub-Saharan women and children as well aboard a rubber dingy.

I made my way to a police station, and for a few moments I simply stood at the entrance wondering what I was going to do. What was I to say? I wasn't a witness. I had no proof. I had heard Sam's testimony but that was all. Sam was gone, and would probably leave Pula that very day. I was feeling a bit silly, but tossed my doubts aside and entered. I gave my second-hand report to the duty officer who asked me for more details regarding Sam's whereabouts and passport information, both of which I didn't have. He asked for a physical description and when I said he was a dwarf who wore a satin jacket and pants with an American flag motif, he raised his eyebrows and looked across the office at a colleague who was listening intently and looked hugely amused. My mention of Malek seemed to tweak his interest, but only momentarily. The officer then asked for my passport details, my current address, and said he would be in touch. After that I put the entire episode away and forgot about it. I'd done what I could which wasn't much, but it was something and I felt better for it.

◆ ◆ ◆

The next morning, after a huge breakfast and several cups of coffee, I began to think of my role and my new responsibilities. Suddenly I found myself in it. I remembered that silly action of Davor's in his apartment-ripping a sheet of paper to show a different plane of existence. But here I was about to enter that different plane. My old life and the memories of it were a different country. Now I was involved in a daring adventure with spirits from the past. With Davor as my guide, I would be interfacing with the dead. Illyrians, Romans, Venetians, Ottoman Turks and sundry others. But what good could I do in the face of spoilers like Malek and his minions. I began to realize that evil, the capacity for evil was much greater in some people than others. The evil I possessed was probably trite compared to Malek's, but maybe I could use it, my own capacity for evil, harness it somehow in my new life. Perhaps you can only fight evil effectively with evil. I realized I was living more intensely than I had ever lived before. I was charged with new life to my fingertips, and it was a great and powerful experience.

Over the next few days I practiced my skills with different ghost sightings. It was here, in the outdoor café overlooking the barred Arena that I had felt a gentle wind just before nightfall and then had seen the three ghosts. They were on the café patio and visible to me but I could tell they were not real, they did not have the appearance of flesh and blood creatures. They appeared faded somehow, but were just visible to me, little more.

The three ghosts appeared to mingle and pass through each other, totally oblivious of one another. Within that charmed circle the physical place was constant, about thirty feet in diameter, but the time was not. The ghosts were dressed differently. One, a Roman centurion in full battle dress was sharpening his sword, the second appeared to be a pirate drinking wine from a leather-skin, and the third, a young Illyrian woman wearing homespun cloth and carrying brown eggs in a basket. They were walking about and through each other, gesturing and performing the separate tasks on their own and within their own time, but within the same space. Three lives from the past, from different eras, super-imposed on each other but not interfering with each other. All of the movements were fluid and natural and, while all this was going on I felt an airy lightness move through me followed by a curious tingling sensation, the way you feel when you bump your elbow hard against something, but it was my whole body tingling, not just my elbow. I don't know if those perceptions of mine can be called fact, but I experienced them and they occurred. I would bet my life on it.

I found that technique wasn't as important as a compassionate sensibility. All of a sudden I'd catch a glimpse of one, of a spirit, just at the periphery of my vision. Almost a shadow, but not quite. I began to realize the interplay, if you could call it that, between them and myself. If you opened yourself up to it, you could move between the living and the dead, between the living presence of people there before you, alive and accessible, and then dead, the spirits of the dead. As I understood it, from what Davor had told me, they wanted help in addressing issues from their former lives. Otherwise, they had nothing invested in the land between life and death but quiet eternal desperation, an eternal limbo. I have to admit that memory befuddled me, because through memory, the dead become alive again, in the objects they left behind, in remembered images, in sounds such as familiar voices and in movement, in the way someone moved when they were alive.

When I thought about the spirits I had encountered, I remembered the journals I had kept for years. When I read them, decades after I'd written them, it was like dipping into a stranger's life, but it was I, I who was the stranger to myself. And if I was a stranger to myself, then how different was that from the strange spirits I would encounter in my travels?

There were all kinds of spirits and ghosts just as there are all kinds of people. There were ghosts that hung around places that they had lived in and just couldn't leave completely. The kind that haunted places. Then there were the grand spirits that wanted a second chance, an opportunity to return to life and correct something.

I had lots of fun with the ghosts. They were harmless enough. They just wanted to be a part of what was happening. Sometimes it just takes a knowing, confident glance and then they stand rooted to the spot. Each of them is uncomfortable when I've seen them and caught them at their game, shadows of the past, sometimes dressed as tourists. The perfect disguise, tourists of all things. These ghost pretenders to life and sentient being. I was trying to understand them, the way Davor said I should. I learned that even ghosts have fears. That's why they're caught between life and peace. Certain things are quite disheartening for them. Dogs and cats, for instance, can smell their non-smell, the absence of it. It struck me as so hilarious to see a group of ghosts fleeing in panic all at once from a small barking dog. They were all of them different, ghosts and spirits. And I was aware of them individually, especially the friendly spirits that surrounded me in my quest for understanding, and they were not to be dismissed. I had the distinct feeling that some spirits around me were vying for ascendancy. That may sound odd, but I believe they struggled with each other to get my attention. They needed me to help them somehow. It began with a grand, heavy silence, a pregnant silence enveloping myriad voices bent on being heard. And then one of the spirits would break through, wanting to engage. Oddly, I wasn't afraid. After all, I wasn't alone. Davor was my friend.

Davor was a kind of matchmaker between the spirit world and the living, material world. In fact he often quoted Sting, saying that we living beings were "spirits in the material." He was a kind of high administrator of souls, connecting people like myself with a counterpart spirit, someone I could help. Not the ghosts of course, but the ones who took the long journey back to life after two hundred years, the true spirits. But Davor knew that any kind of assistance given was fraught with danger. Both from the living and the dead. He often mentioned Malek's name.

I've never thought much about evil. I mean I guess it's a concept like goodness. I needed to think it through. Most people don't get up in the morning thinking that they're going to do good or do evil. They may commit small acts of kindness like giving a homeless person enough money for a meal, or they rip someone off, or steal a purse, but is that evil? I don't know. It seems to me that goodness or evil depends on the scale of the event, whether good or bad, and on its repetition. What the Nazis did to the Jews and others during the Second World War was evil, pure and simple, on a colossal scale. What Malek did to the innocent migrants for sport was evil. What Malek wanted to do to the returned spirits was evil. Why should it matter to him if some lost soul wanted to return and change an outcome that had left them desolate and in a kind of dark limbo. But it did matter to him. He did it for some reason and sooner or later I'd find out. I don't understand evil but it's plain to see the results. But knowing that, knowing that evil exists motivates me to oppose it, and I will. I'll oppose it on any scale.

◆ ◆ ◆

I walked up the hill behind the Coliseum to my apartment. I wanted to prepare myself a light dinner before heading to the library downtown to hear Malek's lecture. After what Sam had told me I was more than a little curious about Malek and his activities. Davor had warned me about him, but I needed to get another reading of the man. What was he about? Had he actually killed migrants as Sam had stated? After what I had seen on Brijuni anything was possible.

As I walked up the stairs to my apartment, the landlord's mother opened her apartment door next to mine, looked at me warmly, and said I had a guest, a special guest that she had allowed into my apartment. She hoped I would understand. Then she withdrew, smiling and pleased with herself.

You can imagine my surprise when I saw who was sitting on the black leather couch.

"Gloria!" I was dumbfounded and totally taken aback.

She rose up from the couch, tiptoed over to me and gave me a peck on the cheek. She asked if I wanted coffee. She looked the same as always, very fit and petite, her strawberry blonde hair done in the latest style. But I felt nothing.

"What are you doing here?" I said.

"Well, since you didn't answer my last e-mail, I thought I'd surprise you. After all, you must be lonely here all by yourself. You are by yourself, aren't you?" She gave me a look that I had almost forgotten, mild curiosity coupled with condescension.

"I have some friends. I'm not lonely. How's Peter? Have you heard from him?"

"He keeps to himself like you. He said to say hello to you. He's in Iraq for a few months."

"I miss him."

"Did you miss me at all?"

"I thought we were through all that Gloria. It's over."

"Doesn't have to be. We can take another kick at the can." There was a hopeful look in her eyes, but I'd seen it before. Another of her affairs had crashed and burned, and I was a known commodity though not an exciting one.

"No." The word felt cold, tired, and spent in my throat. It was the truest word I have ever uttered.

"Well, you can still show me around Pula, can't you? I have a reservation at a hotel downtown. Since I'm here I might as well see the place."

She didn't appear disappointed. She hardly missed a beat. She turned away from me and began to prepare some coffee.

"Sure, we can do that. That'd be fine."

I was relieved that she hadn't brought any luggage with her. I told her about the lecture, and she shrugged and said that might be nice.

◆ ◆ ◆

The Pula library was a large open concept structure, spread across different levels, with floor to ceiling windows offering good views of the street outside. It was early evening. The venue was packed and we had to wait for folding chairs to be brought to us near the back of the library where we had entered. As Gloria and I took our seats, an elderly gentleman was introducing Malek and talking about the work of the Academy of Light Foundation. He said that, as Chairman of the Board, he had never met such an emissary of light before. That was the term he used, and he used it repeatedly. He was dressed like an EU dignitary in a dark gray bespoke suit, crisp white shirt, and crimson tie.

"You are a point of light in our lives. An emissary of light, and we are grateful."

Malek sat smiling behind the lectern with his arms and legs crossed. He was wearing a dark blue outfit buttoned at the neck that was more a uniform than a suit. The buttons were silver.

I have to admit he was an engaging speaker, modulating his voice to match the content of his speech, and using expressive gestures to quietly emphasize his key points.

As always with speeches, my attention drifted in and out, but every now and then I caught a phrase or sentence that struck a responsive chord.

"The grosser parts of our nature want to destroy civilization, want to extinguish the light and leave nothing behind but darkness and a sorry materialism."

As he spoke I could see that he made eye contact with different sections of the audience. When I looked around I noticed that the audience was relatively young and I thought, quite attractive. In the first two rows there were a number of strikingly beautiful women and several handsome young men. I glanced at Gloria and I could see she was impressed. She was twitching with excitement.

"Even the dead, if such were the case, if they could return to the world, would steal the light of our day and destroy our hard won gains, leaving a stagnant, fetid heaviness behind. And others, living interlopers, come here from afar, from the dark regions of the world to push us out, and take our places. They too would cripple the sources of our light. You and I know what has happened recently to a boatload of migrants, the tragedy that has befallen them. We must prevent this by looking at the source, by being proactive and stopping the trapdoors from whence they came. We must stop this traffic of desperate lives that flood our shores. These dark voyages must stop. "

He continued on for some time in the same vein, repeating his key points and calibrating the cadence, emphasis, and volume of his voice to the reactions of the crowd. When he concluded, the audience gave him a lengthy round of applause, and two or three individuals rose from their seats. He was an eloquent speaker but what he said was so abstract and metaphorical. It was bosh. Gloria too was clapping wildly. I hadn't seen her so animated in a long time.

He mingled with the crowd, spending a few moments with individuals and small groups who clearly idolized him. There was a banquet table with wine, cheese, and crackers that people were enjoying. I noticed three tall, burly fellows maneuvered him through the crowd towards the exit when he caught sight of me and waved me over. I introduced him to Gloria.

"Christopher, I am so happy you could attend. And you, dear lady, I hope I did not bore you."

"There was never any danger of that Mr. Malek. Each word was clear and bright. Your audience hung on every word."

"Please call me Malek, just that. I am honoured that you should say that. You must spend more time with us. Are you here in Pula for very long?"

"Gloria is visiting for a week, to see the sights."

"Well then, you are both welcome to join me on a tour. I have a yacht in the harbor that will be out and about over the next few days. Please come.

Let me give you my card. It has my contact number and coordinates, and now, please forgive me, but I must meet with the Chairman and board members."

His bodyguards ushered him away, and I followed with Gloria. We watched as the door of a white stretch limo opened and drove him off. She was very excited and we went to her hotel for a drink. She couldn't stop talking about him. She was clearly enamored. She suggested we call him the next day, but I demurred. I had things to do with Davor and Zora. Besides that, the man was a danger. Now, I believed what Sam had told me about him. He had killed people, desperate migrants, their lives and dreams cut short by his bizarre credo. I tried to dissuade Gloria, but I could tell she was hell bent on seeing him again. We had a second drink together, reminisced about Peter, and then I left for my apartment, and she to her hotel. It was good to be on my own. So good.

♦ ♦ ♦

She called me the next day saying she was free for the day and, could we spend some time together, for she would be away on a tour with Malek after that, before she left for home. I agreed and suggested we tour the Coliseum and stop at my favorite café afterwards. She didn't think much about the Coliseum, saying she'd like to see a concert there, but an empty collection of old stones didn't do it for her.

♦ ♦ ♦

Zora had agreed to meet me at our usual café by the Coliseum. She smiled warmly at Gloria as I introduced her. I explained that Gloria had come for only a short visit and just wanted to see a few of the sights before returning to Canada. I remembered telling Zora that I was separated. Zora's eyes were appraising and reflective, trying to get the measure of Gloria as she sipped at her espresso.

"It is so good to meet you. But you leave in a few days. That is unfortunate. Kristof could use some company."

70

"Kristof? Oh, you mean Christopher. Our relationship is quite independent in nature. As an insurance executive I travel quite often, so distance is a given for us. But tell me Zora, what kind of work do you do?"

I could see that Gloria didn't want to talk about our separation, and I was just as glad. It would have been too awkward.

"I'm an events planner, festivals, conferences, reunions, and the like, " Zora said. "It keeps me quite busy."

"Are you married?"

"I was, but fortunately, that is terminated."

"Oh, I'm sorry."

"Don't be. I'm certainly not."

Gloria smiled wickedly and sipped her café au lait, her eyes sparkling with merriment.

Later we chatted about Gloria's plans to tour with Malek, and I could see Zora was keenly interested in where they might be sailing. She peppered Gloria with questions, but Gloria didn't really know if there was a set itinerary and said she didn't really care. She simply shrugged. Gloria had a way of shrugging her shoulders and looking askance that closed a topic of conversation abruptly, like the metal clasp on a purse closing shut with a loud definitive snap. It was intriguing for me to be in the company of two women who were powerful in themselves in different ways. The two of them were very reserved with each other, wary and careful, like wrestlers in a ring circling each other, though why they should be puzzled me.

◆ ◆ ◆

I walked down to Gloria's hotel the morning of her departure to say good-bye. A black limo parked in the hotel driveway was waiting for an additional passenger for the drive to the airport. We stood together in the lobby, waiting. It felt like the end of something, and I was sad, but there was little to be said. I saw a tear in her eye, or moisture at least, but I knew it was probably rehearsed that morning, like a Hollywood movie ending.

"Did you enjoy the outing with Malek?" I asked, looking into her eyes and marveling at how green and pellucid they were.

"Yes, it was fun, but not what I expected. He was very curious about you, about your background, and about your relationship with someone called Davor, whoever that is. He talked on and on about particles of light. It seemed to me he was lecturing all the time, on display and guarded. He certainly didn't have any love interests though there were enough beautiful people about, men and women, hanging on his every word. I was quite surprised at that."

"Well, I hope this short trip was good for you, regardless. I hope you leave with a few good memories of Croatia."

As I said this, I looked down into her eyes and the most curious thing happened. There were a few sharp flashes of light crossing my field of vision, and then I could see an image forming on her retinas. I thought immediately of Dr. Spehar and what he had told me of Tesla's concept that the image of a thing formed by thinking must by a kind of reflex action produce a corresponding image on the retina that can potentially be projected on a screen if a suitable apparatus or instrument existed. But I was the receiving apparatus, and I could see several images on her retina, happening in rapid succession. Within the space of a few seconds I could see into her mind, into what she was thinking. I looked down into her deep green eyes and saw her on a small bunk making love to the tall Swede I had seen with Malek and his entourage. She was on the yacht. It was so clear, so irrevocably clear to me. I even saw the small red rose tattoo that Gloria had on the back of her hip. It had been a long time since I had seen it, or had wanted to.

I looked away and then back again at her. The images I had seen were no longer there. The limo driver signaled he was ready to load her luggage. I helped her with her bags, gave her a light peck on the cheek, and then she was off and away. Gone. I was surprised at what had just happened. Not at Gloria's behavior mind you, but at my experience with Tesla's innovative idea. I had proven it. I had been able to see Gloria's thoughts as she thought and remembered them.

◆ ◆ ◆

I trudged back to my apartment, somewhat melancholy I have to admit, but with a new, untrammelled resolve. I was a free man, and the world seemed an open book. My work with spirits would begin soon, and I had money in the bank. Later that day I was to meet with Zora to discuss the how and when of my interventions with the returned spirits.

❖ ❖ ❖

She saw me before I saw her, and she waved. The Castle Bar was empty save for the two of us. There is nothing like the attention of a beautiful woman to make you forget a shattered love, the wreck of a misbegotten marriage, love memories turned sour, to make you leave these behind, far behind, and to savor the living moment with one as beautiful as Zora. Gloria Mundi was fading from memory and before me was the promise of new life. Not with Zora of course. She was the goddess of my dreams, the goddess at the gate of my new life. Unattainable, beyond my reach. We were friends, and I could warm my hands before the fire of her dazzling beauty without plunging into the flaming vortex of unrequited love. It was enough for me to sit across from her and sip strong espresso.

Zora looked at me appraisingly for a moment, and then smiled softly before she spoke. "So, Gloria has returned and you are alone once again, but I thought that would happen. What brings us together in a relationship is not the same thing as that which tears us apart. But you are with us, and our work begins here. Everything is in flux just now. Kristof, you must exercise extreme caution. Your itinerary can and will change on a moment's notice. The spirits you will be working with have already left for different destinations across Croatia. I've arranged accommodation for you in the places where you will meet them. I will text you the details once things are set in motion. Our local intelligence confirms Malek's intentions to thwart us."

"But why?"

"Who knows the whys and wherefores? He sees us as a direct threat to him and his host group. We know now that he killed the migrants, leaving only three survivors clinging to wreckage in the water. Somehow he had heard rumours about Brijuni and the returned spirits. From a source near him we've learned he fears the spirits and the opposition they pose to his

73

bizarre philosophy. Total nonsense. For now we must act defensively and lay low. He wants to disrupt our work, but we don't know his methods yet. "

I recounted to her my strange meeting with Sam who had witnessed the migrant carnage and was returning home, fearing for his life. She nodded and sighed deeply.

"We have already moved the survivors to a safe house and will see they reach Germany within a day or two. That was their only wish."

She talked to me of other things then, about the orientation she had given to the spirits and the cultural adjustments they had to make, about her fears and hopes for them. I could hardly believe it had begun. I was ready for it, and asked if she wanted a bit of wine.

I am always amazed at how the smallest action can act like a pivot and change a life. You go about your day-to-day activities, not thinking much of anything at all, and then it happens.

Zora winked at me. She winked at me at 9:08 p.m. in the Castle Bar. I had just brought her a glass of Istrian red wine from the bar where the digital time display read 9:08 in bright red numbers. For days and months nothing significant had happened to me, and then in a single moment everything changed for me. Zora winked at me. And in that moment, in the very second that she winked at me, I believed I had a chance with her, as something more than a familiar friend. The world shifted for me in that moment, like a tectonic plate. It was as if in the blink of an eye, a great door had opened. It was a blink and a door of invitation. I was sure of that. It was a slow blink and not a cursory, common gesture like a nod. The provenance of that blink, the source of it, was from distant Illyrian times, from a well as deep as humanity itself. A stone gate was flung open and beyond it were natural gardens of delight and devotion. A great beauty had blinked an invitation, and it felt like a great new sun shone upon me despite the darkness. Sic transit Gloria mundi.

◆ ◆ ◆

The next evening I returned to Davor's apartment situated on the hill just behind the Arena. I knocked at the great wooden door with its heavy iron studs and waited. A few moments passed, and I knocked again, harder, and with more purpose. Soon the massive door swung open, and there was Davor, smiling and welcoming, despite his habitual wistfulness. I followed him up the dark staircase and into his well-lit kitchen-living room. He motioned to the couch, and I sat down. He excused himself for a moment and returned with a small white canvas bag. I could tell a few objects were within it. He swung it before me like a priest's censer, a mischievous gleam in his eyes, and then laid it gently on the glass coffee table just off the kitchen area.

"For the journey, for your Croatian adventure," he said.

"Once you leave this apartment, go directly home and pack. You must leave early tomorrow morning. Zora will text you your destination. Just take your carry-on with a change of clothing and the bare essentials, including this bag. Leave the rest behind. I warn you that Malek will be sending operatives after you once he finds out you've left Pula. I wish I could be with you, but too much needs to be done here to stop Malek, or at least slow him down. I've given you the bag. Become familiar with its contents. They are your tools. You can figure things out on your own. Determine the best ways to use them. You can do it. You're a clever man."

What was in the bag I couldn't imagine. What were the kinds of things Davor would think I might need? Why wouldn't he tell me how to use them? But then Davor was a strange man, and as I was beginning to realize, so was I. I was very curious about the contents of the bag. We had coffee and talked about my meeting with Zora and where I had been, but little else. And then his voice lowered and he began to speak. But he spoke of nothing but trivialities. The excellent crepes by the Temple of Augustus; the view from the Citadel; the wonderful crimson poppies and dandelions by the ancient Roman theater. He kept rambling on and on. I could tell he was nervous. Usually, he appeared quite confident and would tell me an anecdote or two to illustrate his points, but not tonight. Things had changed for him, and I realized, for me as well.

Beneath our superficial conversation, I was growing more and more curious about the bag. I wondered what was in it and why he wanted me to take it on my journey. Was it heavy? Was it light? At least it wasn't a pig in a poke. There was no movement within it as it lay on the glass coffee table. Nothing animate. But Davor was an interesting man, and so whatever it was, I knew it would be of value to me. He was my guide to an uncertain world, a world growing stranger by the minute. He took the bag from the table and shoved it in my arms. It felt light.

Davor stood up abruptly then and ushered me to his door. Before he opened the door, he looked at me, poignantly, I thought, and then he embraced me, hugging me for the longest time, kissing me on both cheeks, as if it were the last time we would meet, and then abruptly, I was walking home through the cool, night air. I sensed that I was on my way to a far different world.

I hurried home from Davor's apartment. I was very curious about what was in the bag. I couldn't wait to check it out. I scrambled up the stairs to my apartment, unlocked the door, flicked on the light switch, and sat on the couch. I unraveled the drawstring on the canvas bag and emptied the contents on the cushion beside me.

The first thing I noticed were two stones. Odd to see that. They were smooth round stones, beach stones, but quite large like a souvenir from an excursion to the seashore, something you bring home and then immediately forget where you found them. I puzzled over that, wondering over what significance and use they could have as I rolled them together in my hand. And then a dagger caught my eye. I withdrew it from its rich brown leather sheath and saw that the blade, about six inches long, was iridescent and incredibly beautiful. It looked like a Byzantine dagger, something you'd see in a museum. It shimmered green and golden in the light and was wonderfully crafted. The tip of it, when you looked at it straight on, was so tiny and infinitisimal that it seemed that it could penetrate anything. I dared not touch the blade for it looked devilishly sharp. The hilt was wonderfully carved with strange braided designs upon it that looked Celtic. The dagger felt very comfortable in my hand, truly like an extension of my arm. I carefully returned it to the sheath and set it down carefully.

Next I saw a silver arm bracelet, highly polished, with a simple line drawing etched into it of a circle closing in upon itself , growing smaller and smaller, and then stopping. I slipped it over my wrist and it fit perfectly.

Then I removed it and held it in front of the lamplight admiring the exquisite beauty and craftsmanship of the piece. How it could ever be of use to me I could not figure out, but it was a thing of rare beauty.

The last item was a coin, small and polished to a high golden shine. It looked antique Roman with strange markings on it.

I lay back on my bed and thought about what had transpired. That's why he gave me the canvas bag with objects in it, without any explanation. He wanted me to figure things out for myself. He had never once mentioned to me the objects in the bag, what they were, or how I could use them. He was always so playful despite the underlying sadness he carried around with him like a dark, worn cloak. He asked me once how being rich would change my state. Roman gold and glory, money, he said often, had caused more grief than good. He hoped I would use the money well. He had handed me a bank account book, and said it was mine. I glanced in it seeing the deposit Dr. Spehar had promised. Davor said with a smile that whenever I was thinking about money he could see it in my face. He said I had money wrinkles lining my forehead. I didn't have the boldness to tell him that it was always I who had paid the bills whenever we went out to cafes or restaurants. Perhaps that's why I had the wrinkles I thought.

Spirit Voices

Part Three

1667 Dubrovnik, Mia

SOMEWHERE I READ THAT THE past is another country. If that's the case then the future is too, another country I mean. Countries of time, past and future. I was sitting in the plushly upholstered seat of the high speed catamaran heading south along the Dalmatian coast. I was in a mournful, speculative mood because of what had happened. To my left were the dark mountains of the coast keeping their secrets hidden, keeping untold stories from the light of day. It reminded me of the painting by Vlaho Bukovac in the Moderna Galerija in Zagreb, the one of the poet Gundulić dreaming of Osman. At first glance the painting looks idyllic and romantic. But then you look again and see the carnage in the mist, the terrible scenes of rape, torture, and murder. I wondered if some of the spirits I had seen on Brijuni were from the folds and valleys of this very coast.

Davor would know, and I wished he was here with me now. But that was not to be. He was gone forever and lived in the country of the past, and in the farthest country of all, death.

Zora had texted me that Davor was dead. She had said not to return to Pula, that she would tell me when it was safe to come back. Safe. What she hadn't told me was what I knew in my heart, that Malek was responsible for his death. A tragic car accident she had written. A speeding white van, a cargo van with no windows except in the front of the vehicle, had run him down near the Coliseum just after midnight as he was returning from a bar. A hit and run accident. A witness reported that the van was being driven erratically without any headlights on. After he was hit the van sped away. And that was that.

I tried to push the fact of Davor's death from my mind, but try as I might, the pit of my stomach felt hollow with an emptiness I hadn't felt since my father died. Zora had also texted me that I was to meet Mia in Dubrovnik. Zora had told me to prepare myself for the meeting. I focused on that and it helped me, but how I missed him. I missed hearing his anecdotes and seeing the subtle and sad expressions on his face. But I knew I must follow along with the work that I had to do. And nothing would get in the way of that.

The first thing I did once the high sped catamaran, the Krilo Star, had anchored near Dubrovnik was to take a cab from the harbour in Gruz to the ancient walled city, resplendent in the late afternoon sunlight. It felt good to be there.

As I walked with my luggage in tow along the Stradun, the main street within the city walls, I thought more about Davor. That last meeting with him in his apartment, when he had rambled on about various things, perhaps then he had an inkling or premonition of his death. I remembered everything so clearly. I knew it could not have been an accident, a random hit and run. Gloria had said to me that Malek had asked about me, and about my relationship with Davor. Why would he do that? And my American friend Sam Stark had told me about how Malek had killed the migrants. I wondered if Malek knew about what had happened on Brijuni. All these thoughts were sliding and slipping about in my mind. I needed to be clear. I knew I had to be careful and on my guard.

Zora, as always, had arranged accommodation for me. I had an apartment overlooking the statue of the poet Gundulić, near the Church of St. Blaise. I could open my shutters and look down upon the poet as he stood beside a small market selling lavender sachets and olive oil and crafted souvenirs. I was to meet Mia later that evening.

I dropped my bag off at the apartment and walked the splendid walls of the city starting at the Pile Gate. The thought occurred to me how different my life had become. Instead of writing travel pieces for trendy digital or print magazines, I was meeting spirits from the past. Spirits returned from the dead, the undiscovered country that Hamlet talked about. I had never experienced adventure like this before in my life.

Adventure and danger too, I thought. But I felt so alive, right down to my fingertips.

◆ ◆ ◆

A little after eight in the evening, I heard three sharp knocks at the entrance to my apartment. When I opened the door, I saw a small lithe attractive woman with short brown hair and a very fair complexion, the kind that could burn easily under the Dalmatian sun. She was carrying a leather backpack. She looked at me curiously, smiled briefly, and then entered. She seemed a little unsteady on her feet. I ushered her into the kitchen area and we sat opposite each other at the heavy wooden table. I pushed a vase of yellow tulips, just about to blossom, to one side of the table so I could see her clearly. She told me she had been thoroughly briefed by Zora and understood the process we were to follow in our work together. She was slurring her words. Still, I told her that I felt the need to explain to her the overall approach and what my expectations were. She shook her head vigorously in agreement, and then reached into her bag and pulled out a half-empty bottle of plum brandy. She waved the liter bottle about and asked for glasses, and then she slammed the bottle heavily against the tabletop. She was drunk.

"I am sorry, but we cannot proceed," I said. "We will have to begin tomorrow. Around ten in the morning I suggest. In order for me to see the retinal images, your eyes must be clear and focused on the memory images." I stood up, somewhat angry that she had ruined the session. I wanted her to leave.

She looked at me in disbelief and mild irritation, her voice rising. "What? A few drinks and you want to cancel! Surely not. Come, sit down, and we will start."

"No, we cannot continue. You are drunk. Our work would be ruined. Please leave. Tomorrow we can meet again."

"But Croatians drink," she said loudly. "That is a fact of life. Every second Croatian drinks too much. How else could you live in this world without drink? Come," she said, reaching over the table and taking my arm, and pulling it down, urging me to sit.

"I know Croatians drink, but there is a time for that, and tonight was not the time for drink. You need to be sober." I pushed her arm away and stood my ground.

She looked at me in surprise, and then a look of anger suffused her features. She stood up, swung her rucksack over her shoulder, grabbed the bottle, and left in a huff.

♦ ♦ ♦

It was midmorning of the next day when she arrived at my apartment. I closed the shutters to keep out the noise of the small market around the Gundulić statue. A gray pigeon with a wonderfully iridescent neck was perched on the poet's head, and had the poet been alive he would have been glad to have sported a broad-brimmed hat to withstand the pigeon's attentions.

I invited her to sit at the table. Her eyes were bloodshot, but I could see that she was stone cold sober the way veteran drinkers can sometimes be after a spree the evening before. She asked if I had some coffee and smiled hopefully. I prepared a double espresso for her that she drank with two heaping spoons of brown sugar. After a second large cup of espresso she said she was ready to begin. I spent about a half hour speaking softly to her using the progressive relaxation techniques that provided the starting point for our work together. Her eyelids were closed. When I determined that she was ready, I asked her to revisit the exact time that she had returned to life to change. Her eyelids slowly opened and I focused on her retinas. The retinal images she was seeing were projected onto my own, and I asked her to begin, taking special care to mention that when she wanted me to begin my intervention and change the images on her retinas, she was to raise her right hand and drop it, palm down, on the kitchen table between us. She made a guttural sound in her throat and began.

"Vedran would talk to us about a university of good minds, good heads, that didn't need impressive stone walls and precious libraries and learned professors. He said the little acts of kindness and beauty that we spread about was all the stone and mortar we needed to build a true university loved by God.

I once heard him ask a visiting Bishop why the Church couldn't share its wealth to feed and house the poor. He said he believed Jesus would do it. There was a crowd of people around when he asked the Bishop that question. I could see the Bishop was furious, but he smiled through his gritted teeth and said that the people needed spiritual sustenance even more than bread. He said that the house of God on earth required a church that was uplifting, and one that would remind the faithful of the magnificence of heaven and the heavenly father. He glanced angrily at two senior monks who accompanied him as if they were somehow responsible for Vedran's remarks. The monks, one of them tall and gaunt, the other portly and bald, tried to get Vedran's attention but to no avail. He said the people needed bread in the here and now, their stomachs full, before they could admire gold leaf and flying buttresses. The Bishop and his retinue stood silent momentarily, livid and flushed with anger, and then strode away, eager to be gone.

But our Vedran was like a dog with a bone when he set his mind on the truth of something. Common sense, that's what he called it. Otherwise, he was the gentlest of men, and smiled more often than he spoke. He was happy with his life, humming as he walked, and devoted to his Franciscan Order.

When I first saw him I thought what a waste of a man in his devotion to God. So handsome with his thick chestnut brown hair and a strong sweet face. I remember seeing him bathing and swimming at the Dead Sea on Lokrum. My knees trembled to see his golden brown torso, so muscular and fit, without an ounce of fat. What struck me most was his warm, beguiling smile. I made up my mind as I watched him dry himself with his cloak. I could dry every inch of him up and down. I said to my girlfriends that I would have him. They laughed at me saying he was not like other monks and priests. He could not be swayed. Vedran, they said, did not look at them the way the others did. But I set my sights on Vedran, and I was determined to have him all the more. Men are men, and all that is required is patience and time, as with a spider and her web.

Once, during a time of plague, I heard him speaking to a large group on the honey glazed stones of the Stradun. He said that good head thinking meant that everyone would wash and scrub their hands carefully and often. He said that it was important to avoid touching one's face and to keep away from large groups, even at mass. Well, then and there, an older priest shouted that Vedran was wrong, and that it was more important than ever to celebrate mass, especially with others, and to take communion. Vedran stood his ground and said firmly that it made sense to keep clean against something invisible and contagious. The priest went apoplectic and cursed Vedran in front of everyone. Vedran ignored the insult and suggested quietly that the priest give it a try. The priest walked away in a silent fury, his face as red as a boiled pig's head.

For weeks after that I waited for an opportunity to meet him. After Vespers one evening I approached him as he left the Monastery and asked him how I might help him in his work. He smiled his wickedly attractive smile and he asked what kind of work I did. When I told him I was a baker he suggested baking a few extra loaves to give to the poor. I promised him I would.

But each day for several days after that when I brought the bread to the Monastery I did not see Vedran. A senior monk, fat and ugly, took the loaves, thanked me, and gave me a blessing. I wanted Vedran. I did not want a blessing. So I quit that.

As chance would have it I saw him once again at the Dead Sea on Lokrum. I could hardly believe my good fortune. He was swimming on his back as happy as a dolphin. His skin was a golden brown colour that quite struck me with its beauty.

I decided to join him. I eased into the Dead Sea like a water snake and went straight for him. Once near him I pretended that I was in danger of drowning and splashed about in a frenzy of arms and legs, grasping him and holding him however I could. He was strong and immediately swam about and held me from behind, his arm around my bosom, and then swam to the bank of the pool. He pulled me up onto the shore with ease and I coughed violently for a moment expelling the water I had swallowed. I looked up into his hazel eyes and saw his concern and care. I rested beneath him as he knelt above me and spoke to me gently. Behind him the sun shone brightly above clear blue skies. Drops of water fell from him and onto my face. I closed my eyes briefly savouring the moment. He recognized me and then smiled warmly when he knew I was out of danger. He insisted on accompanying me on the short boat ride back to the city, making sure I was fully conscious and alert. We walked down the pedestrian polished stones of the Stradun, and I was so pleased to be walking beside him. Two of my girlfriends saw me and waved, chatting with excitement as we passed. He asked once again if all was right with me. I smiled and nodded, and he was gone, the sun shining brightly on the nape of his neck. The earth trembled suddenly for a few seconds, startling me. My girlfriends felt it too and we laughed, a little nervously.

The encounter only strengthened my resolve to have him. For the next few days I could think of nothing but him, the way he walked, his generous smile, his tan with its hint of rose just beneath the gold coloured skin. I barely slept, twisting and turning with desire through the night.

Three days later I made my way to the monastery and told a caretaker that I had a rosary that Vedran had promised to bless. He offered to give it to him when he returned from his daily work in a nearby village, but I insisted on taking it to his room. The caretaker led me there and I left it on a night table. He escorted me to the entrance opening on to the Stradun and then left. I watched him go and then I hid in a linen closet until night had fallen and all was quiet. Like a thief I waited in the darkness, biding my time. I even slept a bit, so tired from sleepless nights. In the middle of the night, I crept out and made my way to his room. He was fast asleep.

I crept to the side of his bed, lifted a blanket, and lay beside his nude body without touching him. My breathing was heavy with excitement and anticipation. I threw off my dress. For a moment I kept away from him, but then I could take it no longer. I nestled against him and swooned against his naked back, trying to embrace him. Suddenly, he whipped around and cried out in surprise and abject dread, not knowing what was happening, not realizing who was there. I whispered my name and waited. He jumped out of his bed and pushed me away. He kept on repeating no, and firmly kept me at arm's length, trying to keep me away from him. I saw that he was erect. Quickly, he put on his cassock, tossed my dress to me, and pushed me out of his room and into the corridor. A monk was at the far end of the corridor and looked at us in mute surprise. Vedran was breathless and confused. I put on my dress and ran on my tiptoes as fast as I could down the corridor and out a side door to Celestina Medovica Street. I didn't look back.

I didn't see him for a few days after that. Then I saw him talking to a large group of children by the Big Fountain near the monastery. He was telling them that the kindness within each of us needed to get out and find its way back to heaven. He said that helping the poor was one of the best ways to let our light shine. I could see they were listening intently and caught up in his words and the soft, mellifluous tone of his voice. When he looked to one side and chanced to see me, I saw a look of disappointment and infinite sadness spread across his face.

Before long the children skipped away, happy and chatting merrily. Vedran walked over to me, and very quietly told me that he was being investigated for breaking his vows, stemming from the night I had entered his cell. A monk had seen me leaving his room in the dead of night. He said that the Bishop himself was leading the inquiry. Vedran had given them my name. He said it was important that I tell the truth. He said that good mind thinking, good head thinking, required that I simply tell the truth, even if it were difficult for me. I was struck by his compassion for me even after all that I had done. He would only be exonerated if I told the truth. He said he would help me through it, and that I was not to be afraid. Even then I so sorely wanted him, even more than ever. Just to be near him almost satisfied the craving within me.

A few days passed. I was summoned by the Bishop. He sat behind a large, ornate desk flanked by the two priests, the thin one and the fat one, that always accompanied him. They stood and glowered at me. I felt very intimidated and kept my head down. The Bishop outlined the situation, saying that it was very grave, and that if true, if I had been with the Franciscan monk, Vedran, he would be expelled from the Order unless there was some good reason for the dead of night tryst as he called it, with a tone of mocking condemnation in his voice. I did not know what the word tryst meant, but I thought it must be something bad. I looked up at him. His face was severe and seemed to burn within the gloom of the darkened room. He asked for my version of events. I said nothing. He asked again. I was too afraid to say anything. I looked at the stone floor wishing I were dead. My mouth felt like ashes. Then the Bishop rose and spoke in sharp staccato Latin to his priests. He left abruptly, his cassock swinging as he walked by me.

The tall gaunt priest said that my silence was understandable. The fat one smiled. I had been wronged the tall one said, and of such matters he knew from experience that it took time to relieve one's conscience. So, he said I must return for counselling, and that I was not to see Vedran again. I was petrified and still could not utter a word. The tall one leaned forward and drew the sign of the cross on my forehead. My head recoiled at his touch. It seemed to burn on my skin. I nodded and ran from the stale room in blind haste.

Over the next few days, my girlfriends asked why I was meeting with the priests. I shrugged my shoulders and made up a story about a promise I had made my dead father to learn Latin. One of them teased me about Vedran, about how I had failed to win him as she put it. I smirked and pushed her away.

On my third meeting with the priests a strange thing happened. The three of us were sitting on chairs in a loose circle. I was still unable to tell them what had taken place despite their repeated questioning. Perhaps it was shame or fear of what would happen to me, but I could not. I could not tell the truth about my lust. Vedran had asked me to tell the truth but I could not. But the strange thing happened when the fat priest placed his hand on my leg and said there was a way this situation could go away. He said in a kind of breathless voice that neither Vedran nor I would be disciplined or in any way admonished if I were to agree to a small exception. I told him I did not understand what was meant by exception. The tall one said that the exception proves the rule, and that the exception always goes against the norm. The exception is the opposite of the norm, he said, smiling a crooked smile across a twisted, lascivious face. Then he said flatly that I must submit to their desires and allow them to have me. If so, the Bishop would be told it was simply a mistaken encounter, a reasonable explanation would be invented and given, and Vedran would be cleared of any wrongdoing. As simple as that. The Bishop was amenable to reason, and he would be glad to see the whole matter fade away. But I must agree here and now, in this very place, today.

I felt cold tremors rush through my body, and my world seemed to fold and break. I hardly believed I was sitting in a church and that I had heard what I heard. I leapt up and backed out of the room and then ran out on my tiptoes into the sun-swept courtyard of the church, out into the world that was solid and unmistakeable and my own.

Three days later Vedran's body was found floating in the dead sea on Lokrum. They said that his eyes were open and staring into the clear blue skies above him. I learned that he had been expelled from the Order. The local children were desolate and wept bitter tears crying out that the beautiful head was gone forever and where would the light of their kindness go now, now that Vedran was gone."

Mia stopped speaking then. A full moment passed and nothing could be heard save the distant din of the muted marketplace below my apartment. I observed her raising her right arm high above the heavy oak tabletop and then I watched it come down hard, palm down, against its surface. The moment of change had arrived. I focused on the retinal image of her just as the tall priest said that she must submit to them in that moment, in that very place. Mia was breathing heavily, almost panting, and then she took a very deep breath, sighed infinitely sadly, and began speaking again.

"So I did it. I fell. They took me on a small cot beneath a silver crucifix on the wall. I remember that because the Christ figure on the cross held my own pain as I stared upwards at it. I pretended I was somewhere else, far and away from the filthy cot and their filthy touch. But Vedran was alive. A week passed. The priests kept their word and the incident faded away. I was miserable and drunk every day on the plum brandy that my grandmother made. It dulled the hurt but it didn't take it away. It was always there in the morning. But there was something else.

I felt a premonition of something terrible coming. The days of March passed like weary, worn markers on a well- travelled road, and then April began suddenly. Each new day felt like a threat. The skies were crystal clear and as blue as the promise of Spring, but something was looming, something momentous. My intuition told me that I must act. Twice I met Vedran by the big fountain, and he smiled and asked me if he could help me in any way at all. He stood near me but didn't touch me. He could see the misery in my face. I told him nothing of what had happened. It was so good just to be near him, our shadows crossing and then mixing on the flagstones beneath us. I could feel my parched lips form a smile and then fade into oblivion.

The order of events seemed to occur on its own with little effort on my part. Things just happened, and I followed along with them. I contacted a friend in Cavtat and gave him all the money I had in the world. He was to give it to Vedran, and only Vedran, on the evening of April 05 as a gift from a believer. When I told Vedran, he laughed delightedly, saying that I was the messenger of good head thinking. I said that the benefactor loved children and would be happy to see a group with Vedran when he came. They could stay overnight as he would be honoured to host them. Vedran's face lit up, and I could see how he checked himself from embracing me, but then he couldn't help himself and hugged me closely as he would a dear and beloved friend.

When I knew it was about to happen, when I felt how near it was, I ran to Vedran's monastery in the middle of the night. All was still. Vedran had left the day before. Like a thief I made my way in, down the corridor, and crept silently into his room. I slipped under his sheet and pulled it across my face. The smell of him was on it and beguiled me with his scent. I spent the next few hours in a delirium of desire, happy that I had done one good thing at least. The sun had already risen when a heavy thundering sound broke across the city followed by a jolt that shifted everything all at once, cracking the stone floor of the monastery and making a deep crevice next to the bed on which I lay. The fetid smell of the broken earth and its gasses assailed my nostrils. I remember thinking it was April 06 and I would not see Vedran again. I flew to the window and the last thing I saw were huge boulders rolling down the slope of the hill behind the city just the moment before I fell into the maw of a deep, dark pit beside my beloved's bed. It was over."

Mia's face was happy as I looked at her, the retinal images we shared dissolving into a flood of tears as joyous as they were sad. We were both exhausted from our work together and parted soon thereafter.

◆ ◆ ◆

The next morning I walked once more around the walls of the city, just musing and thinking about what had happened. I followed the well-worn path walking in an anticlockwise direction starting from the Pile Gate. The work with Mia had gone well. Now, I waited for a text message from

Zora to find out where I would go next. When I had circuited the walls, I simply wandered about, not looking for anything in particular. It was a sunny day and pleasant. And that's when I saw her, Mia, sitting on a stone bench near the Franciscan monastery. She waved me over, smiling, and with a gesture of her arm invited me to sit beside her. Her outstretched arms were slightly behind her, and she raised her face to the sun, her eyes closed. For a moment neither of us spoke just enjoying the ambience of the place. Then, out of curiosity I asked her if she wanted to stay, here in life, and not go back to the country of the dead.

Mia turned to me and looked at me quizzically before she spoke.

"In the land of the dead you don't have to worry about invaders or about rulers from on high. You don't have the care of vassals and subjects below you. You don't have work to do with each of the changing seasons, something always on your mind and vexing you, never a chance for quiet rest. You are free to enjoy endless springs, summers, autumns, and winters with nothing to do. Nothing, not a thing. Everything is as endless as heaven and earth. Queen Teuta, the Illyrian Queen, sitting on her throne, could have no greater happiness than this. Oh yes, I will return to that place from whence I came. I have come back and with your help have completed what I set out to do. I am enjoying this place and this time here, but not for a fortune and a kingdom would I want to stay."

I was stunned by her words, but it helped me process the residual pain I felt over Davor's death. Her words made me hopeful at a time when I sorely needed it. I was grateful to her for that. Then she stood, patted me on the shoulder affectionately, and left, saying she would see me again.

So much had happened. I walked back to my apartment to pack and to check for any messages I may have received while I was out. There was a text from Zora. Parts of it were enigmatic and didn't make any sense to me. But I would do my best to find out.

The situation here has escalated. One of four Tesla retina scanners has been stolen. Two of our spirit guides are missing along with two returned spirits. Will send directives soon on next destination. Till then be hyper vigilant and be especially careful around vans. The Academy of Light has recently made purchases of several of these vans. We do not know why.

I felt a sense of dread in the knowledge that two guides were missing. People like myself. I was on my own here, in uncharted territory, and Davor was gone. There had been a time when I thought Malek was just a curious guru-type personality with a talent for speechmaking and attracting weak-minded acolytes. But there was an oddness to the man. I remembered the two beautiful women who were with him on one of the nights I had seen him. I realized now they were simply garnish for him, nothing more, something to decorate a table with and attract admiring glances. And this on the same night when he attacked the Italian tourist who had been playing the fool with his denture. That was an indicator of Malek's pettiness, of his silly righteousness. I deleted Zora's text message and went to an Irish pub, on one of the side streets off the Stradun, for a pint or two of Guinness. As I sipped my beer I thought about the vans. Malek certainly wasn't in the business of transporting goods or people. And then the missing guides and spirits, that troubled me. I knew I was fortunate in not needing one of the Tesla retina readers, but other spirit guides would require them. And now there were only two.

I slept in the next morning, checked my iPhone for messages, and seeing there were none, decided to walk around the town once again. The city was quite crowded with tourists from the cruise ships. Small groups of about twenty or more would be huddled around a tour guide holding a small colored flag atop a stick as she recounted historical details of Orlando's column or the Rector's Palace or the large fountain. There were several such groups, and I wondered if they felt a pang of fear if they lost sight of their guide even for a moment. I walked back to my apartment and found a message from Zora on my iPhone.

Hello Kristof,

Make your way to Osijek any way you can and quickly. Once there text me, and I will give you further instructions for your accom-modation and spirit meeting. Everything fine here, but be careful on your journey.

Zora

1533 Osijek, Petar

I met Petar three days after I arrived in Osijek. I was staying at an Airbnb apartment between the Museum of Fine Arts and the Market on Stjepana Radićeva Street. Zora had given him instructions on how to find me. There was a sharp, hard knocking at my door, and when I opened it, I saw a short, muscular man with a ruddy, handsome face and long, fair hair. I noticed at once that his eyes were very observant and he seemed to take everything in, looking about and assessing things. I offered him some wine, a cold meat platter and some freshly baked bread, and for a half hour or so we did little else but eat and drink. He savoured each morsel and nodded in appreciation of the red wine which I poured liberally for him. He laughed heartily and said that two hundred years without a drink can give a man a fierce thirst. I knew that he had accumulated his two hundred years over a much longer period of time, and I was eager to help him.

"Živio," he said, raising his glass in a toast.

"Živio," I replied. I then spent several minutes explaining the procedure, how I would listen to him recounting his story, and how I would be listening intently to him as he spoke, and creating images in my mind to work with later. I asked him to let me know exactly when he wanted me to change an image with a new choice, a new outcome. He nodded in agreement and took a long drink of the wine and wiped his lips with his forearm. I spent a short period of time readying and relaxing myself, and then he spoke.

"The year was 1533, in the autumn. My village, Tenja, was very near here, A little to the southeast. Most people were in the vineyards, gathering grapes. It was a rich harvest and my wife Maria wanted me to help with the picking, but I am a hunter and I could smell the game in the air. My Maria is as beautiful as she is gentle. She simply shrugged and bid me go. I packed some provisions in my rucksack, my bow, arrows, field axe, hunting knife,and set off that very morning."

I laid my hand gently across his wrist and saw him smile broadly at the scenes he was summoning up in his mind and then sharing with me these same images on his retinas. The images, were crystal clear. He took a deep breath and continued.

"Much has changed. In coming here, in walking from Tenja, I didn't see the oak forest that I knew. In my preparation period with Zora I knew of the immense changes, the electric light, the motorized carts, the moving images captured in thin rectangular boxes, and the weapons of course, but the oak forest had been magnificent, a wonder like a great cathedral. The modern developments seemed to me tricks merely, like a dog standing on its hind legs and walking. Clever only.

I made good progress the first day I set out hunting. I stopped to fish and enjoyed trout for my lunch with biscuits Maria had made for me. I wished my friend Tomislav could have joined me but he was committed to help with the grape harvest. His wife is a shrew and not gentle and kind like my Maria. Still, there is a lot to be said for hunting alone. Your senses are more highly attuned. You are ready for anything. A wild boar crossed my path so suddenly and with such speed that I had no time to string my bow. But I took it as an omen, and grew excited at the prospect of what lay ahead for me.

The sun was brilliant above me and the sky was as blue as a robin's eggshell, without a cloud in sight. The grass was so green and spotted with tiny purple flowers that I removed my gear and rolled about in it like I did when I was a boy. Such a lovely Autumn day. I felt so strong and happy to be alive. That first night I slept under the stars by a stream, and wished I could share it with Maria. But a hunter cannot have everything.

The next three days were the best hunting I have ever had. Game so plentiful that even the poorest hunter would have returned with plenty. The game seemed to be coming from the east and heading west. All kinds of game. My arrowheads were razor sharp and my bow ready to be strung within a few seconds if need be. My field axe hung from my belt in readiness. I followed a stream until I came across a tall oak tree with massive branches high up. That evening I fashioned a horn out of birch bark and using it, uttered low guttural sounds, the sounds of a cow crying for a mate. After several blows on the birch horn, I filled it with water from the stream and poured it on the surface of the water to imitate a cow pissing. I did this several times.

Then I climbed the oak tree with my kit and made myself comfortable for the night in one of the topmost branches. Before darkness fell I had time to carve a design on the shaft of my axe. The design was based on a tattoo my grandfather had incised on his shoulder. I remembered it from memory, a small circle within a larger circle both of them with short vertical lines, short bristles emanating from the circumference of the circles and ending in a tiny cross. I had seen and touched them so often that in the carving of the design on my axe shaft I felt my grandfather was with me. Despite my high perch I slept soundly.

The next morning I awoke to the sounds of the gurgling stream below. It sounded like the laughter of young girls. I peered down the trunk of the tree and a vision appeared beneath me. A majestic stag stood far below me next to the stream. The rack of its antlers, as it moved its head up and down to drink, was like the throne of a summer god. For a moment I was mesmerized by its beauty and could not act. Then, I strung my bow, notched my arrow, aimed, and shot. Within seconds I was able to fire two more arrows in rapid succession. My aim was true. I feasted on roast tongue for lunch and the choicest cuts of meat. But what game I saw about me that day! Deer, boar, golden pheasants, and giant hares, a favourite of my Maria. I did my utmost to return to Tenja with only the choicest cuts. I fashioned a litter out of young birch trees to drag behind me as I hiked to carry what I had killed. So much I had to leave behind. Perhaps I was too greedy, but it happens rarely that such bounty is dropped in your lap.

With a hopeful, happy heart I set off for home on the fifth day. That morning I saw a black stork flying west. There was a scent in the air, as of distant smoke, the smell of burnt fields. I was making progress with my makeshift litter, but it was hard going, and slow. I thought of so many things as I hiked. Maria's joyful face, my father's expression of pride, the look of good wishes tinged with envy from Tomislav. And I anticipated the taste of soup and dumplings Maria would cook from the wild game. Along the way I would stop and rest, sometimes laying in the deep grass and looking up at the blue skies. As I lay there I noticed the barest trace of brown discolouring the eastern part of the sky. That was odd to me. But then the smell of burnt ground struck me. I stood up and looking east I saw more discolouring in the skies, and I knew great fires had caused these changes.

Several hours later I was nearing the outskirts of Tenja. All around me the verdant meadows were gone, the fields were wasted and barren. I thought of my grandfather and the huge straw monument he would build at harvest time of a gigantic partridge that would be set aflame to give fertility to the soil the following year. And then I knew as I neared home. My heart fell with the realization of it. The Turks had come and devastated the land, burning whatever they could not take with them. Tenja was gone. Only the smoking timbers of a few of the village houses were left. The vineyards were gone. The remains of several corpses were piled in a mound, but the fires had left them charred and completely indistinguishable. There was not a soul to be seen anywhere. I knew. My people were enslaved or dead.

For several hours I sat stunned upon the ground where my house had been. I wept and then slept and then woke and wept again. But tears accomplished nothing. Maria was gone and my father and my people. All gone or dead. I wandered about in a daze and finally sat by the stream near the blasted vineyard and thought about what I would do. I forced myself to roast some meat and eat. I would need my strength in the coming days. I knew what I must do.

I made my way east following cart tracks on the old road. I knew I had to be careful and stealthy. It would only take a day or so to catch up with them. They would be moving slowly with children and aged folk trailing the long lines heading to the east. I had to be wary of Turkish scouts and warriors skirting the large moving groups. I didn't know what I could do when I caught up with them, but I would find out. My family needed me now more than ever. My mind raced with fanciful ideas, but I was a single man against hundreds, perhaps thousands of the enemy. What was I going to do?

I caught up with them in less than a day. I was careful to avoid their scouts. There were many bodies along the way. The corpses of stragglers who could not keep up, usually the elderly but not always. Their throats were slit from ear to ear. I moved slowly across the burnt ground and finally came to a forested area that afforded me greater protection. I could disguise myself more easily now, blending in with the shrubs and trees, the way of the hunter.

I observed the crowds moving slowly in great lines. I counted several of them. There were hundreds upon hundreds of people slowly trudging forward tethered to short ropes that were joined to a heavy massive rope for a particular line. There must have been several villages captured in the raid. Children and older folk were seated in carts pushed by captives. Turkish warriors on horseback moved up and down the lines whipping anyone who showed signs of stopping or impeding in any way the steady, inexorable movement forward. I could hear cries of desperation and fatigue rise above the throngs of the enslaved. I had never seen such human misery. I recognized no one.

That night I found a small depression in a felled tree where I could hide and sleep the night. With meat in my rucksack and water in my wineskin I was all right, at least physically, but that hardly mattered. I barely slept and woke fearfully before dawn.

I had no plan other than to skirt by the moving crowds to look for familiar faces. I spent the better part of a day avoiding detection by Turkish scouts and scanning the long lines that were moving steadily forward. I would dart from one hiding spot to the next in a constant state of readiness. My unstrung bow was positioned diagonally across my back along with my quivered arrows, and field axe. My hunting knife was strapped to the calf of my right leg. I felt fear but I was hopeful too that I might find someone from my village.

The vast majority of men were at the front of the procession all of them tethered alternately by short ropes to a longer rope, with women and older children behind them. On either side of the rope lines, Turkish warriors urged them on. I had to be extremely careful and keep my distance. For hours I moved in fits and starts along the side of the old road, keeping under the cover of trees and low shrubs, sometimes crawling, sometimes darting, as if I were following game.

In late afternoon they stopped to set up camp. The lines of men and women were organized into smaller, still separate groups and were watched very closely by their captors for any sign of resistance. Once the camp was made they were tied securely again and bound to each other. They were given miserable uncooked rations and water. I heard some of the Turks shouting orders in Croatian. Curt words and phrases along with random whipping and pokes with the blunt end of their lances and the flat side of their swords. Cries of pain and moans of misery rose into the sky. Horsemen with their bows strung were ranged along the periphery. A large tent was set up and dozens of women were prodded inside by overseers. The organized sequence of activities showed me they had done this often.

I crept as close as I could to see if I could recognize any faces. There were none. Suddenly I felt something behind me, sniffing and nuzzling my rucksack. I turned and started when I saw a huge wolfhound standing before me, almost above me. It began to growl menacingly, but fortunately not barking. Very slowly I unfastened my rucksack and threw a chunk of meat to my left side. Just as it turned its head to take the meat, I pulled the knife from its sheath on my leg and drove it deep into the dog's heart. There was a little gurgle coming from its throat and then silence as it fell heavily onto the ground.

I knew I would have but one opportunity and the chance of finding Maria was little indeed. But try I must. Guards were moving in and around the captives, all of whom sat or lay on the ground, bound and tied to each other. I heard terrible cries of fear and despair and pain coming from the great tent that had been set up in a copse of trees just off the road. I watched as a cart with barrels of wine was pulled and pushed by prisoners into the tent. I waited a few hours in misery as I heard the wails of women coming from within the tent. I wanted to let the wine take its effect on the Turks and then strike.

Fortunately the night was dark, with great clouds overhead, the only light coming from fires around the camp. I crawled to the rear of the tent that was unguarded and set against tall pines. Carefully, I took my hunting knife and cut into the tent with just the tip of it a few inches, and then thrust it down. Peering inside I could see the backs of naked women shaking with fear and dread. I sheathed my knife and crawled away to another rear section of the tent and cut the tent again. I prayed God to see Maria's face. And there, bloodied and in shock, there she was. She was standing behind a small group of women, completely silent, with a blank, stricken look upon her bloodied face. In one fell stroke I slit the tent wall, rushed in, low and bent over, and pulled her with me to the outside. But once we were under the trees, she simply fell to the ground trembling and unmoving and stunned. She didn't recognize me. I knew I couldn't escape if I had to drag her behind me. With a pang of sharp sorrow, I left her."

Petar stopped speaking then, and I heard a choking sound coming from his throat. I was ready with the intervention, and I nodded.

"Kristof, this is the moment, just before I leave. Here."

"OK," I said, seeing the image on his retina accompanied by several bright flashes of light, and then the corresponding image projected onto my own retinas. "Go ahead. Now. Make the change."

"In the midst of everything, in the midst of the camp, and in the midst of my pain, I looked at her with an infinite tenderness and told her that I loved her. I swung my field axe up from where it rested on my waist, tore off the leather cap on the narrow end of the wooden shaft, and then plunged the metal spike deep into her heart in one fluid motion. In a split second I saw the trace of a smile grace her features, and then a look of astonishment like the time I surprised her with an amber necklace. She fell into my arms and I laid her on the ground softly. There was a hollowness where my heart had been.

I scurried to an unguarded section of the camp and cut through the ropes that tethered several men prisoners. As I did so there was a cry of alarm and a few Turks came rushing forward. Suddenly, a Turk's face was directly in front of mine. I could feel his drunken breath upon me. My blade was in my hand and as if of its own accord it struck deep into the left eye socket of the man. Great spurts of energy coursed through my blood. As I sped away so did a half-dozen captives I had freed. I saw two of them cut down by Turkish swords, but two others escaped with me.

I ran deep into the woods, separating from the others to have a better chance at survival. I didn't look behind me. I ran until I was exhausted and fell upon the earth in a deserted graveyard, panting and in a great fatigue. I took refuge under an overgrown mound covered in brambles that tore at my face. Beneath the vegetation there was a coffin of stone with a stone roof over it, the size of a doghouse. I had failed. I had killed my beloved Maria. Dazed, I pushed deeper into the stone coffin pushing away the skeleton I shared the space with, and then fell into a deep sleep, exhausted and totally spent. I don't know how much time had passed before I heard a scraping, scuffling sound above me, the sound of a beast trying to tear into my space. The sound of raucous Turkish voices crying out in the darkness was coming closer and closer. Suddenly, I could feel the snout of a huge war dog pushing at the stone above my head. I could smell its breath. It was moving about and sniffing the packed earth to one side of the ancient grave. There were truffles buried in the earth above me. Suddenly the dog stopped its frantic pawing, and I could hear Turkish voices above me, standing on the mound. Clods of earth fell across my face from the weight of the men standing above me. Moments passed and then I heard laughter as they found a truffle and wrested it from the dog. I heard the dog whimper and then run off. The Turks soon left, but I remained alert and motionless in the darkness. I managed to pull my field axe from its sheath on my belt and cradled it in my arms, the axe blade resting coolly against my cheek. The steel was sharp and ready. I must have fallen asleep for when I awoke it was the hour just before the dawn. I made my way west."

"OK, we are finished Petar. It is done" I said abruptly. We were once again fully conscious that we were in the Airbnb apartment on Stjepana Radićeva Street in Osijek. The images on his retinas were of me sitting across from him. I went to the IKEA cupboard and pulled out a bottle of plum brandy that the Airbnb host had left me as a welcoming gift. We had several drinks and then parted in good spirits. Petar was going to visit Tenja for a few days before returning to Istria. I set out to explore Osijek's old town and the Fort, beginning with the Plague Column in the cobbled Holy Trinity Square. Afterwards, I would wait for instructions on my next destination.

When I returned from my sightseeing to the Airbnb apartment, the owner, a very large stout man with a constantly glistening bald head, was waiting for me with a concerned look on his broad face. He lived next door with his family in an adjoining apartment and nothing passed by without his knowing about it. In a low, confidential voice he mentioned to me that two gentlemen had been looking for me and had asked when I would be returning. They said they were close friends of mine from Canada. But there was something about the men that bothered him. Neither of them spoke with a Canadian accent like I did, and they sounded and looked more like formal Europeans than anything else. They were dressed in dark blue suits buttoned to the neck that looked more like military uniforms than regular suits. They had arrived in a large white cargo van without any side or rear windows except for the front windshield which was tinted darkly. The van's engine, he said, had been left running while the men spoke to him. He told the two men that I had gone to Vukovar for the day to do some sightseeing. They asked what kind of vehicle I was driving, and he told them he believed I had flown to Osijek from Zagreb. I thanked my host and said I would be leaving a day early, and that I would of course pay for the extra day I had booked. He nodded and shook my hand firmly and wished me well. I packed up my things in haste and made my way to the bus station, my mind racing with thoughts of all kinds.

I remembered something Davor had told me, an anecdote, while we were having a drink in a hotel bar in downtown Pula. He said that the vast earth and the great starry regions of space were endless and infinite, unlike a human being who is mortal. He said that you can take a man who is a finite being and plop him down like a clockwork plaything amid all those never-ending spaces, and he is gone. Gone. Finished. His whole passage is over, as fast as a swift horse glimpsed through a crack in the wall.

I asked him if he thought the horse in his story was a Lipizzaner, the famous breed from Slavonia. He smiled ruefully, looked at me with infinite sadness and compassion, and then he said "quite possibly."

Within an hour I was on a bus heading west through a fertile plain. It was easy to see how invaders could sweep the region and drive onwards. Through the window I saw maize fields, orchards, and vineyards and ruined castles. I was looking forward to seeing Petar in a few weeks in Brijuni. But it troubled me to know that Malek's men had found me. I was so glad that I had been able to finish my work with Petar without incident.

My backpack was on the vacant aisle seat next to me. I pulled out the canvas bag Davor had given me and felt its contents once again. I did not draw the articles from the bag. I simply felt them as a kind of reassurance for me, like talismans. My fingers touched the two stones and then the

Byzantine dagger in its sheath. I pressed my hand hard against the hilt and felt its latent power. My fingers ran along the silver arm bracelet and felt the intricacy of the designs stamped upon it. I pushed my hand deeper into the bottom of the bag where I found the coin, the gold coin that Dr. Spehar had said was from the time of the Caesars on their march to the Illyrian city of Metulum. How I would use these things I had no idea yet. Davor had said I had to figure things out for myself as situations arose. I smiled at the memory of Davor and then placed the canvas bag into my packsack. The landscape whizzed by, and I settled more comfortably into my seat.

Soon I was dozing pleasantly, half asleep, with the images of broad fields and ancient, crumbling towers flashing by outside my window. The glass of the window was warm with the sun. Sometimes I would forget, and then suddenly, I was jolted back into the flat, stinging reality that Davor was gone. All of his knowledge, his insightful anecdotes, were gone, gone forever, but for the half painful, half joyful memories that were released from the sea of my unconscious. And then, as if to plague and vex myself further, I thought of what Mia had said in Dubrovnik, about death being as wonderful as sitting upon a Queen's throne. I tried to sleep.

1813 Karlovac, Ante

Zora had arranged for me to meet Ante at the Bimini Bar in Karlovac, a restaurant with a sportsman's theme. It was about eight in the evening, and a little chilly. I recognized him straightaway from the description Zora had given me. Even sitting, drinking a glass of red wine, there was a distinctly military air about him. He was handsome with thick, curly, dark hair and the features of a matinee idol. A fit, compact man of middle size and height with a commanding physical presence. He wore a light tailored gray suit and sported a white shirt and a loosened blue silk tie with a tiny fleur de li motif upon it. I felt underdressed with just a black pullover and khakis. As I approached his table he stood up smartly and offered his hand, smiling.

"Kristof, I presume," he said.

"The same," I replied.

He snapped his fingers to summon a waiter. He spoke in rapid fire Croatian, and in a moment the waiter returned with a bottle of Veuve de Clicoq champagne and two fluted glasses. The young man poured a bit for Ante to sample, but Ante waved him off, not unkindly, indicating that he should fill our glasses without any preliminary fanfare. We sipped and chatted amiably for a while before Ante leaned forward and quietly spoke.

"I have waited a long time for this meeting."

"Yes," I said, "The champagne, I hope will quench your thirst."

"I only wish my throat were as long as a giraffe's, as one of the men in the pub said, so I could savour it all the more as it descended," he said laughing, while raising his glass in a toast.

The bar around us was filling quickly for dinner with a merry crowd laughing and talking happily. We decided to finish our drinks and then go to my Airbnb rental apartment a short distance away. There, we would complete our work together and possibly return to the bar later if he wished.

◆ ◆ ◆

The apartment was spacious and on the second floor of a renovated Habsburg building that overlooked the Kupa River. Lights were sparkling on the opposite side of the river as if a celebration of some sort was taking place. Ante stood by the window looking out. I asked him to join me at the dining room table, so we could begin our work.

Once we were comfortable and seated opposite each other I asked him to fix on a thought, an image from the past that was relevant to our mission together. I asked him to relax but to keep his eyes open, and to look steadily at me. As he did so, I felt strong flashes of brilliant light enter my eyes. I recognized this as a precursor to what was to follow. I observed his retinas closely.

Oddly, the first image was of a night sky in the dead of winter. The stars were brilliant and snapping in the cold light and sharp points of illumination were reflected in the heavy carpet of snow that covered the ground. The image was of a man looking up into the December sky as he lay dying. He was gazing into the night sky and smiling in remembrance. The image changed. Suddenly, a woman appeared beside a cabriolet, again in the dead of a winter's night. I asked Ante to tell me what I was seeing and provide some background where he could.

"I went to military school here in Karlovac, as a cadet, and later, I was sent to France for further training. My mother was very proud of that. When she approved of something I had done there was a subtle smile that played about her lips. Whenever I saw that happy expression on her face, I felt like a part of the sun was released inside of me. So very special that smile. My father had died in battle against the Turks at Dubica and had served with great distinction. She often said to me that to die without honour gave a lie to life and the people one loved. My mother often spoke of how brave my father was and gay. He loved joking and making merry."

He paused for a moment as if recollecting some almost forgotten memories. And then abruptly, he continued, his voice tinged with melancholy.

"My favourite season is the winter. Especially on a cold winter's evening with brilliant stars high in the heavens kindling the snow with their light. That's when I remember her best, my Tamara. She was a celebrated Russian ballerina, and always cheerful.

We met in Paris at an officer's ball. Why she took a fancy to me, a young officer amongst so many bright military lights, I will never know. I could see the envy in the faces of so many senior officers as we danced. But attraction is a fickle thing and that night it was reciprocal and belonged to the two of us alone. After the dancing she came close to me, unruffled my cravat mischievously, and then looked up at me in a radiant, captivating smile. She suggested we leave for a walk in the Bois de Boulogne, the night being fresh with new fallen snow. Just as I helped her with her coat and gathered my cloak and hat, an officer of the highest rank stood up and waved me over, signalling me to join him. He was not smiling and neither were the other officers around him, all of them sporting great golden epaulets and serious paunches. I doffed my hat and nodded in salutation, but as he was not from a regiment that I recognized, I gave the ballerina my arm and we left. I was not about to waste a precious evening with military chitchat and formality. Tamara looked up at me quizzically, beaming at me with a wonderful smile, and then laughed as we descended the grand stairs of the portico.

The snow made a crunching sound under our feet as we walked into the park. It began snowing again, with huge snowflakes falling down upon us. Tamara threw back her hood and lifted her face to the starry night sky. I saw her open her mouth and extend her tongue to catch the snow as it fell. I laughed and did the same.

We came to a broad plaza, and she insisted we stop. She wanted to dance, she said, to remember the moment by doing what she loved best. I threw down my cloak and spread it over the snow. She gave me her coat to hold and I stood there, enraptured, as I watched her dance, bare shouldered, as the snow fell leaving indelible memories. Time seemed to stop and later, after she invited me to her hotel apartment, she ordered champagne, and we looked down upon the Bois de Boulogne from the balcony window at the reflected starlight still investing the fallen snow with great dazzling, impermanent riches.

Just before we fell asleep in each other's arms, she showed me her Japanese lacquered jewellery case. Within, there was an incredible assortment of precious rings, necklaces and bracelets, made of pearls, rubies, emeralds, diamonds, and topazes. She lit a candlestick and set it beside the case. There was a rich crimson lining within the container. Then she tiptoed barefoot to the living room to retrieve a handful of ice cubes from the champagne bucket. She dropped these into the jewellery box and we watched spellbound as the ice melted amid the jewels in shimmering and cascading glories of colour. She looked at me with such tenderness then and embraced me saying our moment would never be forgotten. The delight and surprise of that evening is with me forever.

Kristof, let's stop for a moment as I do not want to share with you all of the elements of my night with Tamara. I am fearful lest some of the more intimate images linger on my retinas."

I couldn't help but break out into laughter over Ante's solicitous care of images from his memory, censored or otherwise. I poured us each a glass of Istrian wine and we sat for several moments in contented silence.

He nodded to me when he was ready to return to our work. We looked into each other's eyes and I observed his retinas. Suddenly his face took on a serious look, and I waited for the images to flow. I saw several sharp flashes of light enter my field of vision once again and then I was ready.

"On the retreat from Moscow I was with the third regiment under Field Marshall Šljivarić. We had a very difficult time protecting our flanks from the Russians. We were constantly harried. Ours was a rear guard action defending the wounded and stragglers as we made our way across the Berezina. As Captain of several Croatian platoons, my intent was to have my troops strike and then fall back in several sweeping circular movements. The enemy wanted to engage in set pieces, but our guerrilla tactics confused them. We created havoc as we retreated. What I have always loved about the storm of battle is the calm, still point I find within me. It is as if everything is happening in slow motion and I have more than enough time to strike and retreat and strike again. I especially went for the Cossacks, their lances killing our wounded even as they fought so bravely to the death. I rode back and forth along the bristling, changing line of engagement my sabre raised, shouting encouragement to my men. And then I was struck down by a lance. I fell from my warhorse for the last time, my beloved Inferno. A truer creature I have never met. The lance had gone right through my chest. It was such an odd sensation accompanied by a whooshing sound. I pulled it out with effort, found my sabre, and struck out savagely at an infantryman charging at me. He fell with a cry, and then another rushed at me from the side. I was able to parry his thrust and slash at his throat before I was felled from behind. Around me the battle was raging. It was ugly and bloody and chaotic. I knew the Grand Army would cross but with great casualties.

The sounds of battle died away and I looked up into moist night air. The stars were brilliant. It began to snow as I lay there, and I knew I was dying. I opened my mouth and extended my tongue, catching some snowflakes as they fell. What struck me was the wistfulness of it all. I was departing from this world and felt a melancholy longing. I felt no physical pain, just wistfulness and wonder. My eyelashes trapped the falling snow, blurring the sparkling stars above, and I remembered then that magical winter night and a lacquered jewel case with shards of ice melting and blurring the multi- coloured jewels within. And then I left with one last breath for the dark spaces between the stars.

Now is the moment for your work Kristof. Now, just when I have come home. You must help me to see her before she dies. I must talk with her. She knows I am dead, but not how I died. I need to tell her so she can die in peace. "

I looked deep into Ante's eyes at the retinal images there. I manipulated the images that I had last seen of him as he lay dying in the Russian snows and watched.

He was outside his home looking in through a window.

"Her window was open, and I drifted in with the cool night breeze," Ante continued. "The moon was full and her bedroom was suffused in soft blue light. I had come home as she was dying. She was sitting upright on the bed, her back propped up by large pillows behind her. A heavy down quilt covered her legs. She held a small wooden rosary in her right hand. The tresses of her sparse greying hair fell lightly over her shoulders. Her eyes were closed. Beside her was a tray with uneaten food upon it.

I moved with a breeze behind me and sat on the side of the bed, and bending towards her, I kissed her tenderly on the cheek. Her skin was incredibly soft and cool. Suddenly, her eyes opened and she saw me. She was not alarmed."

"Ante," she said as slowly and softly as a prayer, turning her face towards the blue shadow beside her.

"Mother, oh mother, it is good to see you."

"I knew you would come. I knew you would return."

"Soon, you will receive further word of me. I am gone, but I have served most honourably. The Legion of Honour, fifth degree, Grand Cross, has been given me posthumously. Napoleon himself, I learned belatedly, witnessed my military comportment.

I watched with the utmost pleasure as a subtle smile spread across her lips, tinged in the soft blue light of the air about her. She moved her head towards me and I kissed her on both cheeks. Her eyes closed and she fell back against the pillows, the smile still marked upon her face. A bright silvered light filled the room, and then I left."

A moment passed before the retinal image was that of Ante looking at me from across the dining room table. He was smiling, and I could see he was content. He rose from the table and walked over to the window overlooking the river with its pinpoints of light reflecting on the water. I saw him raise his left hand and touch the window lightly with his fingertips. His hands, I noticed, were remarkably beautiful and expressive.

"It is good to be here Kristof, but I look forward to going back."

"What's it like Ante, what's it like for you back there? Are you really wanting to return?"

I was intensely curious to know what death was like. I had never thought about it much before, but having someone come back to life, a man who could actually tell me, was incredible, and I wanted to know. I wanted desperately to know. Ante turned away from the window and a warm smile lit up his handsome face.

"I grew up in Donji Oštrc, a few miles from here. It was my home, with the people I loved living all about me. The familiar voices, the familiar faces, and even the welcoming slope of the land, its features, as you neared home, warmed the heart. I could run into the homes of my kinsmen and always be welcome and be given food and drink, and good company and laughter. Now imagine, if I had left Donji Oštrc in my youth and had forgotten my way back. In death I am returning home, to my immortal home, that I have not forgotten."

"Hah! Ante, that was my father's village, where he was born. I haven't been there, but I remember my father talking about it. It is the same."

The very moment I told him this fact he ran up to me from the window and embraced me warmly. He was ecstatic. It was as if I had met a long lost brother. We talked long into the night and he was especially curious about my son, Peter, and his military career as a tank commander. He kept nodding his head as if it were a foregone conclusion that a descendant from Donji Oštrc should be in the military. I was really surprised by how exceedingly warm he was with the new knowledge of our common home and heritage. It felt good to belong. I had never felt anything like it before. It was as if we were part of an extended family. We spent a few more hours together before I left for Zagreb. Ante would spend a few days visiting his ancestral home. He was keen on seeing the place of his birth and how it had changed. I hoped he wouldn't be disappointed. He asked me to join him but I had work to do in Zagreb.

◆ ◆ ◆

It was late afternoon by the time I checked into my apartment in Zagreb, took a quick shower, and headed out for a walk. I wandered about Jelačić Square for a time and admired the handsome statue, then crossed the busy street, careful to avoid the blue streetcars thundering by on the tracks. I wanted to get a sense of the layout of the place. There were many small bakery shops offering sandwiches, pizza slices, and sweets of all kinds. People sat at outdoor cafes chatting with friends and looking about at the passers-by. I felt relieved at being here and away from Pula, away from the menace of Malek, still a bit tired from travel but feeling somehow as if I had escaped and was free. It was so good and heartening to be walking about with scores of people around me in the early evening. Strangers to be sure, but everyone friendly and smiling, with places to go or friends to meet. The city beckoned.

One of my last conversations with Davor, so long ago it seemed, intruded my thoughts and bothered me. It was as if a new and terrible reality confronted me through his words. A reality where evil, in various forms and capacities existed side by side with normal, everyday reality. I looked around me and what I saw I believed was good and untroubled. Maybe Davor had been gravely mistaken. Chaos, pain, a craving for destruction, couldn't be found here. Evil spirits weren't drifting about. People were sipping espressos and laughing. Even the dogs were comfortable sitting under their masters' tables enjoying tidbits and special treats, content with the world and their place in it.

◆ ◆ ◆

I wandered about the city, stopping wherever I wanted. And there, just there, in front of the Croatian National Theatre, I was struck by the sight of them. Two large pines thrust their peaks high into the Croatian sky.

They stood on either side of Meštrović's sculptural masterpiece, the Well of Life. For me, it seemed as if the ancient god of the Illyrians rested under their tangled branches. The great god of life, Pan, the goat god. The god of the Croats before Christ, before Catholicism. Keen to feel the experience I crept under the heavy branches of one of the pines to its twisted trunk where beneath it was a small space covered in pine needles. I crouched beneath its heavy branches and sat for a moment in perfect silence. It was an odd thing to do, but it felt right to do it. I was particularly intrigued because earlier in the day I had visited Meštrović's studio in the old town and seen a sculpted head with the title "Moses" beneath it. I laughed to see it, the curious title. It was truly the head of a goat man and god, the god of the Illyrians, the god the Romans called Pan. I remembered for a fleeting moment what had drawn me to Croatia, the chance to become a travel writer. The country was so rich in history and culture. But I had made my choice and knew I could not return to any other kind of life.

That evening I received a text message from Zora to return to Pula. My heart skipped a beat. In a few hours I was back in Pula, the journey there nothing but a blur in my mind.

Anticipation is one of the greatest of aphrodisiacs. Zora wanted to see me. She wanted to see me, and I was hopeful that it wasn't all of it strictly work related. For the first time I felt I had a chance with her, not just as a friend, but something more, something richer, something altogether different. My world had changed. That was a given. There was real danger about. I knew that. Davor, I was sure, had been murdered. It was bizarre to me. Zora would be able to confirm a lot of things for me. That I knew for sure. And in the midst of all of this insanity, there was just the most tender shoot of hope springing up, of possible love between Zora and me. Whatever it was, I wanted to see it through to the end. I needed to. Life was richer now, far more nuanced, and somewhat deadlier than I had ever supposed. I remembered Davor saying that life is either a daring adventure or nothing at all. He was always leaving me with quotes that were like tiny gold nuggets.

When I came down the hill from my apartment I saw her sitting alone in the outdoor café with her back to me. It was early in the evening on a humid day. She was wearing a dark blue dress with tiny white polka dots across it.

I stopped for a moment and just stood there wondering what would happen, what a few hours would reveal about our relationship. Sometimes, I thought, you can blind yourself to reality and perceive what you want to without any regard to truth, to actuality. The moment passed and I walked towards her with a lump in my throat. She turned suddenly to her left and saw me.

She stood, her face beaming, and her arms stretched out for an embrace. I quickened my steps. I held her close to me for a luxurious moment basking in the warmth of the embrace. She sighed deeply and I watched her facial expression change from joy to sadness in a split second. Tears ran down her cheeks. We sat and looked at each other in silence. A waiter approached us, but then feeling the intense emotion around our table from a few feet away, he turned abruptly and left.

She shook her head as if to drive the untoward thoughts away, and then we made small talk until some degree of emotional equilibrium was regained. She wiped the moisture from her eyes with an embroidered handkerchief, and took a deep breath. We were back on solid ground.

"Have you heard from Gloria?" she asked.

"No," I said.

"Will you," she said, very softly, her eyes searching mine.

"No. it's finished. I think she thought there was a chance we could get back together, but it's over. She was looking for security in between lovers."

Zora's face brightened, and she smiled, her dimpled cheeks startling me with their sudden beauty. I had almost forgotten how beautiful she was.

"Well," she said, "after all, she is in the insurance business."

We both laughed, and I asked her if she wanted another coffee or a glass of wine.

"I know this Croatian restaurant that is famous for home-cooked dishes, the Baka Kuha, near the farmers' market," she said. "If you like we could have an early dinner there, and then I would like to invite you to my apartment for some dessert."

The restaurant lived up to its reputation. It was a small venue with two rooms, but comfortable and relaxed. Zora knew the bartender who also served as a waiter. He was a trim, bearded fellow, dressed impeccably, who brought complimentary drinks to our table and moved quickly through the two rooms with a natural zeal in his steps. The fish platter Zora and I shared was delicious. Gradually the restaurant was filled with diners and a low steady hum of contentment filled the space. Every now and then our waiter would go to a storeroom and bring out a saxophone. He would play a riff on it, and then put it away and return to serving his guests. He did it several times. It was delightful.

Afterwards, Zora called a taxi and we went to her apartment. I had a taste of her home-cooked apple burek and it was divine. I was sated from our dinner and drinks at the restaurant and could not finish the generous portion she had given me. Her apartment was small and tidy with photographs of family and friends on the wall. There was a large portrait of Davor on a cabinet. He was smiling ruefully, and it brought back to me so many memories where I had seen that same smile. Zora, seeing me looking at the photo, touched my forearm and smiled warmly.

"The picture captures his essence, doesn't it?" she said.

"Yes," I replied.

"I feel so sad," she said. "No, that's not the right word. Sadness is trite. It is a longing for him that I feel. A part of my life has been ripped away, torn from me forever, and where Davor had been there is nothing now but a hollow longing."

I turned to her and held her for a moment. I heard her sobbing, and then, steeling herself, she pushed me away and said that we must carry forward the rich legacy he left us. We must carry on our work with the spirits. And we both agreed he had been murdered. It was not a hit and run accident. It was murder. We sat across from each other at her kitchen table. I observed her eyes dart to the right and then down, as if remembering something. I waited for her to begin.

"Kristof, you will stay in Pula for a few days and then I will give you instructions where you will go next. We have the returned spirits spread across Croatia. I have matched them with spirit guides who are sharing the three Tesla cameras. The safeguarding of the cameras is vital. Dr. Spehar has advised us that it will take several months to produce just one. Luckily, you are able to do the work without the need of a camera and that has proven invaluable to us."

I nodded and looked away from her. I thought she might be able to detect my selfishness. I felt crass and forlorn. I was miserable. What I had thought might be a romantic evening, our first together, after a fine dinner and drinks, was something quite other now. We were steeped in a fantasia of violence and death mystery. I said nothing. I rose to go.

"Let me call you a taxi," she said. "Please sit."

We looked at each other fondly and in silence as we waited for the taxi. Suddenly, she reached over the table and placed her hand over mine. She smiled then, and with her perfect lips she said, "Kristof, there will be time. Don't worry. There will be time."

◆ ◆ ◆

It was odd to be back in Pula with Davor gone. The place didn't feel the same. I simply waited for instructions from Zora. Davor had been a kind of filter for me. I saw things through his perspective. Now that was over. I wandered about the familiar streets empty and lost. We hadn't known each other a long time, but somehow we had connected, and the world was different for me now, surcharged and exciting. I walked to the small park near the Coliseum where we had often sat, and my heart skipped a beat when I saw who was there.

"Christopher, my friend, how delighted I am to see you once again. How have you been, and where have you been?"

Malek was sitting on the very bench where Davor and I had often sat. Malek was smiling. That damned smile. I kept my anger tethered like a junkyard dog deep within, and forced myself to sit next to him. I pretended to be happy to see him. He took my extended hand in his, and held it momentarily. His palm was cool to the touch and oddly, slightly moist.

"Malek," I said, feigning a light sociability and ease of manner that was difficult for me. "I have been well and touring about this wonderful country of yours."

"Correction. This is not my country. I am from Europe, a different configuration and entity altogether. All of Europe is my native land, my country, and Croatia a small piece of it, but a pivotal piece to be sure."

"I don't understand your use of the word pivotal. How can Croatia be a pivot?"

Malek laughed confidently, and I thought, somewhat contemptuously. He stared straight ahead looking at the changing parade of tourists passing by, the trace of a smile still on his thin lips. The sun was quite high above us, and there were no shadows to be seen. The great Coliseum loomed to our left across the busy street with its mid day traffic.

"Pivots can move things about, quickly and silently. They are necessary to let the light in. Great transformations require pivots. That's how civilizations progress. I would have thought you knew that. I saw you once at one of my lectures. You really must attend more. I think you would find it edifying. Your wife Gloria told me that you were a teacher and an intellectual. Are you Christopher? Are you that?"

I felt the junkyard dog within me straining against his collar. I took a deep breath and turned to look at him.

"Yes, I could see she enjoyed the ambience of your yacht. It was bright in her eyes, the time she spent on your boat. She's returned to Canada now, so I suppose she too will miss the necessary edification of your lectures. Edification and enlightenment go together I guess. And that holds true for both wives and ex-wives, I should imagine."

Malek turned his head over to me, his expression nakedly hostile. His teeth were bared for a second, but only a second, and then he caught himself, and smiled thinly through his anger. I was surprised my words had that effect on him.

"I was sorry to hear of your friend Davor's death," he said. "A stupid hit-and-run accident. Altogether unfortunate. I didn't know him personally, but I knew him by reputation. It seems that he was involved in the dark arts. Is that true?"

"What do you mean by that?" I asked, in a slightly surly tone that I was unable to hold back in time.

"Oh, just that something occurred on Brijuni that was unnatural, about spirits from the dead. Imagine that. Just hearsay, mind you, but an occurrence that was most strange."

"What occurrence?"

"That is for you to tell me, Christopher. Unfortunately I don't have the details. Perhaps it has something to do with the migrant deaths that took place nearby. I don't know. People talk. Surely you know something. Do you Christopher? Do you know something, anything?"

"I know nothing about strange occurrences. I do know that migrants were slaughtered by some maniac or some right wing group."

I knew that Malek was fishing for information, and I knew that he knew more than he let on. He was playing me. It felt strange to me, to be sitting next to him and talking in this way. I felt a sense of loathing rise in me, but I stayed quiet, took a deep breath, and looked up into the clear blue Istrian skies. I remembered looking into those same skies with Davor.

"This part of the world has always known migrants and refugees and invaders. And always they have been pushed back into the sea. They are from parts of the world that are dark and dense and different from us. Little wonder that they seek the bright lights of Europe and the living host to feed on, but that is not to be. Not now. Not ever. They might as well be returning from the dead. We don't want them here. Sometimes the maniac you speak of can be a saint or a hero, someone who preserves the light of civilization at all costs and roots out the darkness. The growing light in the heavens is contingent upon leaders who are not afraid to tackle the dark materialism of our times, the death that must be vanquished now and forever. Can't you see that Christopher?"

I was struck by the power of his words and the soft modulations and seductive cadence of his voice as he spoke. The man was more dangerous than I thought, for he truly believed in what he was saying.

"Perhaps your language can light a fire that can sweep the world with its easy images and fear mongering, but it runs counter to common sense. It doesn't have staying power."

Malek rose abruptly from the park bench in sudden fury, glowered down on me for a tense moment, and called me an insolent fool. My remarks had stung him to the quick. He strode away towards the main street and then turned left. He was joined immediately by a group of four big men in dark suits who nodded and followed behind him. Not one of them spoke.

◆ ◆ ◆

It felt good to be lying in bed in the same Airbnb I knew from my first days in Pula. I propped up my two down pillows and placed them behind my back comfortably. I reached over and took a careful sip of the coffee I had made, taking care not to spill a drop on the clean white sheets. I placed the clear glass cup on a coaster on the bedside table.

I thought about the objects in the canvas bag that Davor had given me. So far I hadn't found a use for them. Strange souvenirs. And yet I remembered Davor had said that things could be silent witnesses. I think that was the term he used. Was there special power of some sort in these material objects? Or were they symbolic only of a lost time, an era long gone? What did they mean? Could they be silent witnesses to actual historical events? An unspoken history that contained truths if I could decipher them.

I thought about the time in Pula when I was given objects by Dr. Spehar. The suggestion was that I could investigate the past more readily through objects that belonged there, that belonged to that time, that derived from there. The time I had gone to the market in Pula I had seen the past as in a vision. I had clutched a Roman gold coin in my hand and seen, in a kind of trance state, a Pula market from Roman times. I could have dismissed what I saw as a waking dream and forgotten about it.

But I chose not to. I chose rather to enter that market scene and interact with it, the gold coin buried in my hand. I could see the market stalls so clearly. I could see the hanging carcasses of meat in the butcher's stall covered in flies. I could see the young woman selling brown eggs. I could see the tethered dog being bullied by a boy. It is so easy to dismiss things that run counter to daily, normal experience. It takes courage, I thought, to leave your moorings momentarily, to give yourself up to an uncommon experience.

The ground rules are simple. Basically, I reflected, there needs to be a sensitivity to the spirit of place, to what transpired there, in that specific location in days gone by. And then, a proactive probing of the images from the past event. All of this is facilitated if the person or medium, or whoever, has an object, a silent witness, directly related to the event. For me, the object was the Roman gold coin. It offered currency of a double sort. I knew it was worth money in today's marketplace, not only for its gold value, but also for its historical relevance, from the time of the Caesars. And then, as a silent witness, it could facilitate entry to a place and time remote from the present.

I had had enough speculation for the present. I reached over and took a generous sip of the coffee, but it was already cold.

1605 Istria, Stipe

Zora had invited me there to help him, but I didn't know what I could do for him. When I first met him, in Zora's apartment, he was quiet and still, in abject agony of some sort. But the agony wasn't of a physical kind. A huge mountain of a man, immensely muscular, with the biggest hands I had ever seen. He wore his hair very long and it fell heavily upon his broad shoulders. I had been told his name was Stipe and after I had explained to him the process we would follow through his memory images to access the right moment, he related his story to me in some detail. He sat bolt upright on the small couch in Zora's living room, taking up half of it, and I sat opposite him on one of the metal kitchen chairs.

I guided him through some relaxation exercises. He closed his eyes for several minutes, and then opened them. I leaned forward on my chair and observed the images on his retinas. A flurry of images came and went. I felt several sparks of light cross my field of vision sporadically and then they stopped. I was ready.

I received his memory images easily without effort. The images allowed me to piece together what had happened. Stipe didn't speak a word. He didn't have to. The images were crystal clear and readily transferable from his retinas to mine. A small band of Uskok warriors led by Stipe had come across and defeated an enemy encampment much larger in numbers. In the camp they had found a child, a boy of about nine, broken, and horribly abused. There were large purple and yellow bruises and welts all over his body. He had a fractured right arm and had suffered gross indignities and wounds to his groin and rectum that made Stipe and his people grow silent in thought for the longest time. They learned later that he was from Poreč and that his family had been killed by these men who took the child as a slave and plaything. Stipe bore silent witness to the boy's injuries in his own tent and bid his warriors to not exact revenge until they learned more about what had taken place. Stipe himself was shocked at the boy's condition and had to leave the camp periodically where he was sick to his stomach at the thought of it.

They learned that the boy had been repeatedly abused and raped by several of Stipe's captives over several weeks. They discovered that the captives, who tried to put the blame on each other for the boy's horrible injuries, were amazed at his behavior and commented on it. He had never cried or whimpered. Even after he had suffered horribly from them, he would sit alone by the fire and hum or quietly sing a song and rock gently back and forth, his arms wrapped around his knees. The only time they had seen him weeping was over a stray dog that he had befriended. One of the men, a short fellow with a livid white scar across his forehead, had noticed how much the boy loved the dog and for a lark had killed the dog and positioned its body next to the boy as he slept. When he awoke and saw his beloved friend, he let out the greatest, most heart-rending moan and wept. It was the only time they had seen him cry. They had thought he would make a fine slave and would fetch a high price in the Venetian markets.

Stipe listened closely when his warriors talked about the boy, and he thought about what to do. He observed the boy hobbling in pain around the camp, but helpful and useful, gathering firewood, or fetching water, and performing miscellaneous duties that he hadn't been asked to do. Once, just as the sun was setting, the boy sang a wonderful song about a golden string that was wound into a ball and led to eternal delight. Stipe had wept when he heard the simple melody, his self control lost in the beauty of the song. His warriors had never seen their commander weep before and they shuffled away in quiet embarrassment.

The captives, about two dozen of them who had been trussed and questioned repeatedly were untied and made comfortable and given polenta and smoked ham to eat. They were asked quietly, to identify those who had raped or beaten the boy. If anyone was found to have lied, they were told they would all be punished, so they were cautioned to be truthful on pain of death. It wasn't long before three of the captives were identified. Their guilt was confirmed through individual interrogation.

The three men were placed separately in small rough weave baskets and raised several feet off the ground and suspended from trees. The baskets were of such a small size that the prisoners could barely sit upright. They howled in protest but to no avail. Stipe would go for long walks, and he was clearly troubled. Before and after each of his walks he would gaze up at the prisoners in silence. He was told that the boy continued to work diligently around the camp and that he had asked that the prisoners be released from their pens and be given food. Stipe pondered this request for some time but then shook his head firmly. He could not allow it. From his tent Stipe watched the boy standing below the suspended prisoners. The blonde haired boy would simply stand as if waiting for something. On some days he would stand and then sing. It was always a song of such beauty and joy that many who heard it began to weep. When the boy did this, Stipe, alone in his tent, would bury his head in his massive hands and shake uncontrollably. Coursing through his body were feelings and emotions that he couldn't understand, try as he may. Around the camp the boy was referred to as the good soul. The warriors loved him and would play games with him. They fashioned a ball out of rags and twine and would kick it to him using only their knees and feet. They carved tiny animals out of oak and little boats of cedar wood with tiny masts to amuse him. They made strange faces and went cross-eyed to make him laugh. Now, these were hard men, and Stipe was more than a little surprised at their silliness.

This slip of a boy with a golden voice left a trail of tears whenever he sang. He was consistent. Each day he would go to one of the guards standing below the baskets of the three prisoners and ask for them to be freed. The guards would look to Stipe and see the iron in his face, and then quietly they would let the boy know it was not to be. The boy, seeing the deference paid to Stipe's wishes, asked to speak to Stipe. Stipe grew confused when the boy softly asked for the three men to be released from their cages. He could not understand why the boy forgave them. Stipe said he would decide their punishment for what they had done to him.

The boy smiled sadly and then noticed a gray tattoo on Stipe's forearm. He was clearly intrigued by it and looked at it intently. It was composed of two circles, a smaller one within a larger one. There was a dot in the middle of the smaller circle. And on the circumference of both circles there were short lines that radiated outward, each line culminating in a dot. There were 16 lines radiating from the smaller circle and 24 from the larger circle. The boy traced his finger around the perimeter of both circles and then asked Stipe if he could have one too. Stipe nodded.

A few days later the three men were released from their tiny basket cells and placed with the others from their band in a common area where they were tied and bound to each other. They were given food and water, and the expectation was that they would all be released once ransom had been paid. In due course the ransom arrived. However, Stipe changed his mind. He agreed to release thirty-five of the captives, but the guilty three he refused. They would not have their freedom. For their unnatural acts they would be punished. Ransom would only be accepted for those who had not hurt the boy.

The following day Stipe summoned the boy and prepared to give him the tattoo. A mixture was made from the soot of burned resinous wood and combined with honey in a small wooden bowl. The boy's arm was pierced with a needle and then the design was applied. Throughout the tattooing the boy smiled, focusing on the work in progress, showing no pain. Finally the tattoo was rubbed and covered with the honey soot mixture. His arm was then wrapped in a linen cloth that was removed two days later. The fresh tattoo was then washed and cleansed. The boy was very pleased.

Four days passed. Stipe was ready. The weather was dismal and rainy. He said it was a good day for punishment, and fitting. He chose for himself a club that he had often used in battle and a dagger that he attached to his right calf. The three men were given any two weapons of their choice, clubs, short swords, daggers, long-handled axes, hammers. They were told that if they defeated Stipe, if they killed him, they would be given their freedom. No ransom need be paid. They could leave the encampment without fear of being stopped. Each of them would be going against Stipe in single combat. The boy stood silent and watched in dismay.

The first man chose a double-bladed axe. He did not want any additional weapon. He was a short, bald muscular man with powerful sloping shoulders, and as soon as the signal was given, he let out a war cry and lunged at Stipe swinging his axe with a wild abandon. He missed on his first swing falling in a heap just beyond Stipe. But he immediately scrambled to his feet and charged once again, his axe at the ready. But Stipe was ready for him, ducked to one side, and then brought his club down hard on the back of the man's head, cracking it open with a lethal swing. Strangely the man turned around savagely and managed to raise his axe for one final attempt, but then simply crumpled to the ground dead on his feet. He was dragged away with blood and gray matter oozing from his head.

The second prisoner chose a sword and dagger, strapping the belt and sheath around his waist. He was a big, bearded man, as big as Stipe, with a massive barrel chest and head. He approached Stipe confidently, moving slowly, knees bent, with both hands firmly on the sword handle. Stipe waited until the man was very close and then swung his great club, just missing him. The prisoner raised the sword and brought it down hard, deeply cutting Stipe's left thigh with the action. Stipe backed away getting the club ready for an attack. He lifted it high and then swung at the prisoner's knees, shattering his right knee and knocking him off his feet. The prisoner held the sword in front of his body, unable to stand. Stipe rammed the club against the side of the sword, sending the sword flying high and behind the prisoner who struggled to release his dagger from its sheath. Then Stipe tossed his club away and twirled around on his feet. He stopped for a moment and then dove upon the prisoner, and in the same instant pulled out his dagger from his right calf and thrust it into the man's heart, killing him instantly.

A few moments passed before the third man, small with a white scar across his forehead, was brought forward. It was just beginning to rain. The prisoner refused to choose any weapons. He fell upon his knees in front of Stipe weeping and asking forgiveness. He turned and cried out to the boy imploring him to forgive him. The boy ran forward and stood between the prisoner and Stipe shouting for him to stop. Stipe towered above the boy, breathing hard. Everything seemed to pause for an instant. And then the boy's soft voice pierced the silence saying that you prove yourself better than your enemy by not being like them. Stipe stood stunned. He gestured to one of his men to take the boy away. The boy wept as he was carried away in the arms of the warrior. Stipe glared down at the prisoner and was as silent as stone. Suddenly, he spat into the man's face. He walked behind the man and took a sword from one of his men. And then in one deft stroke he severed the man's head. Oddly, the man still knelt for a moment, headless, blood gushing from his neck, and then he fell forward into the mud without a sound being made.

After the incident Stipe went to his tent and did not come out for three days. He refused the food his men brought him. He simply lay on his rough cot thinking about what the boy had said. He couldn't sleep. He tossed and turned, writhing about, forlorn and without peace. The memory images stopped. We were back in Zora's apartment and I could see my image in Stipe's eyes.

A new moment had arrived. Stipe had made the long journey to Brijuni. He had slowly travelled through two centuries to have an opportunity to relive one moment, the moment before he decapitated his prisoner against the wishes of the boy. I was there to guide him back through his images, to change the choice he had made. I knew what he had to do. I asked him to return to the memory image just before he had killed the third man. He needed to experience that living moment decisively once again, and to change it. He nodded silently, and I saw the retinal image appear.

It was the moment after the boy had wept as he was carried away in the arms of the Uskok warrior. Stipe had glared down at the prisoner and was as silent as a temple stone. He spat into the captive's face. He walked behind the man as he had before and took a sword from one of his men. And then, instead of stopping himself from severing the man's head as he had done before, he carried through with his action. There was a light swishing sound. The man knelt for a moment, headless, blood gushing from his neck, and then he fell forward into the mud a dead heap, as before.

I looked at Stipe in disbelief. He had come so far, so far from the undiscovered country, to correct a decision, to make a new choice that would give him peace, and he had chosen not to. He had travelled through two centuries of accumulated time to redeem himself, to honor the boy's goodness and purity, and he had failed.

"Why Stipe? Why?"

Stipe looked at me, smiling ruefully, and yet through the sadness, I saw an aspect of triumph as well.

"I waited two hundred years for a chance to change, but when that singular moment came, I could not. I would not. Every cell in my body, in my being, cried out for vengeance, and I could not stop it. The scum needed to die, and die he did. I thought I might spare him for the boy, but that was not to be, not in any lifetime."

I shook my head in disbelief. I rose from the metal chair, walked over to him and embraced him. I felt his hot tears fall upon my cheek. I understood the man and his fate but could not help him.

◆ ◆ ◆

Zora had arranged the meeting with Mr. Šubić. I was waiting for him, seated alone outside in a café directly opposite the Temple of Augustus. It was a quiet evening and few tourists were about. It was too early for dinner. I had ordered a double espresso and sweetened it with four packets of brown sugar. I craved the bitter sweetness of the drink.

He entered the square from the direction of the harbor. He was accompanied by several aides, some perhaps bodyguards, who quietly sat at tables nearby. Mr. Šubić was a slight, small man in his sixties with a wizened face, rather large ears, and thin sand-colored hair. He was wearing a crisp white shirt, long-sleeved, and a dark blue silk cravat. I stood up to greet him and extended my hand. There was a broad smile on his face as he shook my hand and then sat down. There was something special about the gentleman.

"Ah, you remember me Mr. Radelja. Zora has told me of your successes since we met. She has briefed me regularly," he said. His manner was extremely confident and there was a look of quiet amusement in his twinkling hazel eyes.

"Please, call me Kristof. Mr. Šubić."

"And you must call me Šubić. That is my name and easy to remember."

I nodded. There was a sense of gravitas about him perhaps, that made me feel uncomfortable with the thought of using his surname in addressing him. So, I avoided it, and we spoke for a few moments about Zora. I noticed one of his aides went inside the café as we conversed. A waiter came by a moment later and left a bottle of chilled white wine in a silver bucket and two glasses. He poured the wine into our glasses deftly and then withdrew. We held our glasses high and toasted.

I remembered meeting him briefly on Brijuni. Davor had introduced us, and I could tell from Davor's deference to him then that Mr. Šubić was a leader. Neither I nor Davor had been permitted to enter the huge tent where the returned spirits congregated after their fantastic arrival, but I remembered the joyous greetings that had hailed his entry into the great tent. I wondered what strange ceremonies and orientation rites had taken place under the tent's canvas roof.

I saw him shift in his seat and place the palm of his right hand on the linen tablecloth. He looked directly at me with a level gaze. There was to be no small talk. He cleared his throat and began.

"Your consummate skill in working with our returned spirits has been one of the recent highlights in our work. And this without the intervention and use of a Tesla camera. We are grateful to have you on the team." He leaned forward then, towards me, looking close at me, and breaking into a great broad smile.

"Kristof, I am trying my best not to think any untoward thoughts, for fear that you will see the evidence of it on my retinas. I have heard of your prowess with retinal scanning." His laughter resonated in the space around us. He looked about the spacious piazza of the ancient Roman Forum.

"I love this space. It is wonderful here with the Temple and the Town Hall and the fine buildings around us," he said, taking a moment to survey the area. Then he tapped twice on the linen tablecloth as if to signal a shift in his thinking.

"So, I wanted to apprise you on what has been happening. You have been very kind in working with us without demanding a full knowledge of the background to our work. Davor, I am sure, supplied you with some basic facts, but unfortunately he is gone now, and you must be content with my overview." He sat back in his chair and took a drink of his wine before continuing. A few droplets of condensation ran down the outside of his glass.

"Brijuni was the start for us and proved an auspicious beginning. Eighty returned spirits. Eighty souls in search of redemption. Eighty of our men and women, from our far past. You have met and worked with some of them, and to your credit, have succeeded for the most part. Stipe was an exception, but even that was not in vain. He was true to his being though his intent and motivation in returning had been different. Two hundred years it took for him to reconstitute his spirit with our help, in slow, steady stages, and then with your intervention we hoped to be successful, but it was not to be. But, dear Kristof, he had the opportunity, the chance to make amends though the outcome was the same as in his original life. What can you do?" He shrugged then as if to acknowledge the limits of power and purpose, given the facts of human nature. There were things that could not be changed. The fingers of his right hand tapped twice on the linen tablecloth.

"What you saw at Brijuni was something remarkable, the fruit of decades of research and experimentation by hundreds of us, until we finally succeeded in breaking a kind of code. Illyrian spirits, Croatian spirits, returning for a brief time, reconstituted in living flesh for a few months to make a correction, a moral change, a slight deviation, sometimes gentle, sometimes violent, but made nevertheless with good or at least just intent. I believe it was Kant who said that two things filled him with ever increasing wonder and awe- the starry heavens above him and the moral law within him. At least that is my purview of our situation.

What we had not counted on was the interference of Malek. We had been so single-minded in the recovery of our returned spirits, and its celebration, that we failed to look at what was happening on the periphery of things. Before his untimely death, before his murder, Davor had warned us of something sinister taking shape. We dismissed his cautions. Malek was investigated by our intelligence team and deemed harmless, a popular lecturer, until the raft of migrant refugees and their murder, pointed to his involvement. Only then did we think to acknowledge the fact that Malek had learned of something going on at Brijuni, though he didn't know what was taking place or when, but had suspicions. The raft of migrants was an unexpected occurrence and he liquidated them calmly and ruthlessly, with only a few survivors left clinging to the wreckage. His bizarre philosophy or religion saw them only as fodder, as fuel, for a manic drive against something he perceives as evil. He is very dangerous, the more so because he believes what he preaches, and his self righteousness gives him the power to act ruthlessly and mercilessly. He refers to himself as an emissary of light.

We know now that his intelligence has infiltrated our organization and the prime target happens to be the returned spirits and the spirit guides who assist them. So, Kristof, be vigilant, be ready. You are on his list, and he knows you."

At that point one of his aides came to our table and whispered in his ear. He nodded in quiet affirmation at something that was being said and then turned to me again, saying nothing.

I felt a hollowness growing in the pit of my stomach at what he had said. I remembered my conversation with Malek in the small park across from the Coliseum. Around us the tables were starting to fill with diners. Waiters, in black vests, were walking briskly back and forth serving the tables. A small gray cat sped away from under one of the tables as an old couple sat down. Another of Šubić's aides approached our table and handed him a cellphone. He took it, listened for a moment, and then uttered an expletive after which he returned the cellphone to the aide.

"Zora and other administrators have been sending encrypted messages to you and the other spirit guides telling you when to move throughout Croatia to meet with the returned spirits. However, we have reason to believe that Malek's people are fully aware of these movements. So, I have given directives for administrators to be creative in disseminating their appointments between spirit guides and returned spirits. Spirit guides will move independently, making their own accommodation and travel arrangements until notified of meetings by their respective administrator. In this regard, I would suggest you emulate the behavior of the small white butterfly. You see them everywhere in summer gardens, in cabbage gardens, these common butterflies. Their seemingly erratic patterns of movement cannot be anticipated in direction or destination. Indeed, it is far easier to capture an eagle or a hawk than a common white butterfly. These creatures can shift direction suddenly and irretrievably obeying laws of nature that have not yet been decoded. They are elusive, ethereal specks of light, as difficult to follow as sparks from a flame. I have thought about them often. If size and scale could be factored in, and if they could be transformed into warriors, they would be indomitable. No enemy could touch them. Future armies will move that way." Mr. Šubić suddenly lifted his left arm above the linen tablecloth and moved his fingers erratically in the air for a brief moment, and then dropped his arm lightly on the table. He chuckled under his breath and then glanced over to his aides, signaling the meeting was over.

"There is one other thing. At some point, I would ask you to perform a certain action. At Makarska. There are foreign spirits, many of them invaders from the past, seeking release from the sea, from watery graves. They wish to return to land, and I would request that you assist them. I will let you know when, but only if you are predisposed to help in this regard. It has nothing to do with your spirit work with us. It is something extra and rather extraordinary. Extra compensation, of course, will be provided."

"Of course," I said. "Just let me know."

Mr. Šubić smiled briefly and then motioned to one of his aides to take care of the bill. We both stood, shook hands, and then I watched him walk away with his escort. The first stars of the night sky were just beginning to show themselves.

1493 Near Krbava Field, Nikola

When I first saw Nikola I was impressed by his military bearing. He was a tall, thickly set handsome lad with long blonde hair, startling blue eyes, and a sad smile on his lips. He looked to be no more than twenty-three years old, like the other returned spirits. He was smartly dressed in a white linen suit with a light blue shirt, and he sported a dark blue cravat at his throat. It was silken. A short-brimmed panama hat was on the iron wrought chair beside him. His presentation, if you could call it that, was very elegant and insouciant even to the sandals he wore. I prepared for our meeting by ensuring I was completely relaxed and free from any distracting thoughts. I wanted my intuitive capacity to be at its zenith. Zora had arranged for us to meet in a wine bar just outside of Udbina. He was sitting under a grape arbor, the sun spilling through from above, when I approached him. He stood up immediately, spoke a few words of welcome, and offered his hand. It was very smooth, obviously not a workman's hand. I noticed quickly that he had a habit of brushing back his long, thick hair as he spoke.

It was early afternoon and the bar was deserted except for the two of us. There was a pitcher of white wine on the table, some wonderful looking black olives, and a bottle of sparking water. He poured me a glass of wine without asking if I wanted one, and then smiled warmly. I nodded my thanks and then told him how we would proceed. He would recount his tale as I relaxed into it, and then I would intercede at a point I deemed appropriate. Through his thoughts, I explained, he would create memory images on his retinas that I would also see until we were at a precise moment where he would choose a different outcome than the one he had originally chosen. Then, I could begin my work. I asked him to begin. Just before the first of the memory images started, I experienced the several sharp customary flashes of light that startled me momentarily. His retinal images were crystal clear.

"I cannot tell you the reason why I did what I did, for reason cannot exist where passion rules the day. I should say where passion rues the day for I have certainly done that countless times. I was already on horseback, my gear and weapons with me, and moving to the front when I saw her on the balcony just as she turned away from speaking with someone inside. She raised her face to the sun, holding it there for an instant, and then slowly scanned the busy yard below. My best friend Mirko, mounted beside me, saw her too and waved, for she was a beauty. Though she was smiling at everyone in the courtyard, she spoke love secrets to me from the delicate corners of her green eyes. She was high-born and resplendent in a golden beaded dress that accentuated her auburn hair. I made some flimsy excuse to

Mirko and my troop that I would join them soon. Mirko smiled knowingly and cautioned me to hurry. He knew my proclivities well. He left for the front with a knowing look on his face.

I dismounted, tethered my stallion, and signaled to meet her in the courtyard. There was something in the air that encouraged and allowed different codes of behavior from the ordinary. The imminence of battle perhaps. She approached and we stood and chatted beside an old woman selling fine lace. Two of her attendants waited nearby, smiling and whispering softly to each other. The beauty pretended to be examining several pieces of lace as she spoke to me. She invited me to lunch after we had ascertained several families and friends that we knew in common. We barely ate, our appetites not fixed on food. She dismissed her attendants. We arranged to meet in one of the buildings on her father's estate.

From late morning to evening we made love and laughed, and I discovered the scent of lavender beneath her breasts. No explorer of continents unknown could boast of any experience, any find richer than that. The remembrance of that scent I took with me to my grave. The way she spoke was like poetry to my ears.

At dusk I hurried off to join the others on their way to battle but alas was sidetracked along the way. An innkeeper's daughter waved me over, holding up a jug of dark red wine. Behind her was an arbor covered in bunches of golden grapes and great, multicolored vine leaves. She was dark with hair the color of a raven's wing and a body so perfectly endowed that you could fall to your knees and praise the saints by the mere sight of its magnificence. Ah, such beauty, such winsomeness. For a skirt she wore two embroidered aprons, one in the front and one in the back. She took me to a small hut by a silver stream under the quickening light of stars, where, after the necessary preliminaries, she rocked me again and again to my very core. Her lips were soft like ripe purple cherries. She carried with her an odor of sausages and sauerkraut, and I was hungry. And later, much later, just when I thought she was satisfied, she rose up with such delightfully insistent demands that I could not help but oblige. Later, exhausted from lovemaking and from wine, I slept deep into the next morning, and then woke with a start. She was already gone. I grabbed an apple from a basket and raced to find my horse fresh and ready in the barn by the inn. I saddled up and made for the battlefield. I was in a panic from having slept so long when I should have been with the others. My steed seemed to feel my agitation, and we set off quickly on our belated mission. My thoughts raced before me. I was hoping to be with my family on the field as soon as possible. My father, grandfather and cousins would be there, all of them, a brace of kinsmen and friends ready to do battle with the marauding Turks. My head was clear and my arms ready.

When I arrived the worst was there before me spread like damnation across Krbavsko field. I couldn't believe my eyes. It was hell."

For several minutes Nikola was quiet, as if dredging up memories too horrible to bring to full consciousness. He sat there frozen and reflective. I refilled his wine glass and signaled the waiter for another jug. The sun was filtering through the canopy of wine leaves and vines above us, creating a latticework of light and shade on our table. He lowered his head for a moment and then continued his eyes moist with recollection. The retinal image of a battlefield was horrible to behold in his eyes.

"You see the battle was over. The field was littered with the freshly dead. I recognized their faces. So many of our nobles lost forever, gone. The fallen standards and flags lay tattered among the dead. I wandered about stunned and ashamed for not being among them. My legs felt so heavy as I trudged through the bloodied field, and then I stopped suddenly for there before me was my father's body a Turkish lance through his chest. I pulled the lance from him, tossing it away, and then knelt and cradled him in my arms. I wept bitter tears and begged forgiveness from him. I kissed him on the lips and felt the cold indifference that I had never known before in a kiss. A kiss. I stood up and recognized two cousins and my grandfather a few feet away. I reeled away in grief. All around me there were heaps and piles of the noble dead, some decapitated. I noticed a group of peasants with oxen and wooden carts come to haul away the dead for burial. They were silent as they went about their work. Mine was the only warhorse standing about. There were no others. And then I saw Mirko lying mutilated and dead beside one of the captains of our troop. I looked about me at the desolation on the field and cried out in sheer horror and dismay for

I was not among them. I wanted an end to my pain. My tears were gone and would never come again from that day. Tears are nothing but another kind of urine, moisture that means nothing."

He emptied his glass of wine in one swig and then set it down hard against the glass tabletop. I thought it might crack or shatter, but it didn't. He looked at me and waited.

"Nikola, as you've told me your tale, I recognize the pivot point needed for the intervention. We both know why you made the long journey back. And now you and I will return to that pivotal moment where you can change your fate. We will re-enter the past and change it. We will go back and manipulate a single fleeting retinal image and its new memory image will change all. Are you with me?"

He nodded, his face shining with hope and potential redemption. He reached over and placed his hand on my forearm, his grip strong and ready. I signaled to one of the waiters at the far end of the bar to ensure we would not be disturbed. I had given him a wad of cash earlier to ensure our privacy.

I spent several moments reviewing the images Nikola had provided for me. I moved through the images. I asked him to look into my eyes and concentrate on the images, particularly when he saw the woman on the balcony just as she turned away from speaking with someone inside, and then the next moment when she raised her face to the sun, holding it there for an instant. He was listening to a disembodied voice, my voice, as he relived the moment. I asked him to urge his horse on as the woman still held her face to the afternoon sun. I rearranged the retinal images I had received from Nikola and watched him ride away from the woman and the courtyard and his lovemaking towards a new destiny, towards the gratification of an honorable death.

I watched the way his eyes moved and the way his body twitched wildly as it encountered new memories. After several moments the trace of a smile played on his lips. He was dying happily on a battlefield that was strategically lost before it even began. But I had seen the alternative images and memories as I intuited Nikola's future if he had not died at Krbava field. A crushed spirit within a drunken body that carried on for a decade more before it fell indifferently into death. Then his eyes closed.

It was very quiet as we sat under the arbor. A light wind was blowing from the east and the sound of rustling leaves could be heard. When he roused and opened his eyes, I could see the immense relief etched upon his face. He seemed to be energized and vital somehow, in a way that he had not been before. He stood up and came to my side of the table where he embraced me in a great hug and laughed uproariously. Never had I met a man who welcomed death with such ardor and gratefulness. He said he was suddenly hungry for sausages and sauerkraut, ravenous in fact. I laughed and signaled over to one of the waiters. After our meal I asked him what his plans were. He laughed, looked above at the arbor with its grapevines and leaves, and then winked at me. His wink was a mischievous wink, that was plain to see.

"Kristof, it is as if I am on a long belated holiday. I have completed what I set out to do, with your help of course. Now I am looking forward to returning home. But I have several days before I must return to Brijuni and the peace that I crave. This precious time will not be wasted. It is a vast marvel to be alive again, to feel the sun on my face, to see the sun streaming through the vines overhead, to hear the wind move through the trees, and perhaps, if the gods allow, to touch a beautiful woman."

He went silent then, just enjoying the day we shared, pleased with the ambience of the place.

"Would you like to stay then Nikola, if you could? Would you like to remain alive, here?" I asked, immensely curious.

"Oh no, not now. Why would I trade the peace and vast dark richness that is mine for the trouble and strife of living again as I have just done. Certainly, I will treasure these living moments but they cannot compare to the afterlife, now that you and I have corrected what happened to me in life. The next few days are a holiday only, a lark to be enjoyed and then put away forever. No, I will return and gladly so."

"So, where do you want to go? We have money and time."

"To the seacoast, between Split and Makarska. I want to hear our music and sing, and drink red wine, and eat barbequed lamb, and dance."

"Nothing else? The women here are beautiful. After all, you're a young man despite your age."

Nikola started laughing uproariously, shaking his head from side to side.

"But Kristof, you didn't listen carefully enough. I did say I wanted to dance," he said emphasizing the word dance in a low throaty voice.

I watched as he stood up. I watched him walk away from the arbor, and then toss his panama hat high into the clear sky, catching it by the brim on its descent with a mischievous twinkle in his eye. Now we were on holiday time.

410 Solin, Anka

The first time I laid eyes on Anka was in Zora's apartment. When Zora introduced us I held out my hand to take hers, and she recoiled at my gesture as if I had meant to strike her. So, I simply nodded in greeting and sat across from her at the kitchen table. It reminded me of how people acted during the height of the COVID-19 pandemic and the time of social distancing. I saw the trace of a smile flash across Zora's face as she prepared coffee. Anka was a thin woman, young, with olive-colored skin and wonderfully thick dark, curly hair that fell below her shoulders. She was the kind of woman people would call handsome because of her strong, defined features. She was quiet but there was a finely tempered resolve in her face that marked her as a woman of steely determination. She took her coffee black and closed her eyes with pleasure at the first taste of it.

I explained the process whereby she would provide memory images of a moment she wished to change, and I would create and manipulate the pixels that made up the memory image. I asked if I could hold her hand as a part of an initial relaxation procedure. She refused. I glanced at Zora, and she merely shrugged and stirred three packets of sugar into her coffee, so I continued without her hand in mine. I asked her to tell me her story.

"I must begin with the inscription on my tombstone. It reads that my husband had brought me to his home when I was eighteen, and that he had lived with me in chastity for thirty-three years. That inscription was his pride. I had 51 years when I died. That ending was also my beginning, the beginning to my story. From the first day I dared not touch him. And from that first day I was always aware of his body, of where it was in relation to mine."

At that point she stopped for several moments. Her eyes were closed and I could see her eyes moving beneath her eyelids. Hundreds and thousands of images danced across her consciousness. I observed her closely, and every now and then her eyes would cease to move as she recalled a particular moment in time.

"I didn't love him at first. That took time. It was easier to practice abstinence when I did not love him. Much easier. The hardship came when I began to love him, when he made me laugh. Once, he hollowed out a watermelon and fashioned a Roman helmet out of it and then danced around our kitchen with a broomstick for a horse. He was a good man and chaste. It is easy to be good with a stranger, even a married stranger, a husband, but when that stranger becomes a beloved, it is infinitely more difficult to be good, because you begin to think that that goodness is not so good. Once, when he accidentally bumped into me my whole body seized up and I had convulsions on the stone flagstones of our kitchen. I think he thought I was dying and when he cradled me in his arms I passed out. When I awoke the priest was giving me last rites, but it was not a rite that I wanted. No, not at all."

She stopped for a moment and held up her empty coffee cup, signalling to Zora that she wanted a refill. Zora nodded and prepared more coffee. The trace of a smile crossed her lips and then she continued.

"That day was five years after I had come to his home. Things continued as before and I would keep my distance from him, and he from me. But then the priest, the middle-aged one with slick black hair combed back, the one who had given me last rites, asked my husband if I could assist him in the church on occasion. He said he needed help with laundry, with scrubbing the vestry, with polishing the altar ornaments. Of course my husband was pleased and gave me leave to do such work. He was proud that the priest wanted me. For several weeks I would work at the church in the evenings after Vespers, and the priest was happy with my work. It was very quiet and

I would be quite alone, except for the priest who checked with me every now and then, asking if I needed anything, a flat iron or soap.

One day I noticed he was looking at me as I was scrubbing the vestry floor. He was just standing there and staring at me. I asked him if anything was the matter. He asked me if I needed to have my confession heard. I thought that was odd because my husband and I always had our confessions heard every Saturday afternoon. He just mumbled something and then left. But the following week he came to speak with me just as I was finishing up my work. He told me that my husband's confession had troubled him. He said that my husband was sorely tempted with desire for me and that he was very much afraid of sinning in the flesh. He said he needed spiritual help to combat his temptations. I was surprised and told the priest that what was heard in a confessional was not to be revealed to anyone, ever. He looked at me oddly and nodded, saying that in special circumstances the clergy could become an instrument of the Holy Spirit and intervene where needed. That special dispensation included sharing the secrets of the confessional and something more, something truly miraculous, the vicarious assumption of the marital function of the husband. At first I did not understand him. He was using big words. He spoke more slowly saying this unique dispensation allowed the husband to keep chaste while allowing his spiritual seed access to the Holy Spirit through the instrument of the clergy, the priest and the confessor of the believer. He said this special dispensation was a shared secret with the priest, himself, as the go-between. The husband was not to know that the wife knew of his tribulations of the flesh. Only the priest would keep the secret and offer himself up as the physical instrument of the Holy Spirit. Then it dawned on me what he wanted, and for a moment I could not speak. I turned away from him and went to the vestry window and looked at the Square below. I could not move. Suddenly I felt him behind me with his arms embracing me. I felt his manhood stirring and I tried to wrench myself away, but he was too strong and held me, mumbling in Latin and kissing the nape of my neck. Somehow I found my strength and pushed him off and ran out from the vestry and from the church.

Several days passed, and one day my husband came to me asking why I had not been going to help the priest. He said the priest had asked for me to return. My husband reproached me and said it was an honor for me to serve God in this way. I did not know what to say to him. I was ashamed to tell him what had happened. My moorings were gone and I felt lost and abandoned. I returned to the church the next day and went about my work. For the next three days I did not see the priest. And then on a Tuesday, after Vespers, as I was folding laundry in the large closet behind the vestry I heard the door close and saw him approaching me. I flung some garments at him and tried to run past him but could not. I was unable to cry out. I froze in terror, and he pushed me over. I went limp and a part of me rose above the priest and myself on the floor. It was as if I was watching what was happening. In a few moments it was over and he left, saying his work was done for the day. The part of me that was a speck on the ceiling descended back into my body, and I slowly gathered myself and wandered out into moist night air. I can't remember how I got home or what my husband was saying when I came into the kitchen. I simply went to bed and wept hot tears into my pillow.

Over the next days, I could see my husband was concerned for me. He asked if I was ill. I stayed in bed and he brought food to me. He was very worried and anxious. One rainy afternoon my husband came into my bedroom with the priest. I cried out in alarm when I saw him, and pulled the covers around me into a tight ball, turning on my side and folding my knees against my chest. I peered out at him from the corner of my eye. My husband looked at the priest in consternation. The priest stood there for a moment, uneasy and awkward, then held out a crucifix and mumbled a Latin prayer. He whispered something to my husband, and then, abruptly, he left.

My poor husband was so distressed. He tried everything to cheer me up. He stuffed his mouth with cherries and tried to speak, hoping I would laugh as I had done in the past, but I could only look at him stone-faced, watching the cherry juice dribble down his chin. I was impure now and he was not. I did not belong with such a good man. I stayed in bed for two more days and then knew what I must do.

Early before dawn one morning I walked to a small village north of Solin. There, on the outskirts of the village lived an old woman who I had been told made her living by selling herbs and potions. She opened the door before I had even knocked. She was dressed completely in black with a black kerchief tied about her head. Her face was clear, plump, and radiant. She invited me into her small hut, where I sat upon a three-legged stool that she offered, and I could see she was studying me very closely with haunting grey eyes that seemed to penetrate my very being. I told her, with my eyes downcast, that there were rats infesting my home and that I needed a poison that could act quickly and without fail. She nodded. She was silent. She looked at me for the longest time. Somehow she knew. She took my hand in hers and then after several moments, she embraced me sympathetically, and I began to weep uncontrollably in her arms. I told her everything. I wanted to die with my shame.

Then, a curious thing happened. As I looked at her, her face seemed to undergo a series of odd changes. Her face was changing from that of an old woman's to that of a young woman, and then back again to an old woman's face before my very eyes. I became frightened and I stood, and was about to leave when she bid me sit and wait, and I did.

Several moments later she returned with two packets. The first that she opened contained a vial with yellow liquid within it that she said was fatal if mixed with cherry juice. The other was wrapped in black canvas and it held what she said was a Byzantine dagger. When she unwrapped it so very carefully, removing it from its fine leather sheath, I was startled by its beauty. Its magnificent hilt was decorated with infinitely fine patterns. The slender greenish-blue blade ended in a point that was almost invisible. She said that it was particularly effective if dipped in a cesspool prior to its use.

I gave her some silver coins, which she accepted very gratefully and tucked beneath her blouse. As I reached out to take the vial, she said that I must take both items and decide which was the better remedy for my misfortune. I was puzzled, but she insisted, wrapping each of the items very carefully. She invited me for a breakfast of polenta and milk, but I thanked her and said I must leave as my husband would be worried. She kissed me and then I left.

My husband looked at me with such tender concern that I was sorry to have left him even for a day. He told me that the priest I had served had found another woman to help with his chores and that I would no longer be needed in the vestry. Over the following days I could not bring myself to drink the potion the old woman had given me. Perhaps I was a coward and did not wish to die. I had hidden it and the dagger beneath one of the flagstones in our kitchen. I was puzzled over why she had given me both items.

I did not like having secrets from my husband, but I knew it must be so. When we went to Sunday mass I noticed that the priest would not look at me directly in the eyes. His jaw would tighten and he would look away. I saw too the young woman who had taken my place and the abject misery etched into her fair features. I was so sorry for her. She couldn't have been more than sixteen years old.

Time passed. I would watch her walk by our home and see her posture droop as she neared the church, her arms hanging limply by her side. Some days, when I went to market to sell eggs, I would see her in the churchyard hanging laundry, a dozen or so white sheets flapping in the wind. Her mind seemed to be somewhere else, and times there were when she would sink to her knees as if in prayer and cradle her face in her hands. I knew she was weeping.

Once, on a brisk, windy day as I walked by the churchyard, I saw her standing amid the wildly flapping sheets, just standing there, mute and devastated. Suddenly the priest was by the stairs calling out to her to come inside. She walked to the rear entrance of the church as slowly as an old woman. Her eyes caught mine for an instant and I saw the stricken terror of them. I turned away and hurried home.

My husband was away that day. I went to the kitchen and removed the flagstone beneath which was hidden the vial and the Byzantine dagger. I fell to my knees. I ignored the vial of poison. I slid the dagger carefully from its sheath and wondered over its blue-green beauty. The feel of it in my hand was magical. The point of it was almost invisible and the thin blade glinted sharply in the filtered morning light that came in through the barred kitchen window. I simply looked at it for the longest time and then put it away.

Several weeks passed and life continued as usual, each day the same. On market day I would gather my eggs from the hencoop behind our house and walk by the church to the city square adjacent to it. I had walked the same route so many times before." Anka stopped speaking then, and her retinal images ceased.

"Now Kristof, now is the moment when I need your help. Now is the time to change the memory image. Now, instead of going to the market and continuing my life as before, I will take my revenge. That is my choice."

I nodded to Anka that I understood her decision, and I began to create and manipulate the pixels that made up the memory image of her just as she was about to walk to the market. I was in the zone. When I was ready I raised my hand in a signal for her to continue with the new retinal images I had created for her.

"One day as I walked to market I carried the Byzantine dagger with me. I was in a trance-like state. I stopped only once to dip the blade in a common public latrine. It was filthy. No one was about. I continued my walk and entered the churchyard. There, once again, the young woman was hanging the last of the white sheets upon the clothesline. There were three lines of sheets, about a yard apart, all of them moving briskly with the wind.

The priest came down the church steps and stood behind the young woman as she set the last of the clothes pegs on the sheet. He could not see me as I approached him from behind, the white sheet behind him snapping in the wind. Behind me too I could not be seen from the street because of the line of white sheets behind me. I saw him pressing himself behind the young girl quite brazenly. She stifled a cry and then stood stock still in fear and apprehension.

I placed my bag on the ground before me and then carefully withdrew the dagger from its sheath. A white sheet flapped in the wind behind me covering my movements. The dagger shone so brightly in the sun, the blade still wet from its dipping in the latrine. I called out to the priest. He turned abruptly in a dead panic, the white sheet outlining his chest and stomach like a plump pheasant.

Suddenly my arm lifted by itself, and it was as if the dagger was pulling and guiding me to its fell purpose. The thin blade struck out, encountering little resistance even as my wrist turned and tore through his astonished flesh. The dagger sank easily within the soft, yielding flesh until the hilt of the blade rested against the white sheet and the priest within it. Great blotches of red spread unevenly across the sheet in random irregular patterns. The priest sighed quietly, as if someone had whispered a terrible confession to him, and then he fell backwards in a black heap on the ground. The young girl ran off. I wiped the blade against the priest's cassock making the sign of the cross in a crude vertical and then horizontal stroke. I placed the dagger in its sheath and returned home. There, I hid the knife carefully under the flagstone and set about preparing dinner. My husband told me the next day that the miscreant who had attacked the priest was not found. There were no gypsies about. The priest lingered on in a coma for almost a week and then died. It was quite a grandiose funeral, the bishop having been given special dispensation to spare no expense in displaying the most sumptuous of funeral rites."

1477 Tučepi, Franja

I was staying at the Rare Pink Bird Apartments in Makarska, a family run business, and as I looked out from my second floor balcony to the distant islands of Brač and Hvar, I thought about my next returned spirit encounter. It was Franja himself who told me his story. Zora was busy with her administrative tasks, mainly that of matching guardians like myself with what she called "counterpart spirits." The logistics involved in housing and feeding the Brijuni spirits newly become flesh were quite substantial. I was surprised and delighted with how quickly my Croatian was coming back to me. Every day I had a better feel for the language, for the way the words felt in my mouth as I spoke them. I loved the visceral feel of the spoken language, its immediacy, its blunt clarity.

Franja and I met in Tučepi. He was a tall thin man with a shock of long brown hair down to his shoulders. I suggested a walk along the long promenade fronting the sea where we could talk, and he readily agreed. But he quietly insisted that we begin with prayers at the tiny, one-room church of St. George tucked behind the towering modern hotels. It was built on the site of an ancient Roman basilica and was more impressive in its simplicity than any cathedral a thousand times larger. There were a few wooden benches and simple red crosses painted on the walls. After his prayers Franja was beaming with delight and ran the palm of his hand across the cream colored wall to the right of the small altar. From there we made our way past the high-rise tourist hotels and then through a small pine grove to the picture postcard beach. The trunks and branches of the pines were twisted from the strong bora winds that blew in from the northeast. The place was extraordinarily beautiful.

"It began exactly there," Franja said, pointing to a spot just beyond the pebbled beach to our right. "There were five of them, Ottoman officials, come to select a boy from our town for administrative or military training they said. The chosen boy was to become a Janissary. They emphasized how great an honor it was. They select only the best and the brightest they said.

A number of seven and eight year olds were brought before them, nine in all. It was just outside the one-room church on the small hill where they were gathered amid the ruined foundation of the Roman basilica. I remember it so clearly for my son was among them. You could hear the mothers of the children crying and sobbing for they knew they would probably never see their child again. As a teacher I knew there were only two of them who would be eligible, who could pass both the psychological and physical tests that the Turks would give them. My own son Toma, and another, a boy named Anton. Years before I had marked Toma's calf, the calf of his right leg, with a blue rose tattoo, for good luck I said. Before any contest he always rubbed it.

A few days before their arrival I took my son aside and spoke to him of the secret game I wished him to play. I told him of the Turkish officials who would test his knowledge of numbers and soldier games. I promised him special gifts if he would make mistakes and deliberately lose half of the tests that he and the others would be given. But, he must do it secretly and pretend that he did not know the correct answers to the Turkish tests. He would lose so that others might win. At first he refused saying he wanted to win. He shook his head firmly. I had coached him well. He was strong-willed and competitive and loved prizes. I said it was a game to give the others confidence. I promised him finely carved toys and little boats with tiny sails that he could play with in the sea. Finally, he relented and agreed. I told him he must pretend to lose because it was a pretend game. He must be clever and cunning. He must let everyone know that he did not know at least half of the correct answers to the tests. And he must make sure that in the archery contest he would not hit the center of the target. I made him promise me that. And he did, but he did so reluctantly.

The Turkish officials began by saying how fortunate the winner would be, how he would bring great glory to the village in serving the empire. There was a battery of tests conducted over three days. Numbers tests and also tests with toy soldiers pitted against each other. There was an archery contest and a lance-throwing contest. My son kept his word and was ranked third overall. He never once rubbed his blue rose tattoo for luck. The boy Anton gave him a puzzled look on several occasions knowing Toma's prowess with numbers. But he was in the game and he wanted to win and he did so.

On the final day of testing one of the Turks unrolled a great Persian carpet on the grass and in the middle of it placed a splendid golden apple. He challenged all of the boys to get the apple without stepping on the carpet. An hour passed before Anton went to one end of the carpet and began slowly rolling it up until he could reach the apple. It was a brilliant move and the Turks smiled and nodded to each other, in confirmation of his cleverness. They gave him leave to eat the apple. He brought it to his mother who wrapped it carefully in her apron.

The following day the officials boarded their ship and left with Anton. He waved from the top deck of the ship to his parents who were standing forlorn on the dock, his mother inconsolable and his father mute with grief. The boy looked so small and frail standing amid the tall Turkish soldiers and officials. My son Toma waved to him with tears in his eyes. We never saw Anton again.

After he left, Anton's mother would walk the trail from Tučepi to Makarska each morning. There is a vantage point where she could look south towards Asia, or where she thought Asia was. She died heartbroken three months later and his father was carried away by the plague a year after that. My son Toma never once touched the gifts I gave him for the pretend game. It was never the same between us. I think he felt cheated that he did not win. As I have told you he was very competitive."

I asked Franja to walk with me to the quaint sand-colored church built in 1311, to the little hill just beside it where the Turkish contest had taken place. We sat amid the ruined foundations of the Roman basilica fronting the church, and that's where I asked him to relate the story to me once again. I asked him to stop at the point where he first took his son aside and had spoken to him of the secret game he wished him to play. I asked him to look into my eyes so I could see the retinal images as he thought them, and very soon the memory image of Franja speaking to his son was there before me. I concentrated on the images until I had just the right moment, and in that moment Franja did not speak to his son about a secret pretend game. Franja simply spoke of the contest and encouraged Toma to do his best. That was all. He patted Toma on the shoulder three times and saw the great smile break on his son's face. His son rubbed the blue rose tattoo on his leg for luck as he always had. The chosen memory image closed upon that moment and the day changed forever for Franja, and all of his days afterwards.

"My son Toma left with the Turks, their young champion. He was easily the best of the competitors. He did not seem unhappy as he waved from the top deck surrounded by his new family. Time passes. Almost two decades later there was a battle with the Turks and afterwards, the Croatian victors including myself walked through the battlefield collecting our dead for Christian burial. I shuddered when I came across a fallen Turkish warrior with a blue rose tattoo on his right calf. I turned him over slowly to see his face, dreading what I would find, and it was the face of my son Toma, my beloved Toma. Around the warrior were two young men from the village who had died fighting him. These same young men had participated in the contest with my son. Toma was buried among our own."

I observed the memory images as he thought and remembered them. There was a sharp poignancy to them. For the longest time Franja simply stood with a look of infinitely wistful sadness upon his face. Then he fell to his knees, traced his fingers across the blue rose tattoo on the warrior's leg, and wept bitter, bitter tears. And then the memory images stopped. We were once again in modern day Tučepi.

"Franja, tell me what you want to do. We have finished our work. You have a few weeks before you must return to Brijuni."

"Ah, what I plan to do every day for the next few weeks. A hike to Makarska, and then on to Baška Voda along the coast and back here again, and then back again, until I grow tired. Between the mountains and the sea. That's always been my heart's desire. Toma loved it. We often walked that path together. When he grew tired I would carry him on my shoulders. Oftentimes, he would fall asleep, his small hands pressing lightly on my forehead. He was so relaxed his drool would drop upon my face. It was a wonderful time Kristof. Life is a real treat, but I would not trade it for the quiet expansive peaceful chambers of the dead that I will return to."

◆ ◆ ◆

Nikola and Stipe had gone out for the evening to the Makarska promenade. I didn't want to join them for another night of drinking, so I sat happily on the patio balcony and watched as the first stars came out into the night sky. The night was soft and seemed to be full of promise. In a day or two I would be meeting with another returned spirit, Danica, in Korčula, and I was looking forward to the encounter. I wanted my mind to be clear and sharp. The last thing I needed was a hangover. Zora had told me to be ready. Appointments could change in the blink of an eye. In the morning, for exercise, I would follow the scenic path from behind the Biokovo Hotel in downtown Makarska and along the forested path by the sea.

Suddenly, to my right, I heard laughter and voices speaking English. Three men were sitting on their patio balcony in the apartment next to mine on the second floor of the apartment hotel. They were drinking large plastic bottles of Karlovačko beer and in very good spirits. A single light shone above their table. I was sitting in the shadows away to their left. They couldn't see me. I simply sat contentedly and listened. I found their conversations oddly amusing.

Two of them chatted for the longest time about the differences between the metric and the imperial systems of measurement. Every now and then the third man would sigh in disgust and ask for another topic to be discussed.

He was ignored for a time. And then they spent an inordinate amount of time talking about the relative merits of the positioning of toilet paper rolls. Should the dispensing leaf be overhand or underhand? What position served better? They sounded Canadian.

I went inside my apartment for a moment and turned on my patio light and then went out to the patio again. I was interested in meeting them.

One of the men, seeing me, raised his glass and toasted me "Živio!"

I was drinking a soda water and responded, holding my glass high. "Živio!"

"Hi," I said. "I heard you speaking English. Where are you from?"

"Canada," a solid looking senior said. They looked to be in their mid to late sixties or thereabouts, of middle height, with muscular builds. One of them wore spectacles.

"Me too," I said. "I'm from Toronto, from Mississauga."

They introduced themselves in turn. They were three Croatian Canadian brothers on holiday, originally from Northern Ontario. The oldest still lived there, while the middle brother lived in Southern Ontario and the third lived in New England. The eldest spoke to me in a rough and ready Croatian, and said he was eager to learn more. The other two understood a fair amount, and tried as best they could to speak it as well. I could see they were enjoying themselves immensely. They were as happy as three kings. The lights circling the tall palm tree in the garden in front of us suddenly came on and gave a festive air to the evening. The fact that we were all Canadian and from the Croatian diaspora warmed the conversation immediately.

"Where are your friends?" the eldest asked. He was a handsome man, balding slightly and with the white hair of a patrician. He was friendly and sociable, and hugely confident, the kind of man who in his youth you sensed must have been someone not to cross. The youngest was wiry and fit with large hands and a winning smile, an aging athlete I thought. The middle one was hard to read. He had the kind of fitness you get from a gym, and what I suspected was a cheerful, thoughtful disposition. Perhaps a retired professional of some sort, a teacher or a lawyer. I liked them.

"Oh, Stipe and Nikola. Yes, they're out on the town tonight. They enjoy the nightlife here in Makarska. They've been away for a while and they're making up for lost time. I can't keep up with them so I stayed home."

The wife of one of them, fit and attractive, came out to the their balcony and said she was going for a walk and that she could return with more beer if they wished. The eldest smiled warmly at her and showed her the brand they favored. Karlovačko. She said with a knowing chuckle that she was well aware of their beverage preferences. I could tell by her tone that she knew how to deal with her husband and would brook no nonsense from him. She was strong in herself, and her strength matched his own.

We shared stories about Croatia, and then I bid them goodnight, and I went inside my apartment, leaving the balcony light on for Stipe and Nikola.

A few hours later I heard singing. It was Stipe and Nikola. Their voices were loud and strong. I went to the sliding door and looked below. The two of them were walking unsteadily through the front yard. They had an arm over each other's shoulders and they looked as if they hadn't a care in the world.

And from next door I heard the voice of the eldest brother. They were still drinking beer but had turned off the balcony light. "Hey, look at the size of those two guys crossing the yard. They're the ones we saw with the guy next door. They could play for the NFL. I'd hate to meet those two in a dark alley."

I chuckled quietly to myself. Stipe was well over six feet and two hundred and sixty pounds. Nikola was just over six feet tall and two hundred and twenty pounds. Neither of them carried excess weight. They staggered up the concrete stairway under the light of the decorated palm tree, and then spent several minutes trying to insert the key in the lock and cursing vehemently before it opened. I went back to bed.

Stipe and Nikola were up early the next morning, and I heard their cheerful voices as they crossed the front yard heading downtown for coffee and breakfast. I went out to the balcony. One of the brothers from the evening before, the senior of the three, was in the small garden examining a fig tree. He reached up and picked one, and bit into it. It wasn't quite ripe he said with a happy smile to Stipe and Nikola. He tossed it aside into a garbage bin, and the three of them started talking in Croatian. I couldn't quite make out what they were talking about. After a few moments the three of them together headed to the gate and downtown. The senior, whose name I could not remember, walked slowly and with some effort. Stipe and Nikola slowed their pace to be in step with him. I could hear their gregarious laughter as they opened the metal gate and closed it behind them with a clang. It amazed me that in the space of a few moments the three of them could be chatting like fast friends. A member of the Croatian diaspora encounters ancient Croats. It seemed to me then that life is stranger than we often realize. I left the balcony and went inside to make myself a large pot of coffee. I remembered there was a croissant left over from the day before, and some local strawberry jam to enjoy with the coffee.

A few hours later when Stipe and Nikola returned, I asked them what he was like, the man they had breakfasted with. I could not remember his name and that bothered me.

"He is one of us, but from away. That is Martin," Stipe said with an appreciative smile. "He has some hard bark on him."

Nikola simply nodded his head in quiet affirmation. "And very cheerful as well," he said.

♦ ♦ ♦

The next evening I was on the patio balcony having a beer and waiting for Stipe to return home. He had said earlier in the afternoon that he wanted to enjoy a few drinks at several of the pubs along the promenade in Makarska. Our work together was finished he told me, but he said his thirst was not. And Nikola had told me that he had met some German women and with any luck, he would not be returning to the apartment that evening.

It was nearing midnight when I heard the metal gate clang open and anxious German voices asking Stipe if this was where he lived. I leaned over the balcony and saw them. Three young Germans were supporting him as he staggered into the yard fronting our apartment. I ran down the stairs to help them with him. A tall, two hundred and sixty pound man can be very difficult to move in the right direction. Somehow, by pulling, pushing, and carrying him, we got him up the concrete stairs and through the door to our apartment. We carried him to his bed and he fell heavily upon the mattress, breaking one of the corner posts of the bed as he fell.

The three Germans, young cyclists, had seen him come crashing onto the ground from the rear door of a van, a white cargo van that was parked by the closed market area across from the church. The van sped off quickly when the driver saw what had happened. They had said to us later that the interior of the van was all lit up with bright, blinding lights. It was the oddest sight they said. They had wanted to take him to a hospital but he had refused. He had simply pointed up the darkened, narrow alleyway across the street and staggered forward towards the apartment. I thanked the Germans for their kindness in bringing him home, and then they left talking excitedly in German about what had happened.

In the light I was appalled by what I saw. Stipe's face and arms were covered in terrible burns and abrasions. Pieces of skin hung from his forehead and cheeks. I applied balm to his burns, watched as he fell into a deep sleep, and then I went to sleep as well having dome as much as I could to help him.

The next morning found me as surprised by his physical condition as I had been the night before. Apart from a few superficial cuts on his skin, he was radiant with good health. There was not a sign of any burns at all. It was a remarkable recovery.

"What the hell happened?' I asked, after making sure everyone had a large cup of coffee in front of him. The two of us were sitting on our balcony looking out on another fine Makarska morning. Three swallows were flying in high arched curves before us.

Stipe shook his head in disbelief as he recounted his tale. "I had had my fill of drink and was on my way here, a little unsteady. I remember having a pee by the church and then, just as I was about to cross the road to get to the alleyway and home, the side door of a large van slid open and three men jumped out. It all happened so fast. Lightning fast. They grabbed me forcibly and flung me into the interior. I heard the van door sliding closed, and then a locking sound shutting me in. I caught a glimpse of the men getting into a car parked next to the van just as I was thrown inside. For a moment I was stunned. There I was in the dark interior of this vehicle without windows, alone and drunk. I couldn't see anything. I didn't hear a sound.

And then, after about a minute or so, everything was suddenly lit up. Instantly. Bright lights from everywhere, from the interior sides of the vehicle, from the roof, and from the floor. All of the space around me was flooded with incredible light and heat. I was blinded by it, and then it intensified, both the light and the heat. Within a few seconds I felt great pain, and a weakness throughout my body that I have never felt before. I knew it was the end for me once again unless I did something about it. I threw myself against the interior side walls. It was a very small space, and I could not stand erect. I rammed my shoulders hard against the front wall and then the back wall of the vehicle. I did it again and again hoping I could somehow break free. There was a lattice-like steel frame protecting the light sources. I shoved the fingers of my right and left hands through the spaces on the steel network and used that finger hold to support me as I smashed with my feet against the rear door repeatedly. I rammed my feet against the closed door, striking hard with my heels. I used all of my diminishing strength to slam into the door again and again. I felt I was being burned alive. I was in a desperate panic to escape. I pounded away at it. And then suddenly something in the door gave way all at once, and I was free and tumbling from the van to the hard, dark ground by the church. I was stunned and in great pain but free. The van peeled away from me. And that's when I heard the German voices above me, helping me."

As I listened to Stipe I remembered Zora's comments about being vigilant and careful. So they were here now, Malek's people, and they knew about us just as they had known in Osijek. I felt a cold dread move through me. I trembled, remembering an expression my grandmother had used. It was as if someone had walked across my grave. I sent an encrypted text to Zora describing what had happened to Stipe. I also said that Stipe's recovery from the incident was remarkable. Within a few hours he had fully recuperated from his ordeal. There were a few bruises but his flesh was intact and undamaged.

1571 Korčula, Danica

There was a Croatian word Davor had gifted me with. He said it epitomized the Dalmatian spirit. Inat. When I looked it up in my iPhone's Google Translate I found that it meant spite or malice. Another dictionary suggested it meant defiance. And when I offered those definitions to him, he simply smiled and said there was more to it than that, much more. So I left it at that together with the memory of Davor until I met Danica. As always, Zora had made excellent arrangements for travel and accommodation. The high speed catamaran from Makarska had been swift and efficient and very comfortable.

It was a dismal afternoon. The spirit of the day was dampened by light, constant drizzle. There wasn't enough strength in the gray sky for a full committed rainfall. I had a small Airbnb near the very center of town, near the Cathedral. On the way to the apartment, I purchased some bread, cheese, smoked sausage, and the local Grk wine that Zora had recommended. I decided I would have an early dinner before Danica arrived. It wasn't the kind of evening to go out for dinner.

As always, I remembered to prepare myself for the encounter with the relaxation technique Dr. Spehar had taught me. I touched my iPhone and noticed it was about half past six in the evening. I made myself comfortable on the living room couch with my hands resting on my lap. I began counting with each exhalation I made. After a few moments I looked down at my hands wondering if I would see a movement or twitch in the right or the left hand. Seconds passed, perhaps longer, before I saw a tiny twitch in my right forefinger. Then, in a fluid motion I saw my right arm move upwards from my lap, my elbow bent at a ninety-degree angle to my body, until my hand hung suspended before my eyes. I was not trying to control its movements in any way. In fact I encouraged whatever movement it wished, and if it pulled away I went with it, knowing it would eventually return of its own accord. After a moment, in short, stepwise movements, my hand neared closer to my face, and at the same time, my eyelids began to close. I wasn't trying to control it. I was simply going along with it in a relaxed, insouciant way. Then I felt my hand touch my chin, and I fell deeper into a comfortable, easy trancelike state. My hand fell slowly to my lap and rested there. I lost all sense of time but I must have been sitting there like that for a full half hour. My eyelids opened gradually and as my face turned toward the gray light of the window, I noticed my head turned in stepwise movements, slowly and inevitably, without any conscious willing on my part. I was ready.

There was a sharp knocking at my door at around eight in the evening, and there she was: Danica. A tightly knit woman, more handsome than pretty I thought, and lean and fit. She had chestnut brown hair and her skin was like burnished copper. A noblewoman from ancient Korčula.

She was wet from the rain. I offered her a towel from the bathroom that she gratefully accepted with a cheerful smile. She dried her hair before me, and used her fingers to roughly comb her hair. She was very good looking I thought.

Though my Croatian had improved by leaps and bounds since I had arrived in Pula, I noticed a subtle smile cross her lips as I spoke, and outlined the process we would follow in our work together. After I had finished, she nodded and said she was ready. We sat across from each other at the small kitchen table. A glass chandelier that lit up the kitchen hung suspended from the ceiling between us.

And I knew I was ready when short random flashes of intense light flashed in front of me, blinding me for a moment. I closed my eyes tightly, and then opened them wide.

As she looked into my eyes the first image that was transferred to my retinas was that of a small stone house, obviously a burnt out house, but similar in size to some of those solid dwellings I had seen in walking from the harbour to my Airbnb apartment. But, the stone house I was seeing on her retinas was a roofless shell with nothing in it, nothing at all. And then there arose the image of an old woman sitting inside the stricken house. It looked as if she was dying. She was breathing in rapid, shallow breaths and she held her legs folded close to her chest. She was in great distress. As I looked into the memory image and felt its pain, I heard Danica moaning and weeping.

Suddenly, she spoke. "The old woman is my grandmother. I had not yet been born. It was during a great plague. 1529. That is where she lived, and that is where she died. The house was burnt, and the roof was removed. It was common. Thousands of our people had died. My mother often took me there to remind me of our past. She said that if you remember a person they cannot die until they are forgotten. She said she could feel her mother's spirit there, and so could I. I would often climb the wall of her house and drop down into the ruin and sit and savour the space within, and my grandmother's spirit.

The images from her memory flowed rapidly and with great detail. Only once or twice did I have to ask her to slow down so I could fully see and understand what was taking place. My memory was cataloguing every image completely, both its colour and minute detail. Then, I asked her to comment on what was happening, from her perspective, so I could know the exact moment that she wished to change. Her voice was low and measured as she spoke.

"You can start from the moment I smash the glass vase on the stone floor of my bedroom. At that very moment in time, when the glass shatters on the floor, at the sound of it. That is when my new choice begins. From that precise moment. Tell me when you have it, yes?"

"OK," I said. "I've got it. You can continue now."

The images were clear and sharp. I watched her sweep the floor with a twig broom and collect all the shards and tiny splinters of glass. She made sure she missed nothing. Then she removed her dress and sat naked and cross-legged on her bed, the dustbin of glass before her. Her face had a gaunt, strained look of fierce resolve. I had never seen an expression like that in my life. I didn't know what to expect, but I felt a grim foreboding in the pit of my stomach. I waited.

Then she took some body crème from the nightstand by her bed, and rubbed her hands thoroughly with it. Meanwhile, I sat mesmerized across from her in the small Airbnb kitchen, looking into her eyes and seeing the image of her on the bed where she sat. I was creating the very image I was seeing. I was crafting a memory. She had made her choice. Instead of sweeping up the shattered glass from her bedroom floor and discarding it, she placed the dustbin on her bed.

Suddenly, she scooped a handful of the ground glass from the dustbin and inserted it into her vagina, slowly and carefully. Her eyes were fixed and determined, with a strange, unearthly cast to them. She had chosen defiance. She would not submit to being raped so easily. I had not expected it.

"Stop, stop, Danica!" I cried out, seeing what she was doing, shocked at the image, at the memory I was fashioning from her despair and desperation. I began weeping until the image was blurred with my tears.

"You must go on," she said quietly and in a low, tired voice. She continued to draw her cupped hand across the broken shards of glass in the dustbin, gathering it, and with delicate fingers pushing it gently into her vagina. She did this again and again, her eyes half closed and looking upwards, her expression blank and remote. I saw tiny droplets of blood showing beneath the white sheet. I was stunned.

"Please Danica, no…no! You must stop. This can't be. Stop! Stop this horror."

She seemed to move forward towards me, her elbows and palms flat on the kitchen table. For a moment we were back in the Airbnb apartment, the image and memory of her sitting cross-legged on the bed, centuries before, dissolved in my tears. She was looking intently at me, and then a look of annoyance and anger spread across her face, and she spoke harshly.

"Be a Croat! Holy Mother of God! What, have modern times bred out your courage? Do you think life is Moreška dancing and music and rich food? Everyone must pay. Everything has a cost. Only a coward runs away. Be strong! I will tell you plainly. The year was 1571. Our husbands and sons were away fighting Turks elsewhere. Our Venetian Governor had run away and just we women were left to defend our city. My children I had secreted away with a servant girl. They were safe.

The Turkish pirate, pig that he is, had told me to expect him that evening, to pay his compliments in my husband's absence, he sneered. I spat at him full in the face, my chin raised high. I was not afraid. The pig laughed and bowed low in mock courtesy, saying he would shake the foundations of the palace with his lovemaking. He said to prepare myself. So, that is what we are doing. Do you understand? I am making ready for the thieving pig. Now, let us go back to then from now. Now. Now."

It took me a few moments to collect myself and begin again. Danica looked steadily into my eyes until we were there again, the image memory of her on the bed, just as before. I could feel myself trembling slightly as she continued. I was there with her, once again. I steadied myself and felt her pain and anguish and indomitable courage. She would be ready for the invader, whatever the outcome. She nodded at me and smiled tightly at our conspiracy. The smile was one of vengeance and retribution and justice.

A new image took shape. I could see the thief enter her bedroom, smiling and unsteady on his feet from too much drink. Danica lay on the bed beneath the sheet. There were two soldiers behind him, awaiting his orders. He turned and waved at them dismissively to leave. The pig wanted privacy.

"Your turn comes later after I have warmed the bitch's bed. And you, my lady, are wise to offer your submission so nobly." He stood at the side of the bed, looking down at Danica, savouring the moment of his triumph. He undressed quickly and slipped under the sheet, laying his sodden weight on top of her, pawing her roughly. She pushed him away smelling the stink of him, holding him off for a moment. He slapped her hard repeatedly across her face, and suddenly she went still, as if leaving her body. He pushed himself into her, laughing all the while as he entered her. He pummelled himself wildly within her and against her, and then stopped. It was a pivotal moment, changing everything. A strange, surprised look spread across his face followed by one of abject horror. Danica smiled back at him as he screamed in pain like a beast caught in a trap. He leapt from the bed crying out in terror, his hands covered with his own blood. His men rushed into the bedroom and seeing the bloodied sheet raised their swords and struck her again and again. She didn't scream as her vision misted over in a brilliant red colour followed by black curtains closing in on her from the sides of her perception. She was gone.

There was no image that I could see. Everything was black. Then I looked across at Danica, and we were back again in the Airbnb kitchen in Korčula.

"Our business is finished," she said. "Now we can go anywhere we wish, and do anything we want. Thank you Kristof."

Her face was serene, and she looked as if she had come home from a long journey that had left her exhausted but fulfilled. I was very tired from the intervention and decided to return to Makarska on the next catamaran.

♦ ♦ ♦

It was a silly encounter, but still dangerous I thought. A bar brawl of all things. The police had been called and I was fretful that Malek would learn of it, and cause trouble of one sort or another to myself and to the returned spirits I worked with. Already I was sure he knew of Stipe's close escape from the van. We were lucky that Stipe and Nikola had left the bar before the police arrived.

Nikola told me what had happened, quietly and dispassionately, shaking his head in disbelief as he did so. He described the action in detail. The two of them were drinking beer by the waterfront in Makarska, looking out at the stream of passers-by. It was early in the evening. It was at one of those outdoor pubs on the promenade under an awning overlooking the small tourist ships at anchor. Flatscreen TVs showed clips from European football clubs. Several customers watched the action, mesmerized by the quality of the play. Across the small bay was the Promontory of St. Peter's. Tourists were ambling by, scouting out where they would dine that evening.

Stipe had been wearing a Dinamo Zagreb football jersey and Nikola himself sported a Rijeka jersey, part of the clothing and gear they had received from Zora when they had arrived in Brijuni. They were not football fans. They knew nothing about football. Pure chance. Harmless enough, but a small, loudmouthed drunken customer sitting at the end of the bar along with several of his friends, took great exception to the jerseys and started mumbling and sending dark looks their way. The little man was encouraging his large friends to do something, saying they were being insulted. After a few more drinks, the mumbling escalated to curses directed at Stipe and Nikola, and the questionable morals of their mothers. At first both Nikola and Stipe didn't understand that they were the focus of attention or why.

But, after several moments they noticed the menacing stares and looked at the glowering group by the bar. They looked at each other and shrugged their shoulders.

An old man sitting at the table next to theirs pulled at his own t-shirt with his thumb and forefinger, thereby suggesting that their apparel was the cause of the drunk's anger. He also pointed to the football play on the widescreen TVs, but from where Nikola and Stipe sat, they were unable to see it.

The small boisterous man, paunchy and red-faced, slammed his fist onto the surface of the polished oak bar. He was wearing a Hajduk Split jersey. Then he stood up, a little unsteady on his feet, and left the bar area with several of his huge companions in tow. They stopped at the outside table where Stipe and Nikola sat, and just stood there, the six of them, saying nothing. Nikola raised his beer mug as a toast to them, and smiled. The little man was furious at the gesture. Stipe sensed something was not right. He pushed his chair back and readied himself for action.

Then things took a menacing turn for the worst. The little drunk spat at Nikola full in the face and then he stepped back allowing his five much larger companions, three almost as big as Stipe, and two of average size, to confront the pair. Well that was that. Both Nikola and Stipe were out-raged as you can imagine. They leapt to their feet like inflamed demons, and then it started in earnest. As Nikola spoke to me, he relived the action, gesticulating wildly, and swinging his arms back and forth. He was clearly excited, but remembered every detail.

Stipe grabbed the first man by his neck and crotch, and despite the man's size, lifted him up and over his head in one spectacular movement, and then slammed him hard against the glass table-top shattering the glass into small fragments and bending the black metal frame of the table. Simultaneously, another attacker tried to punch Nikola, but missed, falling to his knees. Nikola grabbed him by his ears and then drove his knee into the man's groin. The man fell like a stone, writhing in pain. Stipe, meanwhile, leapt at the man he had thrown on the table and pounded him mercilessly with his huge fists. The fallen man was unable to defend himself against the punishing onslaught though he tried desperately to cover his face.

The tourist traffic was suddenly melting away, some tourists running down the promenade and others running across the street, desperate to get away from the brutal fight. The little man who had instigated the confrontation edged further and further back, and then scurried away on his toes frantically, knocking into a waiter emerging from the restaurant kitchen behind him, carrying a full tray of beer. The half dozen glasses flew high into the air and then shattered on the floor, the draught beer forming puddles everywhere. Two of the little man's companions leapt on Nikola pummelling him with their fists until he fell backward onto another table. Stipe whirled about in a fury ready for an attack by the last man, who waved his hands in surrender and then ran off. Then Stipe turned and fell on one of Nikola's attackers with a vengeance. He grabbed him in a chokehold and then flung him down onto the wet floor. Nikola pushed the man atop him away and then stood ready to deliver a blow with his forearm, but suddenly the remaining two assailants ran from the bar in desperation to get away. Stipe and Nikola looked about waiting for any other challengers, but there were none. One of the waiters was on his cellphone calling for the police, but the brawl was finished. Sensing trouble if they stayed, Stipe and Nikola hurried back to their apartment a few minutes walk away.

I met them in our shared apartment and that's where Nikola recounted the tale to me. He and Stipe were still puzzled by what had happened, but I knew it had been because of the football jerseys they had been wearing.

"They fought you because of football," I said.

"What is football?" Stipe asked.

I turned the television on with the remote and found a sports channel where a football game was on. I put the remote on mute. "That is football," I said. "It is a team game and many cities in Croatia have their own teams. Some of their supporters have a grudge against rival teams."

Stipe and Nikola looked at each other in mute surprise and then continued to watch the football game.

"So, they fought us over a game where they kick a leather ball back and forth over a field of grass? Is that what you're telling us Kristof?"

I explained the game briefly and watched the expressions on their faces change from surprise to anger.

"So," Nikola said. "Because of our shirts, because of the city team, because of the colours, they insulted and attacked us. Over a game and a little leather ball. Yes?"

Stipe rubbed his head in dismay. "Oh my people, my country." Stipe said in a tone of incredulity. "We do not have enough enemies encircling us, that we have to fight each other over a child's game. Is this true Kristof?"

"Well, yes," I said. "If you put it that way. I suppose it is like that."

Then, they both started laughing, mildly at first and then developing into raucous knee-slapping laughter. I joined them, and we laughed until tears came to our eyes. I had forgotten how good it was to laugh with friends. We kept the television on but continued to watch it without sound. We drank beer until we were too tired to drink any more. The next morning we woke late and drank copious amounts of coffee.

I walked out to the second floor balcony of our apartment and surveyed the town of Makarska below. It was a wonderful place, with the islands of Brač and Hvar in the distance beyond the sea. To my left and down the steep hill was the Venetian steeple of the church and the small local market beside it. And there, just below me in the front yard of the holiday apartments where we stayed was the tall thin palm tree decorated with lights that were turned on in the evenings. It sported a life of its own. I noticed too s squat wide palm tree in a nearby neighbour's yard immediately to the left of the property, and beyond it down the hill a wildly lush palm tree waving its fronds in the wind. It was the closest thing to a home that I had been in for a long time. The next morning I received an encrypted message to return to Pula immediately.

32 BC Off Mljet, Marko

Dr. Spehar had instructed me to meet him at a small wine bar near the Pula Forum. When I entered the bar I saw him talking to a small but powerful-looking man at a table near the kitchen. He was balding with a fleshy face, and a powerful upper body. Dr. Spehar pushed a chair in my direction. He introduced the man as Marko, and I shook his hand. He was wearing a tight green and yellow NK Istra 1961 football jersey. My hand disappeared in his welcoming grasp. Dr. Spehar related his story and the event I was to guide. Marko raised his wineglass to the ceiling light and we followed suit, toasting our venture. He seemed intrigued, but not overly so, by the furniture and objects in the bar. I saw him touch an electric heater that was on and then pull his hand away instinctively. He was amused. A man from the past, but one not overwhelmed by modern trappings. A two hundred year incubation period had anticipated and cushioned the strangeness.

Later we went to my apartment and prepared the groundwork. The image magic was about to begin. I sat at the dining room table with Marko across from me. Dr. Spehar sat on the couch shelling and eating pistachios. For several minutes Marko and I simply relaxed with our eyes closed. No one spoke. The only occasional sound was a pistachio shell being cracked open, and then dropped into a glass ashtray. He held my wrists in his huge hands, and I felt his great physical power. I opened my eyes. Then I saw his eyelids open wide. I looked at him closely and saw a flurry of retinal images before me. Then, suddenly, for several seconds, sharp electrical flashes crossed my line of vision, and then stopped abruptly. I was getting accustomed to the experience which always preceded the sessions with returned spirits. I felt completely relaxed. I looked again at the retinal images in his eyes. I knew the images were ancient ones, and drawn from his memory as he remembered them. As he stared into my eyes, I received his memory images clearly until I began to feel the warmth of an old sun upon my skin. The images were extraordinarily strong and Marko did not have to speak. I felt great power in my memory and intuition and simply let go, comfortable in the time and space around me.

Suddenly, I was there with them, the three of them. They were adrift in the sea clinging to what was left of a piece of the foredeck from the ship. From my vantage point, I was suspended a few meters above the clear sea, observing them. They could not see me. I was a spiritual presence only, but I was in their time and space. It was the very first time I had manipulated retinal images in this way. It was quite marvelous to me to be there. Living history. Oh, if my son could see me now. Oars from the broken galley were floating on the turquoise blue waters. Shredded bits and pieces of sails floated about them along with dead bodies from the sea battle. Marko held fast to the timber with one arm and with the other, held his friend Vinko above water. Marko was speaking softly to Vinko trying to calm him. It was obvious that Vinko could not swim and was deathly afraid of drowning. Davor had told me a day earlier that the two of them were galley slaves hailing from the same village in Lika. A few meters away a Roman consul whom Marko recognized from his ship hung precariously on to a small barrel that was bobbing in the sea with the motions of the waves. The Roman was swallowing a lot of sea water in his efforts to stay afloat.

I could see the Roman was exhausted from his ordeal and cried out to Marko. "Help me, help me. This barrel is slowly filling with seawater and it will take me down to the bottom with it. Help me! "

I observed everything closely. Marko said nothing, knowing that the makeshift raft he and Vinko were clinging to could not support the partial weight of more than two without sinking. He shook his head. The Roman moaned heavily between his cries for help, and tried frantically to stop the water from entering the spigot hole in the barrel.

Several tense moments passed. The swell of the sea carried them up and down. Vinko was beginning to panic, slipping into the water, wanting to push himself up onto the twisted boards of the raft. He was flailing about. Marko was urging him to be still, trying to assure him that all was not lost. He could see two ships on the horizon, but could not tell if they were Roman or Illyrian. He supported Vinko and held him closely within his powerful grasp. He was telling him they would once again be in their village, to have faith.

The Roman, becoming desperate as he gripped the sinking barrel, shouted out to Marko. "Help me! Help me and you will be a free man. I promise you your freedom if you save me. No longer will you be a galley slave!"

Vinko, his eyes wild with fear, was pulling at Marko, dragging him down, further down into the water, striking at him madly. Marko scanned the distant horizon, caught sight of the ships, and was just able to discern a rust colored Roman sail. In seconds his life would be changed. With a powerful punch he struck Vinko and pushed him away from himself, away from the raft. There was just a single pivotal moment of calm within the surrounding chaos where Vinko realized what was happening and gave Marko such a look that would follow him for the rest of his days. A look of incredulity and disappointment and bitter betrayal. He watched Vinko slide away, slide away from him and down into the clear sea below them, feet first. He sank surprisingly quickly with his arms upraised towards Marko, as if in supplication.

The Roman was treading water crudely, splashing and sinking and barely able to stay afloat, his barrel gone from his grasp, sinking into the sea below him. Marko swam up to him with short powerful strokes and grabbing his tunic brought him to the safety of the raft. Not a word was said as they clung to the timber and waited for the ships. The rescue took place and the Roman was as good as his word. Marko was a free man.

Now, as I hovered over the deep crystal clear waters, and at precisely the same moments as Marco held on to my wrists in the Airbnb apartment, my work began. Image work, memory magic. I moved in time to the very instant before Marko made his decision to be a freeman. I held his retinal image within my own eyes, just after he saw the rust colored Roman sail on the horizon. And just before he made the choice to abandon Vinko. In that single moment choice was reinstated. I manipulated a few memory images and Marko's rebirth was a reality. It had taken him two centuries to revisit a moment of profound choice, and now it was come again, and changed forever.

Marko was in the sea with Vinko. Vinko was panicking and the Roman was treading water and freedom for Marko was in the offing if he chose. The moment came and passed, and then a change was made. Marko punched and pushed Vinko into quiescence. The Roman sank remarkably quickly, about five minutes before the Roman ships arrived. The rescue ships picked up several galley slaves clinging to wreckage, Marko and Vinko among them, and within a few days they were working the oars on another Roman ship heading north. I was surprised at the brilliance and clarity of the images before me.

I held on to the retinal images and waited while Marko conceived new ideas, new thoughts, that were transferred to new retinal images in his eyes. I held them in mine and learned what had happened. Several months after the sinking of their galley off Mljet Marko and Vinko escaped from their captivity near Solin and made their way inland to their mountain village near Medulum, an Iapodes fortress. Dr. Spehar had told me that the Iapodes were an Illyrian tribe. There, Marko and Vinko narrowly escaped capture by Roman scouts and legions moving their cohorts on Medulum. One column of Octavian's legions marched on the mountain heights while the other advanced through the valleys to avoid ambush and surprise attacks by the Iapodes.

Marko and Vinko hid at a place known as 16 lakes for a few days to escape the Roman scouts. Marko told me in a tone of great reverence and awe that the 16 lakes were the fabled lakes of yore where the great Illyrian poets went to die. Marko spoke very softly then while I observed his retinal images simultaneously. I was spellbound as he recounted his experiences.

"Their wonderful poetry fell on my ears and lips at an early age and I was lucky enough to know some of them. They were a special breed, these warrior poets. They wandered among our Illyrian tribes and were welcomed everywhere. They sang of love and war and the passage of time. They were fearsome warriors as well as poets, and honed their songs as sharply as their swords. When it was time for them to die, they made their way to the lakes. I was fortunate enough to accompany one of them to this sacred place. It was a great honor. He was as light as a bird and easy to carry. He never stopped reciting his poems and I would memorize as many as I could, and he would laugh and drink brandy to ease his pain. He died as easily as an oak leaf falling from the highest branch."

And then a flurry of retinal images showed Marko observing three Roman scouts burying items near one of the waterfalls there. After the Romans had left Marko and Vinko uncovered what they had buried. They found dozens of gold coins, a silver armguard and some fine jewellery.

The Romans won their expedition, executing the Illyrian leaders. Meanwhile, Marko, Vinko, and their families hid in caves and escaped the devastation and enslavement of nearby Medulum by the Romans.

The images seemed to fast forward in time from that point. I felt Marko's powerful hands grasping my forearms as we looked into each other's eyes. My intuition was running rampant. I had never experienced this new development before. Days, weeks, months, years, decades, centuries, raced to the present, flashing by. Images of Marko's son and Vinko's daughter on their wedding day. Images of families descending from that first union. Images of descendants living in the hills and mountains of the region to this very day. The memory images were wonderfully clear and bright as I looked at Marko across the table from me. He was beaming with delight. It was the first time in my life that I had ever experienced such a marvel.

Dr. Spehar was full of compliments after the meeting, saying it called for a celebration. After a night of serious drinking, Dr. Spehar graciously paid the bar bill. Early the next day Dr. Spehar came to my apartment and bid me farewell once again, making me promise to be careful as I made my way to my next destination. He asked me to sign three invoices from a joint operating expenses account that he had opened up to simplify accounting procedures. I duly signed, and then he gave me a wad of cash right there on the street fronting my apartment.

Marko, with a wry smile, said he was going to be a tourist and visit the Coliseum and a few of the Pula sites. Meanwhile, Zora had texted me to come by for a visit at our favorite café. I felt a surge of emotion and happiness as I made my way to what she had called our café.

◆ ◆ ◆

Zora was sitting at one of the outside tables facing the Coliseum. She introduced me to an English friend of hers from London who taught English in Pula. We chatted pleasantly about London for a time. Then the English teacher signaled to the waiter who was standing by the restaurant entrance to serve us. Zora's friend politely asked for the daily menu as opposed to the set menu, showing off her knowledge of different Croatian menus. The middle-aged waiter took a deep breath of naked exasperation and handed her the set menu.

"The daily menu is finished for today. This is what we have." He spoke brusquely, dropped the leather-bound menu heavily on the table and returned to the entrance where he stood and waited for us to peruse the set menu and decide what we would order for our late lunch.

Zora's friend was more than a little taken aback by what she perceived as rudeness on the waiter's part. "How rude," she said, "to be so blunt. Surely, he could be more civil. After all, we're the reason he has a job."

Zora suddenly began a mini dissertation on Croatian history and the many invaders who spoke in so many different tongues and had come with so many different manners, none of them civil. I sipped my red wine and mused on the consequences of imperialism and language and a waiter's choice of words.

Zora pushed the set menu away and said flatly, "What did the waiter mean by his bluntness if it was indeed that? Did he even realize that he was being blunt? The bluntness is there I would say because it is essential to the cultural DNA of the Croatian character. Remove it and you remove the sticking point of Croatian courage, of Croatian fortitude. Blunt language can clarify issues. Fancy rhetoric can distract and disarm and render you defenseless in times of great peril. Communicating, in many instances needs to be crystal clear so that there is no confusion about what is meant. So, if our waiter or local guide, whether male or female, is sometimes apparently or even obviously blunt, bear with them. It is why Croatians continue to exist in this contested corner of Europe."

The English teacher frowned unhappily, glared at the waiter standing by the entrance, and took up the set menu, eager to order and change the topic of conversation.

◆ ◆ ◆

A day later I was back in Zagreb. No rest for a white butterfly. Zora had arranged for me to meet one of the returned spirits, a woman named

Marija, under the tail of the Jelačić equestrian statue in Jelačić Square. Zora had somehow left me a handwritten message slipped under the door of my Airbnb apartment very near the square and close to the Dolac Market. Somehow she had located me though I hadn't sent her any text messages or e-mails. I wondered how she had found me because I was moving about as Mr. Šubić had instructed me. Every couple of days I would change my Airbnb apartment, always within walking distance of the main square. Zora's message had said to look for a woman carrying a jar of honey.

Marija was a tall, slim woman with olive coloured skin, dark hair and a gentle face. She had high cheekbones and a mouth like a rosebud, model material. As I approached her she raised the jar of honey towards me so I would see it clearly. I nodded and smiled. She placed the jar of honey in her shoulder bag and then waited for me to speak.

I introduced myself and said that we could go to my apartment and begin the intervention there. I knew nothing about her. I asked if she was hungry. She said no. She asked if she could have a coffee first, overlooking the square. She liked the ambience of the place she said. We sat outside at a café with a large awning above the tables. She seemed very content as she sipped her espresso and looked about the busy square. People were hurrying about, many of them trying to catch one of the blue city buses that crossed the square in both directions.

"Let's go for a walk before we go to your apartment," she said. "I want to walk along Tkalčićeva and see how it has changed." As we walked she let out a small cry of surprise. "Look it is gone. The stream is gone. It used to run right here, and now it's gone. And the bridge too, Krbava Most, is gone. Hah! What strife took place here."

"I read in a tourist book that the stream runs underground now. It is still there, but out of sight, and beneath us," I said.

She stopped walking for a moment as if to take in everything around us, to absorb it, the many tourists making their way up and down the storied street, the restaurants, the bars, the small gift shops.

"So many things happen and they are forgotten in time, but the mystery still runs, like the stream under us," she said.

She looked towards me and smiled, her face bright all of a sudden and tinged with sadness, with the recognition and changes wrought by time.

"Are you happy to be back?" I asked.

We continued walking and I saw her reflect on what I had asked. She looked directly ahead at the throngs of tourists passing by. "Happy is perhaps not the right word to use. I have returned to make a change, that is all. Just that, and then to return home. The people I knew and loved here are all gone from sight, like the stream under us. But the home I left to come here beckons me and I long for that. I won't be here long. I will return to that place of dark wonder soon. Do you understand?"

"No," I said. "I don't understand."

"The afterlife is different than you think and luckier."

"How so?" I asked.

"Just the experience of it. You leave your body behind and move without form into a formless realm. Altogether different. A spirit world. After you die you become what you were before you were born. The circle closes and then opens once again. You were at Brijuni. You saw. Returned spirits, such as I, took on old forms, bodily forms that we had known, and entered the living state again. For a time."

I pondered over what she had said, but I still didn't understand it. She saw me shrug in quiet consternation, and then she smiled warmly. She was incredibly beautiful, and there was compassion in her smile. We walked up the street, and then she stopped.

"Kristof, do you mind if we meet tomorrow instead of this evening. The night is so fresh. The faces in the crowd are like apparitions to me. I just want to walk alone among them. Is that alright with you?"

"Of course," I said. "We can meet at the same café again for a coffee at ten o'clock in the morning. No problem."

I watched her for a moment as she made her way up the street. She walked slowly with a quiet sense of contentment and ease as if she were visiting a place she knew well and loved. I saw her turn once and wave at me.

I made my way back to my apartment. Just as I was about to unlock the outer door that fronted the street, I glanced behind me and just caught sight of two men coming down the stone steps of the Dolac Market. The life-size bronze statue of a market woman carrying a basket on her head stood behind them. The marketplace was deserted. They were tall and youngish and fair, and dressed in dark blue suits buttoned to the collar. They walked past me looking straight ahead and not at me as I fumbled with my card key. Something didn't feel right. I hesitated and simply stood there waiting, watching them walk away. Finally I entered and walked up the two floors to my apartment. It was dark and so I used the light on my cellphone to insert my second card key into the door lock. I looked behind me but there was nothing but the small elevator next to the stairwell. I shrugged at my groundless fears and then locked the heavy door behind me.

My Airbnb apartment was identical to so many others I had stayed in across Europe. Trendy theater posters, IKEA furniture, a whiteboard with recommendations for local eateries, and a tearaway map of the city. I lay in bed for a while thinking about nothing in particular and then fell into a deep sleep without any dreams.

The next morning I showered and shaved early and made my way to Jelačić Square with time to spare before my rendezvous with Marija. A few minutes before ten I sat in the same chair I had sat in the day before and waited. I didn't order any coffee though I dearly wanted one. The city was humming with activity. An Asian tourist group, about a dozen people, merry and happy, stopped in front of the Jelačić statue and took photographs. I continued to wait. After forty minutes had passed I left.

I walked around the Square for a bit and then returned to my apartment, hoping for a message under the door from Zora. Nothing. I remembered the two men I had seen the evening before, and I grew uncomfortable at the recollection. Perhaps it was just a coincidence, but they had been dressed like Malek's people. The same dark, formal suits buttoned to the neck. I threw open the large window overlooking the street below and watched the crowds walking by along Tkalčićeva Street. I made a pot of coffee and found a sports channel on the TV. For the rest of the morning I watched Croatian soccer with the sound off and drank coffee. I needed to think and the silent action on the large screen helped me.

Mr. Šubić had suggested erratic movements to shake off the chance of being followed. To move about like a small white butterfly he had said. I

smiled at the odd imagery but it made sense to me. I needed to leave Zagreb
I decided. But where to go next? I could decide that at the bus terminal I
thought, but I had to leave the apartment now. It was far too comfortable.
I packed and left a note for the owner. As I was closing the outer door
on the ground floor, a flower vendor turned to me, gave me a brilliant
red carnation, and asked me if my name was Kristof. I said yes and she
handed me a note. It had two words written on it, the name of a town on
the Dalmatian coast. Several hours later, after a long bus ride with a short
stopover in Split, I was sitting in a seaside café in Baška Voda enjoying a
cold beer and a light, freshening breeze blowing in from the sea.

I was just about to order an octopus salad when I saw a familiar and
portly figure approach my table.

"Hello Kristof. Hello my good friend!"

Dr. Spehar was impeccably dressed in a three-piece sand-coloured linen
suit. He wore a crisp dark blue shirt open at the collar. I was surprised and
delighted to see him.

"Ah, the good doctor! Hello," I cried out. "So good to see you."

We spoke of many things as we sat. Of Zora, of the loss of Davor, of
the new troubles we were facing. Our conversation jumped sporadically
from one subject to another. We were excited to be together once again and
talking. We were friends. A waiter came and took our orders. An octopus
salad for me and grilled sea bream for Dr. Spehar. When the food arrived we
stopped speaking for a time and ate our meals slowly and with great pleasure.
Afterwards, Dr. Spehar asked me about Zagreb and what I had experienced
there. I told him about how my returned spirit, Marija, had not shown up
for our scheduled meeting at the cafe. I even mentioned my suspicion and
fears concerning the two men I had seen by the market. He nodded at this,
cleared his throat sharply, and then began to recount what he had learned.

"Yes, unfortunately, I am the bearer of bad news. Marija has disappeared,
and we fear she is gone," he said.

"What do you mean disappeared and gone?" I stammered, taken by
surprise. "I was with her last night."

Dr. Spehar leaned towards me, his elbows resting heavily on the tabletop.
His voice was almost a whisper. "Marija was abducted from Ribnjak Park

late last night. Two men were seen dragging her from the Park to a white van stopped on Ribnjak Street. The eyewitness said she was thrown forcibly into the van, and then it sped away. We believe you too were targeted, perhaps by the same men, but you were able to escape this morning, and for that we are most grateful."

"Thanks to Zora and the red carnation message," I said. "And I never got the chance to help Marija. I don't even know what she wanted to change. What a waste, what a terrible waste," I said. The lights were beginning to come on around us. The restaurant was filling with diners, looking happy at the prospect of fine dining in one of the most beautiful settings in the world. The sea was darkening as I looked past Dr. Spehar and wondered what we were going to do.

Dr. Spehar signalled to the wait staff. Our waiter brought our bill and Dr. Spehar paid, leaving a substantial tip for which the waiter was exceedingly grateful. Before we parted he asked me to sign a number of invoices covering my operating expenses and his own. I also signed a form giving him an advance on his expenses from a joint account. I thought it curious that we should be doing this accounting at a restaurant so late in the evening, but thought nothing more of it.

Endgame

Part FOUR

Pula

ONE DAY I FOUND A note under my door. The penciled note was beautifully written with excellent penmanship. It was from Malek, requesting a meeting.

Please meet me at the park across from the Coliseum at 2:00 p.m. this after-noon, to discuss mutually beneficial activities. Our relationship has suffered from a failure of communication resulting in a lack of understanding. I hope we can correct this. Hope you will join me if you are free.

The note served a two-pronged purpose. Malek was letting me know that he didn't need advanced technology to communicate with me, and that he knew where I lived. The threat was there certainly, but also an invitation to join him in his mission. He wanted an alliance.

I prepared some coffee and toast for a light breakfast and took it out to my patio balcony overlooking the small garden. A single sparrow was enjoying the birdbath at the far end of the garden. I knew that in Malek's philosophy, if you could call it that, there were some very simple truths. Simple and deadly. I had to be on my guard. I knew what he was capable of. I smiled warily at the prospect of meeting him.

As I approached him at the designated hour I looked about to see if there were any members from his usual entourage hanging about. I saw no one. He was sitting alone, his legs crossed, with an engaging smile on his face. There was nothing unusual happening in the park. Several tourists were walking around chatting happily. A man was reading a newspaper, his lips moving quietly as he read. Two young children, about eight years old, were tossing a red, white, and blue rubber ball back and forth. It was a mildly overcast day with just the barest threat of rain.

He looked at me and nodded, and then looked straight ahead again. "So once again we are here at this park. It has become our park. I know that you have some misgivings about me, about the ideas that I carry forward, but I ask you to listen. The ideas are more important than me. I am simply an emissary. Whatever shortcomings I may have must not obfuscate the ideas themselves."

"Certainly," I said, "but it is important that people do not suffer because of ideas."

I watched him smile then as if a small child had uttered some foolish, baseless remark. He continued to look straight ahead and not at me.

"Ah Christopher, people have always suffered because of ideas. How else could mankind progress without transformative ideas. It is the way of the world. But please listen. Allow me to tell you a story. It may be a fiction, or it may be true, but nevertheless it is based on ideas. In the beginning of time, long before human time, there were two celestial kingdoms. There was a kingdom of light, and there was a kingdom of darkness. Two solitudes. The two kingdoms existed side by side without any mixture between the two whatsoever. Separate and contained, each kingdom.

But change is inevitable, even with celestial kingdoms. One day or night, as the case may be, the kingdom of darkness attacked the kingdom of light. That momentous aggression created the world we know. The ancients referred to it, to our world, as the Smudge.

Think of this situation Christopher, as a dividing line, between light and darkness. It became the primal responsibility of all those on the side of light to pursue and recover the particles of light that were imprisoned in the substance of darkness, in the material world, in the Smudge. On one side there were people who were virtuous and reasonable. On the other side there were those who were sustained by vice and brutality.

The people of light were relentless in their pursuit to free the light that was caught in the material world. They believed that the light of the heavenly spheres ruled the universe, and with that knowledge they penetrated the substance of darkness to recapture the light that had been taken from them. Are you with me so far?"

"So far, so good Malek. I understand what you're saying. It's a binary thing, light and darkness. Sounds biblical," I replied. His discourse amounted to a lecture and took me away from the pleasant, green park, and the children laughing, and the light breeze swaying the branches of the trees overhead.

"Excellent. Now, imagine if you will, the horror of the kingdom of darkness returning once again to plague our world, the very world that we have been cleansing of vice and brutishness. Imagine spirits returning from the dead, from the substance of darkness, to resume their mockery of life. That is what we are after. That is our ultimate goal. Somehow the dead are with us once again, somehow they have harnessed bright filaments of life. These returned spirits hold the keys to the victory of the kingdom of light. The light within the spirits, the light energy they carry, is the stuff and essence of star creation and precious beyond measure. This very day they walk about Pula, and other parts of Croatia. This we know, but we do not yet know enough. And that is where you can help us."

Malek stopped speaking then, and turned to look at me with an imploring expression on his face. He placed his hand briefly on mine. It was very cool to the touch despite the day's warmth.

"But how can I help you? What you've told me sounds very esoteric and imaginative, but what can I do?" Just then a red, white, and blue ball bounced directly in front of me. I snatched it in the air and tossed it to the boys playing catch. They waved back in thanks.

"Come now Christopher. I have sources that inform me of your involvement in the strange goings on, that began at Brijuni. Don't even bother to deny that. And your relationship with the deceased Davor is common knowledge. Davor organized the Brijuni event. I know that you know things that can help us greatly. I can assure you that money is no object. You will be rewarded beyond your wildest dreams."

"I can't help you," I said, watching the expression on his face change instantly from earnestness to sullen anger. He was livid. The small scar on his cheek was slightly raised and etched in white.

I stood up to leave. He smiled at me with dead eyes. As I was walking away, I heard him mutter these words.

"It would be a pity if we lost the lights of a new dawn because of your decision. Good-bye Christopher."

I hurried through the park, puzzled by his last remark, and returned to my apartment.

The next day I awoke early and puttered around my apartment. The important thing is to think like your enemy. Malek's obsession centered on the returned spirits, and on their utter destruction. That I knew for certain. But I needed to know more. It was a dismal day, gray and overcast, with a slight chill in the air. I decided to stay home.

I walked out to the small garden area just below my apartment. I took a small rubber ball with me, found a place to sit on the ground with my back against a brick wall, and then began to toss the ball against another brick wall, part of a garden structure, about ten feet away. My ball would strike the opposite wall and then bounce back to me, with just the one bounce at a halfway point between where I sat and the other wall. I'd throw the ball, wait for the bounce, catch it, and then throw it again. Very soon I got into a rhythm that felt comfortable.

I remembered Malek's story about the kingdoms of darkness and light and the opposition between the two. I think it was more than just an interesting anecdote for him to tell me. I think he regarded it as truth. He was on the side of the kingdom of light and he wanted to get back what he believed had been stolen by the kingdom of darkness. The yellow ball bounced easily and seemed to channel my thinking. I'd catch it and throw it back against the wall with hardly any effort on my part. My right hand would rise up to meet its return trajectory, gently cradling it in the palm of my hand, before throwing it again. The returned spirits had come back from the dead, the kingdom of darkness, but in order to travel back to life they needed light, very special light, precious light, light that could create stars and human tissue. It was a marvel and I had seen the returned spirits made flesh. I had seen them issue forth from the figure eight circle of light before my very eyes. Malek was after something. It wasn't only the gratification of having people suffer. The curve of the ball as it floated in the air and then bounced back was soothing to my eyes. Fluid yellow curves moving back and forth. Again and again. The bounce of the ball made the slightest of sounds. Malek wanted the destruction of the returned spirits, to be sure, but there was something more he wanted, much more, and it had to do with the light they brought with them. Somehow, he wanted to capture that rare concentrated light, the light of the heavenly spheres I mused, the light of the universe itself. That's why he hunted them so ruthlessly. It was the light of creation that he was after. Hah! Suddenly I missed my catch, and I watched as the yellow ball bounced several times to the far end of the garden and came to settle beside a small potted palm. An old brindled cat walked towards me, sniffed the air, and then returned to where it had been sitting by the garden shed. The day had gotten warmer although the sun was still hidden from view. I felt wonderful.

I went upstairs to my apartment and made a pot of coffee. I turned on the television with the remote and put the sound function on mute. I've always thought better with something flickering in the background whether a TV or an artificial fireplace. I placed two large cushions behind my head and lay down, content with a lazy day and my place in it. I was just about to get myself a coffee when I saw a newsflash on the screen. I turned on the sound. Two boatloads of migrants had been found dead in the waters off Veli Brijun. There were no survivors. The bodies had been riddled with bullets and included women and children. All of them were wearing life jackets. The rubber rafts were a shredded, mangled mess. It was hoped that some cellphones could be retrieved from the bodies to determine what had happened. One report commented that this was an unusual occurrence and that until recently migrant routes had favored the pathways from Greece and the Balkans. News clips showed the bodies lined up on the beach waiting for transport to a morgue. Each of the corpses was in a black body bag. Three of them were pathetically tiny. One reporter blamed unknown right wing elements. I thought immediately of Malek. I knew he had to be behind it.

I grew tired of watching the same tragic footage again and again on the news report so I turned the television off and Googled the word migrant. I scrolled through a long, dated list of news items until I settled on what European states were doing to stop the migrants from coming. What hadn't got a lot of attention was that European organizations were paying African states like Niger massive sums of money to criminalize migration, and block migrants from coming. In effect, they were financing the creation of new Southern borders, borders that were being pushed further and further away from mainland Europe. The pushdown was destabilizing African states but cutting down on migrant flows drastically. There weren't any high profile statesmen seeking long-term solutions. There was no cohesive strategy to deal with the migrants. Some were even discussing floating walls in the Aegean Sea. Great barbed wire fences on the mainland were already in place, with local vigilantes patrolling the perimeters. The world was a mess and desperate people, tens of thousands of them, perhaps hundreds of thousands of them, were still trying to reach a paradise that didn't want them. Things had changed, things were looking grim.

I poured myself another coffee, sat on the couch, and looked out onto the garden below. I was trying to make sense of it all. State actors can be as bad or worse than individuals. I thought about Malek. He was pathetic. His capacity for evil was such that on the lower end he could smash a stranger's denture, and on the other end hit and run over a better man than him, like Davor. Malek's evil was rooted in pettiness and rounded out by murder. In his quest to capture the light of the returned spirits, he would eclipse and override any boundaries opposed to him. Murdering migrants was just a sideshow, and one that would play well to any far right supporters if the truth came to light. The Academy of Light was a travesty of anything good and decent. I took another sip of my coffee but it was already cold. Outside in the garden the brindled cat caught a mouse in its forepaws and played its deadly game with it. I knew quite clearly, and a little sadly, that the best I could do for any migrants who made it this far was to expedite their journey north to the fabled northern lands they dreamt of. I had to help them push north for there were no options open to them here in Croatia, and neither did the migrants want to stay.

♦ ♦ ♦

I was nearing Zora's apartment when I caught a glimpse of Mr. Šubić in the back seat of a black limo as it sped away from the quiet upscale street where she lived. It was followed closely by a brown Range Rover with dark tinted windows. I quickened my steps and within a minute I was knocking at her door. She seemed to be in a daze as she opened the door and invited me in. I followed her to the living room and I sat in the large leather armchair beside her bookcase. She sat on her couch, with an air of despondence, and looked at me with such wistful and sad eyes that I knew something terrible had happened.

"What is it?" I said.

Zora looked out the window and began speaking in a tired, worn voice. "Mr. Šubić has left me with a cellphone. It was from one of Malek's people in Split. It seems there was a confrontation between a group of Malek supporters and Mr. Šubić's aides. The incident occurred after a lecture by Malek at a library there. When Malek left quickly in his limo, a few harsh words were exchanged between the two groups, and one thing led to another. The end result was a minor brawl in an alley behind the library that was fortunately dispersed before any police came. Afterwards one of Mr. Šubić's aides collected this cellphone that had fallen by the curb. All of its data is being analyzed of course, but there was one disturbing video concerning one of our spirit guides, Franjo, from New Zealand." At that point Zora placed the cellphone on the glass coffee table in front of her and pushed it towards me.

I hit the play function and waited and watched. At first there was nothing but white intense light and I couldn't make out anything, but slowly I could see two figures emerging as shadows formed against the blinding light. A young woman was lying on the floor in the background and appeared to be unconscious. In front of her was a tall, dark, handsome young man staring defiantly at the camera and leaning forward, his knees slightly bent. For several seconds there was no sound or movement at all. But then things changed rapidly.

Suddenly, the man, wearing a tight-fitting Croatia football jersey, was making vigorous movements and stamping his feet, while at the same time shouting rhythmic accompaniment in a language I didn't understand. But there was no mistaking the challenge and slow movement forward. He was menacing and wild and intense in a controlled manner. He had curly black hair and a muscular build. The video showed him slapping his hands on his chest and arms with great fervour, while slowly and inexorably, moving ahead . His tongue was sticking out fiercely, and I could see the whites of his bulging eyes clearly. His progression forward was furious, with violent gestures throughout. At the very last moment he lunged forward in attack and the camera suddenly lost focus, with excited voices in the background, Malek's people, shouting in utter despair and terror. Then there was the sound of heavy gunfire erupting suddenly and then everything went dark.

It was about to replay when I turned it off. I didn't know what to make of it. I turned to Zora in consternation.

"What happened on the video? Who is this spirit guide?" I asked.

"That is Franjo. He is Croatian Maori, and those, we believe, were his last moments. He was very brave and protective of his fallen colleague, and went down fighting in that enclosed space filled with intense light. We are trying to determine where it happened, but from the gunfire heard on the video, we suspect he was murdered together with the other spirit guide, a woman named Ana, seen earlier on the video. She fell unconscious before she was killed, we believe, as a result of the deadly lasers of light within the enclosure.

Mr. Šubić was told by other spirit guides who knew him that Franjo was always joking and very cheerful, eager to help others in whatever way he could. The video shows him performing the haka, a famous Maori dance. His father was Croatian, a fisherman from Korčula, and his mother native Maori. His grandmother on his mother's side was a Dame and decorated by the Queen for her work in education. Two strong lines, befitting a hero like Franjo. He told his friends here in Croatia that back home the Maoris call Croatians tarara, meaning fast talkers. The two cultures in New Zealand are complementary and close, and have been for well over a hundred years. Our Franjo was one of the first spirit guides from the diaspora to be recruited for our work with the returned spirits. He was a natural."

◆ ◆ ◆

So much had happened in such a short period of time that I was thunderstruck when her e-mail pinged on my iPhone. A voice from the past that wouldn't leave the present. I sat on my couch and read the text several times, with ever greater dismay.

Dearest Christopher,

I can't help thinking about the good times we had. I can't help thinking about our son Peter who is living proof of the vitality and strength of our marriage. It can't be too late for us, not for the life that's left in us. You don't have to reply to this message. Just think about a new start. You may not even want to, after how neglectful I've been, how selfish and hurtful. But those days are over and done. I want you to know that I've never given up hope for us. Never. Don't be surprised if I drop in on you again. Maybe I'm being too pushy. It would be absolutely wonderful if you extended an invitation for me to join you. Oh, by the way, I'm taking a Croatian language course online. Bok.

Love, forever, your own,

Gloria Mundi

No matter how many times I read it, the threat was there. I couldn't believe it. She might actually be returning to Croatia, to my new life, after I thought my old life was mercifully finished with. I had to put it out of my mind. I deleted it. I wouldn't reply. To reply was to engage in a possibility that I would not allow nor permit. Those days were gone. Gone.

◆ ◆ ◆

It was just after my morning coffee when I received the call on my cellphone. The local police wanted to see me in connection with the report I had given to them regarding Sam Stark and Malek and the migrant shootings. They said a car would be sent for me within the hour. I was surprised at that because I had nothing additional to tell them. It was a second-hand report I had given them. I assumed Sam had left the country, and that was that. I thought of calling Zora but decided against it. I didn't want her to be involved. I knew she was extremely busy with looking after logistics for the returned spirits. Two officers showed up at my door and escorted me to their car. Within ten minutes I was entering the police station.

One of the officers behind the front desk asked politely if they could take my fingerprints and perhaps a photograph. When I asked him why he shrugged and said it was simply a formality. That struck me as odd, and I asked him if I was a person of interest in the case. He said that I was not at that moment. He asked again with what I thought was sincere politeness if I would please comply. A little reluctantly, I agreed. He asked if I had seen Sam since I had given my report. I had not. He asked if I had heard of the recent migrant killings, of the two boatloads of migrants who had been shot and killed in their rubber rafts. I said I had certainly heard of the murders but nothing beyond what the media had reported.

About an hour later, after further questioning of a general nature, and the fingerprints and the mug shot, they asked if I would help in making an identification. I had no idea what they had in mind but I followed them to the basement of an adjoining warehouse beside the police station. It was dark and dank inside. I felt a sense of foreboding.

One of the officers turned on the lighting. It was powerful and cold institutional lighting. There, ranged before me, were dozens and dozens of black, zippered body-bags. An officer took my arm gently and guided me to an area on the far side of the warehouse where several very small body-bags lay atop a stainless steel table. Slowly, he unzipped the bag and I saw the corpse of a small girl no more than four years old. Her face and tiny hands were the color of ivory. A red wool shawl that still looked damp was wrapped around her shoulders. Her legs were gone. I shuddered involuntarily and looked away. I was almost sick to my stomach at the sight of her mutilated body.

"Why, why are you showing me this?" I cried out. "I did not know any of these people."

And then, the officer, without speaking a word, guided me to another of the bags, and carefully unzipped it.

I was horror struck when I saw the face. It was Sam Stark. His eyes had been burned out or gouged out somehow. His little body was naked with clear signs of torture, as if a laser light had etched crude indistinct designs on his skin. The wounds on his chest were puckered in but they looked as if a drunken tattoo artist had tried to draw the stars and stripes of the American flag on his skin. There were no signs of bullet wounds, none at all. It was terrible, and I fell to my knees. Somewhere, far behind me it seemed, as if in a tunnel, I heard one of the officers ask if that was Sam Stark. I said that it was. One of the officers helped me to my feet.

From there I was escorted back to the police offices where I was questioned still further. They wanted to know how Sam Stark's body was found among migrants whose bodies were riddled with high caliber bullets. I said I didn't know and suggested they contact Malek in that regard. They said that they were conducting separate lines of investigation and all leads. I asked if I was going to be arrested. They said I was free to go but to stay in Pula until further advised. I nodded and left, my mind churning in anguish. It was not that Sam Stark and I were that close. We were acquaintances only, but I liked him. He was a decent man who had fallen under the influence of a murderous populist, of Malek. The sight of the broken body of the little girl and Sam's own would haunt me for a long time to come. An officer drove me back to my apartment in silence.

I spent the remainder of the day thinking about Malek. What I began to realize, albeit belatedly, was that Malek allowed time for his victims to become very frightened, fearful of the threat alone that he and his followers posed. That's what he was doing with me now. I was sure of it. He would wait and wait and wait, doing nothing, savoring the atmosphere of fear that was built up and accumulated over time. He enjoyed it. He knew that fear was a common, cheap form of torture that served him well. It cost nothing and was self-inflicted. He simply had to feed it, slowly and intermittently, until the victim was almost incapacitated from visceral fear, fear that you could smell, fear that robbed you of your capacity for action, fear that hit you in the pit of your stomach and made any kind of escape impossible. I remembered that Davor had told me once that fear is a gift you give your enemy.

Rovinj

It was an impromptu, late evening meeting that Zora had arranged at Mr. Šubić's request. The three of us met at an upscale restaurant on the outskirts of Rovinj, near a campsite. Zora had told me the cold and warm appetizers were the best in Istria. The place felt just right.

Apart from the security detail we were the only diners that evening. I counted eight bodyguards who were nearby and constantly roving about, alert and focused. They were dressed casually and were of different body sizes and demeanours. A wide range of delicious appetizers lived up to Zora's comments. The grilled calamari was the best I had ever tasted. There was an imaginative flair in the way the dishes were presented. A nervous waiter brought some after appetizer drinks and some freshly cut fruit, his hand trembling as he set down the drinks and small plates and cutlery from his tray. He knew the heavy security was there for a reason. I saw Mr. Šubić smile at him, clearly seeing his distress, and he made a point of thanking him warmly. The waiter hurried off.

We sipped at our drinks and made small talk for several minutes, until Mr. Šubić lightly tapped the linen tablecloth with his fingertips. He was, as always, impeccably dressed, this time in a light, finely tailored gray suit with a crisp white shirt open at the neck. He was not a handsome man but he certainly had style and presence and commanded attention. His voice was softly cadenced as he began to speak.

"First of all, I need to provide you with some essential background. I will get right to the point. The gist of it is that Malek is using shipping containers against us. When you think about it Malek's use of the shipping containers is brilliant. These intermodal containers have been designed and built for transporting freight from ship to rail to truck. They're as common as cabbage, and moreover, they're ubiquitous. They're hidden in plain sight. Doesn't raise a single eyebrow. Brilliant. Transportation costs are dramatically reduced and there's no need for warehousing. The man is cunning and efficient.

Basically there are two common sizes of containers that have been standardized across the world. They can be twenty or forty feet long with heights of eight and a half or nine and a half feet. The standard width is eight feet. Each of the eight corners on a container has a twist-lock fitting for hoisting, stacking, and securing cargo. They can be hidden easily under tons of other containers. Any evidence they may contain can be shipped overseas as easily as signing a shipyard invoice. We suspect they also may be used to dispose of migrant bodies, but we have no proof to date.

However, as regards returned spirits, based on the retrieved cellphone video, and the actual container found in Rijeka, the inside of the container has been customized and rigged with powerful lights and lasers that when operative, we suspect, proved fatal to the spirits. We do not know why or how it worked, but it did. The experts were surprised at the use and efficacy of the lighting configurations. It was quite unusual in its composition and included special lasers whose function they were not able to determine just yet. They hadn't come across anything like it before. We believe the combination of heat and light proves devastating to the spirits. Nothing was left of them other than a dark residue or smudge on the container floor. These were the only remains.

It's interesting how we discovered our information. The biggest container yard in the country is at Rijeka. Apparently, several white vans, similar to the one used in Makarska in the failed kidnapping of the returned spirit named Stipe, have been tracked by our investigative team. One of our lead investigators, Toma Marković, went down there to take a look around. He is from Rijeka and had several friends among the staff there including the Shipping Manager. As chance would have it that day he had to babysit his six-year old nephew Niko. It was totally unexpected and so he took the boy, who is autistic, along with him. And that's where chance and good fortune favored us. Because of the boy's autism we had a major breakthrough. The boy was bored and getting hyperactive and restless, so as Toma was talking with the Manager of the shipyard the boy asked if he could play on the computer, something he had become very adept at. Toma knew he loved number games, especially those involving statistics. So, the Manager opened a document listing all of the containers in the shipyard by weight. And here is where it gets very interesting. The boy was fascinated with the data on shipping container dimensions, but particularly on the three relevant weights of containers that are painted on the outside of container doors when in service.

Basically, there is the Tare weight which is the weight of the container without cargo or contents. Then there is the Payload or net weight of the cargo or contents that a container can hold. And finally, the maximum Gross weight which includes both the Tare weight and Payload. To give you an example, the Tare weight for a twenty foot high cube container is 2230 KGS, the Payload, 28250 KGS, and the maximum Gross weight is 30480 KGS. Niko loved it and spent several hours examining the numbers, looking for discrepancies, and finally he found one and showed it to his Uncle Toma. There was only one container that didn't figure, that seemed odd and out of place in a sea of containers that had consistently hard data.

The container, a standard twenty footer, had a Tare weight of 2185 KGS and a Payload of only 550 KGS. The maximum Gross weight was 2735 KGS. The boy excitedly reported it to Toma. At first Toma dismissed it thinking perhaps it was a mistake when the data was input into the program. The Manager concurred. It didn't make sense. But the boy insisted on seeing it for himself. He began to cry and whine until the Manager agreed to show him the container in question. It was under a stack of four identical containers. Toma, fortunately, had a special warrant to search any of the containers that he deemed of interest, and of course the Manager was his friend. Toma told us that Niko was howling in excitement with the anticipation of seeing the inside of the container in question. When it was opened for viewing they saw row after row of lighting, on the sides, ceiling and floor of the container, all under a kind of steel mesh grid that covered and protected the curious looking lights. The lights were very unusual in their structure. The documentation on the container indicated it belonged to the Academy of Light Foundation, Malek's foundation. There were several other containers listed under the Foundation name as well, but there was nothing irregular in the weights of the containers. They were standard. It was a major breakthrough and we owe it all to the little boy Niko. Our hero. When Toma asked him what he wanted as a reward, the boy shyly pointed to a lobby display of miniature trucks, ships, and tiny containers by the front entrance. With the Manager's permission Niko was given the toy miniatures that he began to line up, one after the other, around the perimeter of the lobby.

But back to Malek. Forgive me if I seem impressed. I am. You need to take the measure of your enemy and know what you're up against. In effect, he's taken a closed corrugated steel or aluminum box and converted it into a killing zone. The small Payload, we believe, was to allow for only the combined physical weight of a few returned spirits. Once inside the container, the lights and lasers eradicated even their weight.

And something else too that we believe Malek possesses. There was an empty bracket at one end of the container that obviously had held some sort of apparatus. Our speculation is that this apparatus, whatever it is, captures the spirit essence of the returned spirits seconds before they are smudged into oblivion. This light is the very essence of life. That explains Malek's obsessiveness. If he has control of that, he becomes a god. He can close the gateway we've accessed to the past, the figure eight gateway used by the returned spirits. And he can do much more than that. He can destroy anyone, anything, anytime.

It took us a while to figure out why he favoured vans. He wanted a means of transport that could initiate the killing process. The vans were essential in abducting the returned spirits and the spirit guides as a preliminary step to destroying them in the shipping containers. We have the video of our spirit guide Franjo being shot to death in a container as he attacked his captors. His actions must have surprised them. He was very brave in the face of imminent death.

Malek is using a two-step process in the capture of his victims. We don't have a full picture yet but it's developing, and we'll get there soon. A few days ago the bodies of two spirit guides, one an Argentine Croatian, and the other a Croat from Vukovar, were found lying at the base of the Tesla statue at the intersection of Masarykova and Teslina streets in Zagreb. A smashed Tesla retina scanner camera was found by the bodies. That was Malek's way of telling us that he knows about our use of the scanners. We have a leak in our organization. We know that for certain. As for the migrant killings, they were all done at sea using high tactical weaponry. Pure hate fuels his motivation, and the migrants are nothing more than a subordinate target. Who knows, he may have captured other migrant groups and used his ordinary containers to dispose of them. Believe me, we are doing our utmost to find migrant boats, determine their chosen destination, and transport them north. It's perhaps not the best solution, but for now it's the most expedient one.

Just now, I must confide, we are losing the battle. The traitor in our midst knows precisely where our returned spirits, spirit guides, and operatives are, throughout Croatia. Until we plug that leak, we can't move ahead in our work."

He stopped speaking then, lifted his chin up, and looked at us closely for a moment before a sad smile broke across his face.

Obviously, I thought, Mr. Šubić used his considerable influence to keep the matter hushed up. I was impressed with Mr. Šubić's analysis. I realized then that the leaders of this world had to be focused on strategy and tactics in assessing their enemies. Compassion for their victims came later, with victory. I watched him tap the tablecloth with his fingers twice, and then signal to one of the members of his team. It was time to leave. Within moments Zora and I were in a range rover heading back to Pula, both of us quiet and somewhat awestruck with the new knowledge we had.

• • ◆

The driver asked me where I wanted to be dropped off, at my apartment or downtown Pula, or wherever. I was just about to speak when I felt Zora's hand brush my knee, ever so lightly. It was in those small unconscious moments of hers as when she touched me in an offhanded manner, that encouraged me to think we could have a relationship. She said to the driver we could both be driven to her apartment. I looked at her, somewhat puzzled, and then stared straight ahead, my heart in my throat. Someone said once that to travel hopefully is better than to arrive, but when hope and arrival are complementary elements to each other, then nothing can be finer in this world. We had come close before.

Soon, I was sipping a fine Istrian red wine that she had poured for me in her third floor apartment. My emotions were raging within me. I didn't know what to make of her invitation. Was it simply a glass of wine or two, and then a somber taxi ride back to my apartment? Or something altogether different, something wonderful and beautiful? I didn't know, but I didn't want to make a mistake and be mortified if I were wrong. I felt like a teenager again analyzing every word she said or any gesture that she made. I didn't want to assume anything. Assumptions can be deadly to relationships. Fortunately, I didn't have to wait long to find out.

Zora sat opposite me, I, on her couch, and she, on a wooden rocking chair, with a coffee table between us. The living room lights were on low illumination. It felt romantic. She took a slow drink of her wine, all the while looking at me through her wine glass, and then with an elegant, circular gesture of the glass, she placed it on the coffee table, very carefully. She had come to a decision that was about to change her life and mine.

She stood up, walked over to me, took my hand, and then pulled it lightly to her, encouraging me to stand with her. She turned away, turned the light off, and then guided me to her bedroom, still holding my hand. At the entrance to her bedroom, she turned to face me and gave me a soft, enchanting kiss, so soft, and barely touching my lips. Without thinking, I looked deeply into her eyes, looking for an image, a memory.

"Don't look at me like that," she said, with mild irritation in her voice, but still soft and tender. "What you are looking for isn't there yet. All you will see on my retinas is the present image of me with you now, in this moment in time. We have to create new images together, new memories that we can co-create together. Do you understand what I'm trying to tell you Kristof?"

"I think I do. For a brief moment I guess I lapsed into work mode. I don't know what I was looking for. I just want to be with you, that's all." I could hear the hopeful tone in my voice.

Then she smiled with her perfect mouth and kissed me again, a long soft kiss that lingered for a brief time, ever so brief, and then left like a small exotic bird alighting on a branch and then flying away to a distant wood. I stood there, in the entrance to her chamber, and felt my eyelids close. She guided me gently into her room, and we stood at the foot of her bed and embraced. There was no need to rush. We undressed and fell under the sheet and duvet, and for a moment, we simply lay together, not touching, the small space between our bodies charged with desire and anticipation. Around us the darkness was complete. There was no light to distract us.

It felt to me like I was falling through space untrammelled by anything, despite the fact that I knew I lay on Zora's bed in perfect stillness in her apartment in Pula. Seconds passed and then we touched. Our limbs entwined, and it was as if a great and urgent heat encircled us. Our hands and thighs and lips were instruments of that heat and of a desire that was boundless and free. Her body was a dark form upon the darkness, as mine was to her, and there was nothing that we could see. We could only touch and the light was in our touch and nowhere else. The light was contained in the passionate darkness that held us and moved through us. I wondered over the emotions I was feeling. Everything was so new and innocent. I felt an immense strength and power that was matched with her own.

It seemed to me we were in a rich fertile place, a place where vines and exotic plants and a canopy of tropical trees hung over and around us, a place where strange birds and the creatures of the night circled around us. It felt as if we were alone in the universe that spilled about us and infused our passion with its nascent wonder. The world was ours within the orb of that room in Pula.

When it was over, we lay breathless beside each other and I felt her fingers caress my cheek lightly, and then she laughed, and so did I, astounded at our belated encounter in her apartment in Pula. We had come through. I knew then that our bonding was knit with a joyfulness and a tenderness that would see us through any difficulties that lay ahead.

Split

I decided that very morning to take a bus to the coast. I would go first to Split and then determine where to go next. Perhaps Trogir or Omiš, or Cavtat, or any one of a number of towns where I could lay low and wait for instructions. I was following Mr. Šubić's advice to imitate the actions of a white butterfly with its erratic yet purposeful movements. I needed to keep under the radar of Malek and his people. And at any point Zora could contact me with a plan for me to follow and a destination. It was nebulous but it made sense.

It was very busy and lively at the Split bus terminal located near the harbor when I arrived. It was mid-afternoon and humid. People were milling about, some waiting by the platforms for their buses, others queuing to buy tickets, though maybe queuing isn't the right word. There was a tight, messy clump of people in front of the bus teller's wicket each vying for the ticket seller's attention and talking simultaneously. All very normal and chaotic.

I kept my luggage close to me. I had one large suitcase and then a backpack strapped across my shoulders. The canvas bag was in my backpack. I bought a small bottle of water to keep hydrated and looked for someplace to sit and decide on where to go next. I was comfortable with the uncertainty. It felt adventurous. I saw a table and vacant chair outside a snack restaurant and sat down. I was just about to take a drink of my water when a young woman from behind the counter shouted that I needed to buy something if I wanted to sit there. I ordered a čevap and looked around. The place had become incredibly busy. Besides the buses there were several cabs nearby. A couple of the cab drivers were actively looking for passengers, talking to people standing by the platforms, hustling for work.

The important thing, I thought, was to keep my wits about me. I scanned the faces in the crowd. Most of them were locals with strong Slavic features, but there was a scattering of young tourists with backpacks in the mix. I didn't see anyone who looked unusual or out of place. I took a sip of water and went to work on my čevap. It was excellent and the bite sized pieces of meat within the soft, fresh bun hit the spot. I had had a light breakfast before I left Pula, but that was all. I still hadn't decided where to go next, but I knew it would be somewhere south.

Call it a sixth sense or whatever, but I glanced over my shoulder and saw three big men scrutinizing the faces of people standing by the platforms as they walked. They were dressed casually and wore trendy athletic outfits and brand new white sneakers. They took their time, and I saw one of the men share a cellphone photo with the others. The man with the cellphone had a startling purple birthmark that covered the left side of his face. It resembled a hastily drawn map of South America. They were at least four platforms away from me when I decided to move. I wheeled my luggage in front of me and without taking a look back, I walked towards the washroom, marked WC on the signing several meters from where I stood.

I hurried into the lavatory. There was no attendant on duty. I left my bag on the attendant's stool and shouldered my backpack. I knew I had to be quick. I rushed over to the turnstile and pushed one of the four revolving arms that were fixed to a vertical iron post but it wouldn't give. The mechanical gate allowed entry to only one person at a time and in only one direction. I pushed harder but to no avail, until I realized I needed to deposit a five kuna coin in a slot before I could get in. I searched for a coin in my pocket but I had nothing there but my luggage key. An elderly man behind me asked politely if he could get by. I moved away and he dropped a coin in the slot and entered.

I reached into my backpack and into the canvas bag Davor had given me. I had suddenly remembered the Roman gold coin that was in there. I knew it was valuable but I had no choice. I was frantic. I dropped it into the coin slot and pushed the horizontal steel arm. Fortunately it gave way and I was about to enter, but my backpack prevented me from moving forward. I was stuck there. I shifted my shoulders around until the backpack dropped to the floor. I pushed again and was in. I grabbed my bag from beneath the turnstile and went to one of the stalls, latched it securely, and then stood on the toilet seat. I could hear other people coming into the lavatory and using the urinals and washing their hands at the small sink. Someone knocked hard on the door of the stall, but I said nothing. I craned my head to one side and peeked through a tiny crack in the door. I saw one of the three men who I had suspected were following me. He bent down and looked in the space at the bottom of the door, but he saw nothing. I held my breath and waited. Someone said loudly that nothing worked really well in this washroom except for the coin slot. There was sudden laughter and then silence as they left. I stood crouched on top of the toilet seat for at least fifteen minutes and then very slowly stepped down and undid the door latch. I was alone. When I left an old woman was sitting on the stool where I had placed my bag. I asked her where my bag was. She said I had taken a chance in leaving it there. She opened a small cupboard behind her stool and pulled out my suitcase. I reached deep within my pants pocket and gave her a crumpled ten kuna note. She looked up at me in grateful surprise. Very carefully I made my way out of the WC and towards the ticket office. I didn't see any of the three men I had seen before. I purchased a ticket to Makarska on a bus that was just about to leave. I sat in the back of the bus on a window seat and as the bus was pulling out of the platform area, I looked out to see the man with the map birthmark standing by a kiosk and looking about. I ducked low into my seat and slithered down, making myself as inconspicuous as I could. A middle-aged woman in an aisle seat across from me looked at me suspiciously and then turned away shaking her head slightly at my antics. But I was free and away.

Omiš

I couldn't have been more than thirty or forty minutes from Makarska when I drove through Omiš, but I decided to stay the night. I was in no hurry. I had no one to meet in Makarska for a day or two. I found a hotel near the water and booked a room.

The town, situated between the mountains and the sea, was magnificent. A river cuts through the gorge there making the place the stuff of dreams. One of the mountain summits above the gorge looks as if it's turning its head towards the sea. I remembered having read about Omiš back home. A small band of pirates, the Narentani, had ruled the coast here for centuries despite their small size in numbers. Venice paid tribute to them in order to avoid the sacking of their ships. By the river, there were tourist places where you could buy tickets for a river cruise up the river, the Cetina, and marvel at the dominant position the pirates would have held from atop the towering mountains of the gorge. There, they could rain arrows down upon their enemies from the strategic heights. My imagination ran rampant. In pirate days, the Narentani with their small ships could dart around the larger

Venetian ships, attack them, and head upriver where the Venetians could not follow them because of the shallow draughts of their boats, and if they did follow, they did so at their peril, for then they could be attacked at will by the Narentani. I walked through the ancient streets and felt a kinship because the ancestry company I had joined in Canada had identified some of my ancestors as coming from this area. I smiled at the irony of it. Here I was, a Croatian Canadian, ambling about the ancient town of my forbears. I wandered down to the beach area and saw scores of tourists enjoying the sun-filled beauty of the place. Later, I found a small food kiosk where I enjoyed the best čevap I have ever eaten. I sat in quiet contentment at one of the small outdoor tables and savored the food and the day.

Around three in the afternoon I walked up to the fortress tower through a stone stair walkway, bought an admission ticket from a sleepy clerk, and ascended the circular metal stairs. I noticed that the vertical height of the stone stairs, the risers, was quite high. When I thought about it I realized that, in pirate days, the additional height variation from normal stairs would have been useful when running in haste, and perhaps alarm, up towards the tower. I was the only tourist about and stopped every now and then to peer for the longest time through the small, narrow windows where I could look out to the sea and the islands. Near the top of the tower I did the oddest thing without thinking. I spat on the circular inside wall and smeared the spittle across it. I remembered that the ancestry company I had joined had asked me to send them, by post, a sample of my spittle so that they could determine my ancestry. And I remembered Dr. Spehar had also made the same request in Pula. My DNA, I mused, was now a living part of the ancient tower. It felt good to be alive and spitting. I guess I've always found amusement wherever I could get it. Perhaps the pirates did the same. The view from the top was magnificent.

I spent the rest of the afternoon and early evening in free and easy wandering. I decided to walk along the river, on the roadway following it, moving deeper and deeper into the gorge. Then, I found a path beside the roadway that followed the meandering river.

It wasn't long before I had a sensation of people behind me, following me. It was just a feeling, but when I turned to look, there was nothing but shrubs, brush, and trees. But my senses were heightened and I knew I had to be vigilant. I stopped and scanned the trail behind me, standing quite still for a moment or two. When I proceeded on, all was well for several minutes, and then again I felt that sixth sense of someone there behind me, stopping whenever I did, but getting closer to me. And then I heard a bustling sound in the bushes to my left. I felt a wave of panic course through me then and so I stepped off the trail and into the woods. I was scrambling madly and looking for a way out. Suddenly, there was a light push against the back of my shoulders and I found the trail again. It was growing dark quickly.

Strangely, I felt as if someone was helping me somehow. I was alone, physically. Yet it was as if someone guided me forward through the forest. The river was to my left I was certain, but I could not see it for the trees. The only light I had was the illumination from the built-in flashlight of my cellphone. I shone it on the rough path ahead of me, but my hand was guided somehow automatically and I simply followed the movement in my wrist. Soon I was walking through low ground, a kind of shallow valley and the night air felt cold all at once. There were goose bumps on my arms and I sensed I was being closely followed. Behind me, I heard some commotion. It seemed as if several people were in the bushes behind me. I thought I saw the shapes of several men darting in and around the bushes. Suddenly, I heard voices from ahead, crying out and yelling. Loud male voices from several vantage points across the town. There seemed to be dozens of them crying out to each other in warning. The voices were strong, virile, and warlike, urging each other on. Curiously, I thought I heard among the voices those of Ante and Petar. It was bizarre, but it sounded so much like them. That's when the people I thought were behind me seemed to fall away until there were no sounds anymore. I believe they thought they were outnumbered having heard the voices from the town. They were gone, and I felt waves of immense relief pass through my body. I stood for a moment unable to move.

But my guide, the presence I felt earlier, pulled on my wrist and led me forward. The hand felt small and soft, a child's hand, but strong. I was pulled through a dark depression, to a lit area, a parking lot illuminated with orange light, and beyond that, a café. Once I was near the café I felt safe and turned off the tiny flashlight. I was shaken by the experience and I didn't know why.

Every fiber of my being felt I had been followed in the brush by people with evil intent, but I knew deep within, that I had been assisted by a friendly guardian spirit, and those strange familiar voices from the town.

I breathed a sigh of relief and ordered a double espresso at the café where I was the only patron. It was situated on the outskirts of town. I felt safe now that I was under the light, but thankful for the help I'd been given. A paved road led back to town. Just as I was walking back to my hotel room by the sea, I turned instinctively and saw a young girl, of about twelve, thirty paces behind me, just visible. Oddly, she was dressed in old fashioned clothes similar to the costumes you see at local festivals. She waved at me, smiled rather sadly, and then as surefooted as a goat, bounded up the steep mountainside effortlessly, in leaping strides. It was quite remarkable watching her ascent. Finally, I lost sight of her as she disappeared into the covering darkness of the night.

Makarska

I arose very early after a sleepless night. It was still dark. I prepared coffee and took it on the second story balcony of my apartment overlooking Makarska. There were few lights illuminating the city. I couldn't see the islands beyond the small sheltered bay. I was restless and needed to be out and about even in the gloom of night. I don't know why but I emptied my canvas bag of its precious contents except for the two stones, slung the bag over my shoulder, and set off. I crossed the yard in front of the apartment complex and closed the metal gate quietly behind me. I didn't want to wake anyone. I walked down the steep narrow roadway, across the main street, and past the church and market area. There was no one at the small market, and all of the stalls were closed.

It didn't take me long to be by the beach. I turned right and walked in the direction of Baška Voda. The night sky was lightening somewhat. I glanced behind me and noticed human figures in the far distance, joggers, I thought. They were wearing exercise gear. But remembering Zora's advice to exercise caution, I started running hoping that I was just being paranoid especially after a sleepless night. Looking behind me once again I saw them speed up towards me. I knew it couldn't be by chance. I picked up my pace and then sprinted.

I looked back. They were gaining fast on me, and I knew I couldn't out-distance them. Three young guys, Malek's people I assumed, running along the shingle beach, knowing it was just a matter of time before they closed in.

It was still early in the morning, almost daybreak, and there was still no one else about. I was winded and decided to make a stand. Up ahead there was an outbuilding made of concrete blocks just above the beach area. I ran to it, turned to face them, and waited. I was cornered. I reached into my canvas shoulder bag and pulled out the two smooth stones I had lugged across Croatia. Fat chance I had to protect myself with that. There was nothing else. I had emptied my canvas bag of the Byzantine dagger and silver Roman armguard earlier and placed them in a dresser drawer. This was it. Two stones. They were larger than the beach stones I was standing on, but they weren't huge. I held one in each hand and waited for them to get closer. They were tall men and fit. I inhaled deeply, waiting.

They stopped about ten feet away from me and began to laugh, all three of them. The tallest one smirked and looked to his companions, the two of them waiting for him to take the lead and do something. I had seen the tall one before. I remembered his purple birthmark. I had seen it in Split at the bus terminal.

"Oh my, what have you got there? Two stones and three of us. Toss them back on the beach and come with us quietly. No harm will come to you. Promise. Come."

I watched them fan out and stand equidistantly from each other, closing off any chance of escape I may have had. A concrete wall was behind me. Their expressions turned grim. I felt the weight of the stones in my hand.

"Come now," the leader said, growing somewhat annoyed at the farcical standoff. "You don't have a chance. When stones can speak you can call for help, but not now."

The moment he uttered those words, an avalanche of belated understanding descended into my consciousness. I knew what to do. Finally, after weeks of carrying the stones in my canvas bag, I knew their portent. I had figured them out as Davor had assumed I would. I held out my arms like Christ on the cross and and then rammed the two stones together. They made a loud sharp, hard sound. An odd sound. I repeated the motions again and again, smashing the stones against each other with all my power, hearing the sound reverberate in the still of the early morning. The clarity of stone speech come alive. A strange clacking insistence of stone, not to be dismissed, but to be heard, and never to be forgotten.

The three men paused to look at each other in wonder, thinking I'd gone mad. The beach was very still in the suspended silence that hung between the knocking of the stones as they made contact with each other. And then a huge rumbling undercurrent of sound emanated from the shingle beach. The waters, as they rolled back from the beach and back into the sea, made an incredible sighing sound, woeful and utterly weary. As the waves pulled back, more and more tiny stones were exposed and moving. Hundreds of thousands of stones grated and grinded against each other, some submerged in water, countless others not. A pivotal moment hung in the balance between possibility and reality. I wouldn't have believed it if I hadn't heard it, a sound expressing longing and ineffable sadness. But then I was to see it too, as the reality of myriad stone pebbles rose from the beach and into the air above it.

There was a look of incredulity on the faces of the three men. They were stunned at the sight of the suspended stones. For a long moment nothing happened. Nothing at all. The men simply stared at the dense conglomeration of pebbles not knowing what was to come. I stood there and waited. I threw my two stones into the sea and waited.

It began with a single pebble. It whizzed from within the mass of stone and struck the lead man on the forehead, surprising him with its velocity. A trickle of blood ran down his face, and I watched him as he touched his forehead and looked at the blood on his fingers in utter amazement. Then he looked at me and shook his head in disbelief, but only for a moment because a sudden fell swoop of random pebbles rained mercilessly upon his face and body. Abruptly, he fell to his knees raising his arms in a futile defense. Then he fell forward his face buried in the pebbles. More and more pebbles fell down upon him until he was completely buried in uneven blankets of stone, layer upon layer of stone, covering him in a shroud that disappeared quickly, leaving nothing but a mound on the beach.

His two companions, who had watched his death in horror, tried to escape. They turned, but ran headlong into waiting curtains of stone that forced them to their knees. Each tried to protect his face but to no avail. Soon they were covered. There was a great buzzing and humming sound of thousands upon thousands of pebbles striking the two bodies until they too were buried. A faint red mist hovered above where they lay for an instant, and then disappeared. Finally, with a great hissing, sibilant sound all of the stones simply fell to the ground and became part of the seascape once again.

I hastened back to my apartment in the morning light, my mind reeling with what I had seen on the beach at Makarska. My body's natural adrenalin was still coursing through my veins. If only Davor had been with me to witness such an event. What a tale we could share.

Brela

I woke early once again and was taking my coffee on the small balcony overlooking the sea and the not so distant island of Brač. The air was fresh with just a hint of the summer heat to come in a few hours. There were few people walking on the promenade below my apartment. An old man in a straw hat was walking a small brown spaniel who lifted his right hind leg to pee on the vertical dockside posts every few paces. I was much impressed with the capacity of the spaniel's bladder.

I had booked the place the day before while on the bus from Split. Brela was a small town but incredibly picturesque like so many of the other tourist destinations along this storied coast. I would stay one more night and then take a bus to somewhere else, to a destination I hadn't yet decided on. That was my plan but a single text message from Zora could change all that. I wanted to stay clear of Malek's people. I knew there would be others coming after me, like the three at Makarska two weeks earlier. I sipped at my coffee and gazed at a distant sailboat with wine colored sails. I sat and daydreamed and thought about nothing in particular. A seagull landed softly on a floating dock where three boats were moored, and craned its gray neck around.

A knocking at my door shook me from my reveries. There seemed to be an urgency to it. Three knocks and then silence. Three knocks once again and then silence. I hastened to the door and saw that it was chained. I stood there waiting. Another three knocks. I ran to the kitchen and grabbed a butcher's knife from the counter. I stood to one side of the door and slowly opened the door, still chained. I held the knife behind my back. I waited.

"Yes," I said. "What is it?" I looked to see who was there.

"Sorry to disturb you sir, but I have some information for you. Can we speak?"

He was a short, lean man who looked to be no more than eighteen. He had strawberry blonde hair and his hairline was already receding. He wore a white t-shirt, light blue jeans and athletic sandals.

"Who are you?" I asked.

"Mr. Šubić sent me. Please check your messages sir. There should be a message."

"OK, wait a moment."

I turned away, walked to where my iPhone was charging and checked it. A message from Zora said that one of Mr. Šubić's aides would be briefing me that morning, and not to worry. He is one of us she said in the text.

I returned to the crack in the door and looked at him closely for a moment.

"How did you know to find me here?" I asked.

"You've been under surveillance ever since the Makarska incident on the beach."

"I had no idea," I said.

"That's good. We didn't want you to know you were being followed. It's safer for you that way sir."

I took a moment to return the knife to the kitchen, and then I unhooked the chain and opened the door to him. It seemed to me he was very diminutive for a watchdog or a bodyguard role. I noticed he had peach fuzz on his chin. He smiled at me as if knowing what I was thinking.

"Are you alone?" I asked, as I ushered him into the small living room, and with a gesture pointed to the couch where he could sit. I sat opposite him on a well worn faux leather armchair.

"A colleague of mine is outside and out of sight."

"So, what news?"

"Briefly it is this," he said, as he leaned forward with his hands resting on his thighs. His back posture was ramrod straight and, I noticed now for the first time that he had a military bearing despite being a compact young man. "You are a high priority target for the Malek organization. Our intelligence confirms that Malek's operatives have learned that you are a spirit guide, and that they have known this for some time. That is why you were targeted in Makarska. But we have also learned that they are now aware that you possess a unique skill set. Unlike the other spirit guides who require a Tesla retina scanner to do their work, you have the capacity to perform the work without a scanner. That puts you in double jeopardy. They would most likely try to capture you alive to conduct tests, to find out how you do what you do. But if they could not abduct you, we are certain they would render you inoperative." He stopped for a moment to gauge my reaction to his comments, but I was smiling at his choice of words.

"By rendering me inoperative I take it you are saying that they would kill me. Correct?"

"Precisely sir. I mean just that."

"It's nice to be clear," I said.

"Yes, sir, it is."

"So, what else?"

"Malek has considerable resources, manpower, at his disposal. His operatives work in small teams of three. All over Croatia he has positioned dozens of these teams to be on the lookout for returned spirits and spirit guides. They can be redeployed, of course, once targets have been identified, so that additional personnel can converge on a specific location immediately. They seem to favor white panel vans, at least initially, to capture target personnel and take them away to some as yet unknown location. The vans themselves are equipped with powerful lighting and laser devices that render captives incapacitated and malleable. Part of this intelligence, of course, comes from the experience and testimony of one of your own returned spirits, the man called Stipe." At that point he stopped and waited a moment before speaking.

"My colleague and I will be providing your security."

"Just the two of you," I said.

"Yes, but we are in close communication with special mobile teams located in major centers throughout Croatia. We are just the vanguard, the tip of the arrow. You will be safe."

"Why didn't I see you then, in Makarska, on the beach?"

"We were only assigned to your security detail as of yesterday. The Makarska incident occurred before our assignation. I'm sorry sir."

"Me too," I said. "By the way, what's your name?"

"Tomislav," he said.

"Is that your real name?" I asked.

"Very real," he said.

"What's your last name?"

"That's not necessary Sir."

"OK. By the way, the other guy, your colleague waiting outside, what's his name?"

"Krešimir,"

"Really?"

"Yes, sir."

"Isn't that a king's name too?"

"Yes, of course. We are well named. There is power in a good name."

I laughed, shook his hand, and walked him to the door. He smiled then, gave an abbreviated salute, and left.

Makarska

My mind was racing with new ideas as I walked around the small promontory of St. Peter's near the promenade at Makarska. It helped to clear my head as I walked the well-worn ancient circular path. I thought about the past. I knew the returned spirit Franja and his son must have loved it here. Certainly, the trail in his time would not have been as groomed as the one I hiked on in the brilliant mid-morning sunshine, but he would have seen the same vistas as I beheld and loved it as much if not more.

What I reflected on was that Davor had given me special objects from the past, silent witnesses, that contained the hard memory traces of events long gone. That's what he had gifted me, with the small white canvas bag and the power it contained. These objects belonged to people in the past and were used by them, or associated with them somehow. Without telling me how the objects were to be used, he was counting on me to figure things out for myself. Perhaps circumstances confronting me would determine how the objects could be used.

The two round stones, the Roman gold coin, the silver armguard, the Byzantine dagger, these were all powerful objects from the past, from the ancient times of some of the returned spirits. As material objects, they could not accompany the returned spirits who had become flesh and blood creatures through the Figure 8 gateway. But, the returned spirits would have hidden them away in their own times, and secreted them for reuse by others in modern times.

Davor had told me that everything lives. So, I surmised, these objects somehow contained life in their own way. I didn't know how, but they had helped me, and I was living proof of their power and potency. That was enough for me. The one thing I knew for sure was that in order to use them, I had to rely on my intuition.

I knew now the provenance of the objects in the white canvas bag. The gold Roman coin and the silver armguard had come from Marko. Quite possibly, he and his friend Vinko had hidden the objects in one of the caves near his mountain village. Somehow, Davor had found the objects. Most likely Marko had told him where they could be found. I was certain that the same was true for the other objects. The returned spirits would have informed Davor about them. I had used the precious gold coin to enter the bathroom turnstile at the Split bus station. That was an expensive WC visit to be sure. The Byzantine dagger was from Anka and had been secreted away under the stone tiles of her kitchen in Solin. She had used it to kill the priest she had told me about. The kitchen and Solin itself were now an architectural Roman ruin, but the dagger had been found beneath heavy stones. Anka knew instinctively where it was and her precise directions to the dagger's location were superior to any GPS that could have been used. The round stones were the gift of Franja from the beach at Makarska, and they had saved my life when Malek's agents were after me. The two stones, I mused, spoke volumes. These returned spirits had told Davor where the objects could be found, and he had treasured them knowing their intrinsic worth. I did not know when I would use the dagger or the armguard, or if indeed I would use them at all, but I knew that when the time came my intuition would guide my hand and heart.

Now in my walk I was nearing the statue of the saint on the height overlooking the Makarska harbour. For luck I decided to climb the small hill and touch the bronze statue. It couldn't hurt, I thought, to do my utmost to gather as much luck as I could. I needed it. I climbed up the steep, little hill that stood beneath the statue and touched it. I stood there for a moment looking across at the splendid city of Makarska. It was the most beautiful place I had ever seen, and it took my breath away.

I received a text message from Zora to remain in Makarska for the time being. She said she would call me soon and update me on what was happening. I charged my iPhone and made myself a pot of coffee and took it out on to my balcony where I could enjoy the morning sun and the early coolness of the day. I loved being here, a place where I could gaze at the not so distant islands of Brač and Hvar and speculate on what might be happening. After an hour or so, I became bored and decided to shift my perspective.

I slung a backpack over my shoulder and decided to hike to Baška Voda, and on the return leg I could pick up a few things at the small local market by St. Mark's Church. I wanted to be doing something while I waited to hear from Zora.

With a bounce in my step I walked down the steep hill, crossed the road, stepped down past the church and market, to the promenade. Waiters were beginning to put out breakfast menus for the tourist trade. A few seagulls were flying low over the water and the docks looking for their own breakfasts. I continued walking past the restaurants and high-rise hotels that lined the shore. Along the way there were many souvenir kiosks that had not yet opened. To my left, beside the pebbled beach, there were several picturesque twisted pines that lent an air of mystery and magic to the place. The sky was as blue as a promise kept. Within minutes I was on the well-worn trail to Baška Voda happy to be out and about. I was just walking by a small olive grove surrounded by an ancient stone foundation when my iPhone sounded. I found a flat stone where I could sit and take my encrypted call. The reception was good.

"Hello Kristof. How are you?"

"Not bad, and you?"

"Kristof, we have had some setbacks in our work. You need to be advised."

"What has happened?" The tone of grave concern in her voice was unmistakable.

"We have lost some of our returned spirits and spirit guides. A total of three returned spirits and four spirit guides so far. We fear there will be more losses soon. The locations of our security teams have also been compromised. Nine bodyguards have been killed.

We've suspected for some time now that we have a leak in our organization at the highest level. We have taken every precaution but we have still not identified who it might be, or if there are several traitors in our midst. Who knows? Malek's agents seem to know our whereabouts and they can strike at will. They anticipate our every move. They're picking us off one at a time. For the time being we've stopped all spirit work until we plug up the leak."

"What can I do?"

"Go to Zagreb. Find a safe place and wait until you hear from me, and no one else. Do not let anyone, including myself, know where you will be. Is that clear? If someone tells you otherwise, and claims to be with us, do not believe them. Understood?"

"Yes."

"Good-bye."

"I miss you Zora."

"Me too. Good-bye."

Zagreb

I raced back to my apartment to pack and leave. I stopped at a bakery to pick up some pastries for the trip to Zagreb. Within an hour I was on a bus heading to the Capital.

On the way there I booked an Airbnb apartment overlooking Petar Preradović Square, named after a warrior poet. Flower Square, I discovered later, is its more common name. From the bus station I took a taxi to the apartment. It was good to look down from my third story window and see throngs of people ambling about and enjoying themselves amid the colourful flower stalls and cafes. The ambience of the place was warm and inviting. Everything was so ordinary in the best of ways. People were laughing as they sipped their cappuccinos and chatted with friends. An old woman, dressed completely in black and hunched over with age or ailments, entered a church on the northern side of the Square. I noticed three pigeons alighting on the head and shoulders of the bronze statue celebrating the famous poet, living creatures gracing the inert memorial of the dead. There was an air of normalcy that I sorely craved. For the next four days I barely left the apartment other than to pick up food and drink at a basement grocery store located in a mall on the western periphery of the Square. I hunkered down in my apartment watching soccer games and movies, bored and anxious but content, waiting for a call from Zora.

Early on the morning of the fifth day I heard from Zora. I was sitting sprawled out on the couch but sprang to my feet immediately at the sound of my iPhone ringing. Her voice was soft and tremulous, in a tone I hadn't heard before. She spoke tersely.

"Malek has been moving his forces quickly. A total of ten returned spirits have been lost. The bodies have not been found. We believe they've been smudged. Eight spirit guides have also been killed, and three of the bodies, she recounted, show signs of torture. Our security forces, our bodyguards, to a total of twelve, have also been murdered. Apart from the returned spirits, we have recovered all of the other bodies. It is as if Malek knew the precise whereabouts of all of our people, returned spirits, spirit guides, and bodyguards, all of them. All. To be safe we have stopped all contact with our people for the time being. Only face-to-face contact is permitted, this call being the exception over the last few days. We do not yet know who we have lost, who is dead, and who is hiding. He's winning. Malek is winning. Several boatloads of migrants are also unaccounted for. We do not know how many. Malek is on a murderous rampage, and he needs to be stopped. I'm leaving shortly for Zagreb to identify our spirit guides at the police morgue there. I'll text you the address shortly. I want you to meet me there tomorrow at three in the afternoon. You will help us determine if your bodyguards are among the dead. I believe you met them on the coast. Am I correct?"

I swallowed hard before I began to speak. My mouth was dry. "Well, I met with one of them, a young man named Tomislav. I did not see the other, but Tomislav told me his colleague was called Krešimir. That is all I know."

"I will see you tomorrow at three."

"OK."

Her call left me in a state of stupefaction. I walked over to the large bay window overlooking the Square and saw, without seeing, the people milling about, the people drinking coffee at the cafes, the people briskly walking in the cool morning on their way to work, without any knowledge whatsoever, of the calamitous turn of events in my world. And why should they? The world was as indifferent to individual human suffering as children in a playground skipping over black ants in a sandbox. Malek had changed everything. Malek had charted his course in the light of his worst desires and was making speed. Knowing a thing is evil and avoiding it is not enough, I thought. Davor had told me once, in one of his inexhaustible quotes from who knows where, that a person who doesn't punish evil commands it to be done. I sure wished Davor was with me now.

◆ ◆ ◆

I barely slept that night. Tossing and turning, I thought about Zora and what she must be going through. I thought about our love and how little time we had spent together, and how precious it was regardless. I thought about the returned spirits, and wondered if any of those I had worked with were among the lost, or smudged. What a word, I mused. A Malek word, casual and deadly. What other new words would he coin that defined evil in new ways under the banner of light, the Academy of Light. Unable to sleep, I bathed and made a pot of coffee. I pushed the living room curtains aside and looked at the Square below, sipping my coffee, as the first glimmers of the day broke from the eastern skies. Not a soul was in the Square. Then I sat on the couch and waited for the afternoon to come. I napped fitfully through the morning with sporadic dreams marked by struggle and flight.

Zora was already there when I entered the police lobby. She looked distraught, but kissed me lightly on the cheek and squeezed my hand. We sat beside each other on gray metal chairs, and waited, neither saying much until a young, muscular, sandy haired police officer approached us and took our names. He left for several minutes and then returned asking us to follow him. He escorted us down a flight of stairs to a basement area that felt damp and cold. He pushed open a double door and slowly we walked forward, somewhat tentatively. I had a momentary flashback of seeing Sam Stark's tortured body in Pula.

There, before us, were several stainless steel tables aligned in three rows under strong fluorescent lighting. On each of the tables there were two bodies, a total of eight bodies per row, each wrapped in a zippered body bag. I felt a hollowness in the pit of my stomach as I looked at the grim sight arrayed before me. Next to me, I heard Zora take a deep breath, and touch my arm briefly. And then the sad, grotesque procession began. The officer motioned for us to follow him along one side of the row of tables. Each of the bags had a number encased in a transparent pocket just above the zipper. He would bend over, unzip the black body bag, and wait for a sign of recognition from either of us.

Zora recognized all of the eight spirit guides, one after another, and gave their names to the Officer. Three of the spirit guides showed clear signs of torture beneath the pallor of death causing Zora to choke up and look away momentarily at the concrete floor. I recognized two of the spirit guides whom I had met at a café in Pula with Zora. I did not remember their names. I also recognized one guide I had seen in the video that Mr. Šubić had provided Zora. Franjo, the Croatian Maori who had fought bravely to the end against Malek's thugs. But I made clear to the Officer that I did not know Franjo personally. I held Zora's arm by the elbow to offer support if she needed it. She was strong and identified nine of the security officers, the bodyguards. I was unable to identify any of them.

After we had completed examining the three rows in the large room, and a total of twenty four corpses, I was more than ready to leave. I had had enough of the look and smell of death. I wanted to be out in the open air. I turned abruptly to leave, but the Officer said the examination was not finished. He escorted us to still another adjoining room, though considerably smaller. Within it, there was a single row and three stainless steel tables. I followed Zora as the Officer unzipped the bags and we continued our examination. These were all thought to be security personnel. Zora looked at each of them and shook her head negatively.

Because she was standing in front of me as the last bag was unzipped, I could not see the corpse's face. I moved in front of her and took a cursory look at the body on the table. I wanted to be out and gone. But then I felt my body shudder involuntarily in a spasm of recognition. It was Tomislav, my bodyguard. Despite the pallor of the corpse, I recognized the thinning strawberry blonde hair with the receding hairline. He looked so young, with a face somewhere between a boy's and a man's. What a waste, I thought. What a colossal waste. I remembered him saying that he was doing his job if I didn't see him. I knew there was foul play in the death of such a man. I gave the Officer his first name, and said that I did not know his surname, but that I knew he was named after a Croatian king, Tomislav.

I wanted to be out of there as soon as I could. I left the morgue rooms with a bitter taste in my mouth and walked upstairs to the lobby. Zora joined me ten minutes later.

"Will you be staying in Zagreb?" I asked.

"No. I am returning to Pula immediately. I must consult with Mr. Šubić. I want you to stay here in Zagreb until you hear from me. Stay where you are now and remain there, staying indoors apart from essential trips to the grocery store. Once I have arranged security for you I'll be in touch. Kristof, I want you to exercise extreme vigilance and keep your door locked. Trust no one. Understood?" As she spoke I was struck by how cool and measured her voice was. Identifying the bodies had been a sobering experience for her, but one that had left her stronger. I thought then in a sudden grim epiphany that if a person isn't afraid of death, then what is there to be afraid of. I was so happy to be with Zora, even in a morgue.

"Yes, of course," I said.

She kissed me gently on the lips, smiled sadly, and then left the lobby without looking back. I followed her for a moment and then turned towards the taxi rank a few meters down the street. Things had taken a grim turn. Malek's actions had ratcheted up and the image of rows of the recent dead stayed with me for some time. Within fifteen minutes I was back in my apartment.

♦ ♦ ♦

The knock on my apartment door, later that evening, was quiet and tentative, as if the visitor hadn't quite made up his mind to disturb me. After the three light knocks there was silence. A long moment passed. And then three rapid knocks, louder and more definite this time. I unlatched the door chain partially, and opened the door just a little, still keeping the chain in place.

What I saw in front of me appalled me. It was Spehar, but not the portly Spehar I knew, not the fastidious, stylish dresser with a ready, engaging smile and a cheerful disposition. This man was fifteen pounds lighter, unkempt, and wearing a baggy stained suit. There was an abject look of pure misery on his face. His once trim beard was a scraggly, untended mess and his smooth bald head supplanted by splotches of hair of uneven length. Only the bushy eyebrows were the same.

"Please Kristof, let me in. I must talk with you. Please."

There was a whining tone in his voice that I had never heard before. I could see that he was trembling. I hesitated for a long moment, remembering Zora's dire warning, but this was Spehar, Dr. Spehar, my friend and confidante. He was one of us. The warning couldn't apply to him. I undid the chain and flung the door wide open.

"How did you find me? What has happened to you? Why have you come?"

Spehar barged in and locked the door behind him. He raced over to the
window overlooking the Square, looked out for a moment, and then drew
the curtains closed. He seemed to be in a panic. I asked him to sit, and
he did, sitting on the very edge of the living room couch, staring straight
ahead, waiting.

"Dr. Spehar, what is it? You must tell me."

His chin fell to his chest, and for a moment he was silent, his mouth
moving, but with no words coming out. And then, in a torrent of words,
he began his tale.

"I have betrayed our cause. For a fortune, I have sold out," he said.
And then in a kind of rapid fire, cryptic monolgue, he spat out a number
of words and phrases that didn't make any sense to me. "Malek. Containers
at Rijeka. Captured light of returned spirits. Smudges. Ten souls. Migrant
deaths. So many deaths. Spirit guides gone. So much evil. The prism.
Malek." He babbled on and on, and then stopped suddenly. He raised his
head, looked at me tenderly, and then wept. He wept uncontrollably, his
whole body shaking in a paroxysm of grief.

It took me about an hour to calm him down. He had been wandering
the streets of Zagreb for several days, lost and troubled. He told me he had
given Malek information on the activities at Brijuni and the whereabouts
of returned spirits, spirit guides, and security personnel. In exchange for a
fortune Spehar had betrayed all of us.

"I didn't know there would be so many killings," he continued. "Malek
didn't need to kill so many. He had the information he needed, but he
wouldn't stop. And even the migrants, poor miserable souls. Why them?
What had they ever done to him? He called them a footnote to history.
He said he would rid the seas of them, load them all onto containers and
sink them. He said they would make fine ballast. He thinks he's invincible.
When I realized what I had done I was horrified. I needed to warn you.
I followed you from the police station where you had met up with Zora.
I had been tracking her to tell her what I had done, but when I saw her, I
couldn't. I was too ashamed. I fear for you. Malek knows of your capabil-
ities. He wants to use you, and if he cannot, he will surely kill you. And
one thing you must know is that if he asks that you swear an oath to him

you must realize at once that he means to kill you then and there. He is twisted and enjoys playing stupid cruel games. You are not safe here. You must flee. Seek help from Šubić. He is the only one who can protect you."

Then, he grew very quiet as if suddenly remembering some ineffable sadness that rendered him incapable of speech. He sat staring into space for the longest while and then stood up. He looked at me fondly and said he must leave, and that I should follow him within the half hour. He talked about a dangerous shift in power, and how Malek was soon to be all-powerful with his capture of the ten spirits.

And then in the saddest, most pathetic of tones he said very quietly, "If you could see your way to giving me some money, for expenses, I would be forever grateful. I must leave to see my family one last time. You see, I cannot touch the money Malek has given me for what I have done. That money is cursed and rotten, as I am."

I gave him several hundred Euros that he stuffed into his jacket pocket. He took my hand and kissed it lightly, and then flashed a wan smile and left, leaving the door open behind him. It was a pitiful sight to see him like that, so nervous and agitated and defeated, nothing like the happily humming Spehar that I remembered. I went to the window and watched him as he hurriedly crossed the Square and made his way north to the main street of Ilica. Oddly, his arms hung straight down by his sides without any movement whatsoever as he walked. And then he was gone. Less than an hour later I left the apartment as well, my bag in hand.

Brijuni

I arrived on Brijuni mid afternoon. The sky was overcast with light clouds but it was a pleasant day nevertheless. There were only a few people on the private excursion ferry chatting away happily. Security to get to the island was very tight, and I had to present my invitation and picture ID a number of times. I also noticed a number of speedboats cruising about. I didn't know quite what to expect. I wandered about stopping at the church of St. Germaine to see the murals and the Glagolitic writings, the precious printing and script of the early Croats. History was everywhere, and I felt proud of my heritage and what I had done, the services I had performed for the returned spirits. I walked back to the ancient olive tree I had once napped under, and from that vantage point I could see a dozen or so people in the field preparing for a celebration. There were dozens of lambs on spits being barbequed. A party atmosphere was in the air. I simply sat under the olive tree and watched. After an hour or so, I saw a group of costumed musicians tuning their small stringed instruments, the tamburitzas. When they were ready they began to play old folk songs. I remembered loving the sound of the tamburitzas when I was a boy, at concerts, and now as a man, I thought of the sound as being like the sound of an intelligent person thinking, if you could transmute thought into sound.

Slowly, over a few hours, the broad field beside the Mediterranean garden was filled with Croatians wearing folk outfits and costumes from around Croatia. There was laughter mingling with music and high spirits. Small folding tables and chairs were being set up and spaces cleared for dancing. A large white tent was being erected in an open field. I wondered when Zora would be coming, or if she was already here. Some thoughts just come to you unbidden and you can't shake them even if you wanted to. But I knew she was very busy.

Torches were being lit all around the periphery of the field as evening fell. Dozens of men and women were working on the final touches of three huge bonfires that were just about to be lit. Suddenly, at the far end of the field, I could see it, a large figure 8 suspended somehow against the darkening skies near a grove of pines. It was exactly like the one I had seen the last time I had been on Brijuni. The outlines of the vertical figure 8 began to grow brighter in the darkness. I couldn't begin to explain it, but there it was in front of me once again.

Just then I hear a familiar voice, and there was Mr. Šubić standing in front of me. Four men who looked like bodyguards flanked him. I recognized them from Rovinj. The light from a nearby torch illuminated his face. He looked ecstatic.

"Kristof, welcome. Tonight the spirits return, and we are here to witness this event. Not all of them of course. We have lost a few. But many more have survived and now it is their time to depart. The vast majority are happy with their brief encounter back to life, though not all." And then abruptly he moved away from me to greet some others who approached him. His entourage followed him closely. He waved good-bye to me, flashing a warm smile.

I nodded in farewell, thinking immediately of Stipe. He had come back to change one incident in his past. He had come back to spare the life of a single person, a rapist and a coward. The boy, the good soul, had asked him to spare that life, a rotten life, but a life nevertheless. And when the chance came, after two hundred years of thoughtful incubation, he couldn't do it. He was unable to do it. He had to avenge a child that didn't want to be avenged.

◆ ◆ ◆

I stood near one of the three bonfires, feeling its warmth on the front of my body while the back of me was chill and a part of the cool night. I looked and reflected on life and death and my role in this strange, bizarre, wonderful episode of my life. Entire trunks of massive trees were being set ablaze in the bonfires. I watched as thousands and thousands of sparks pierced the night sky, rose and fell erratically, and then died. It was all so mesmerising. Despite our losses we had triumphed. Most of the returned spirits were celebrating on this magic night, on their brief foray back into life, and then later in the evening, they would go back, back again into peaceful death. Wonderful bonfires, with their flames shooting up into the cold night sky, were tickling the thin night with myriad fingers, their sparks alive and then dead, just like the spirits enjoying the fire now, its warmth, its power, its fortitude. I watched and watched, entranced.

Sparks in the cool night air. Holding life in a fleeting cat's paw and then a quick release, not quite abandonment. Blazing, furtive sparks of fire seeking utter darkness, utter loss. Wild impetuous sparks whose direction or path could not be reckoned.

From ignition, from birth, to quiet destruction and loss, the way of a spark, the way of a life, regardless of the trajectory, is the same. The sudden, small burst of flame moving high and higher into the night sky, moving with erratic finality until there was the sudden absence of movement, of inherent power into a nothingness, a void, an abyss of loss, a nadir turning on a pivot until the mysterious workings begin again. It was strange for me to be thinking this way as I looked into the fire, but perhaps not so strange.

Everything is alive as Davor said it was. It may be the past, the present, or the future, but it's all alive. I felt like I could glide through the night air, the mystical cool night air, and see all sorts of things. I could see the fireman moving away from the bonfire and walking deep into the darker darkness of the trees where he could take a pee by the trunk of an old poplar. Columns of intense fire were driving upwards illuminating the night. What I saw around me was happy and good. I spent some time skylarking about, content and free, before I turned and left, hoping to find Zora.

At each of the three bonfires I saw returned spirits, some silent, some talking quietly, as they stood on the periphery. They too felt the warmth of the fire on their faces and chests, and the cool of the night on their backs. I walked among them, and then I heard laughter and singing and music coming from the large white tent in the Mediterranean garden. The sound of their joy beckoned me to join them. I pushed away the canvas flap and entered the tent. I was immediately struck by its brilliant and decorative artificial lights. It was like a moveable palace.

Large banquet tables filled with food and drink and decorated with flowers and ribbons festooned the tabletops. Many of the spirit guides were sitting with the returned spirits they worked with. . I looked around for someone I knew and there, at one of the far tables, I saw several of my own returned spirits, my friends. Ante stood and waved me over. He found a folding chair and beckoned me to sit. No sooner did I get there than Stipe rose up from his seat like a huge colossus and embraced me in a crushing bear hug. He lifted me off the ground and held me there for several seconds laughing raucously in my ear. I saw Nikola whispering something in Mia's ear, and they both laughed uproariously. I saw Anka and Danica refilling wine glasses for Marko and Franja. Everywhere around me there was such merriment and good fun. Petar thrusted a large glass of red wine into my hand and I raised it high and toasted my friends. Wild cheers erupted from our table. I realized that I had arrived at a place where I truly belonged. I felt its love. The absurd necessity and pride of tribalism, I thought.

The noise within the tent was incredible. A small group of musicians playing tamburitzas moved from table to table smiling at the happy, good-natured groups. Waiters carrying large platters of barbequed lamb entered the tent and served the tables leaving more than enough for all. The aroma of the lamb made me swallow involuntarily. Life is good. But so, according to the returned spirits, is death.

After the wonderful supper and merriment a sudden silence descended on our table as we realized that this was the last time we would meet like this, perhaps ever. I could see by their demeanour that the returned spirits were readying themselves for the journey back. A certain wistfulness was in the air.

Several of us walked outside, feeling sated and happy. We sauntered about, not going anywhere in particular on the grounds, but content that we were there together. I didn't quite know what to say. How do you say good-bye to people you've come to love? How do you close a door that may never open for you again? What can you say to soften the hard texture of the moment?

Suddenly, I felt a heavy, powerful arm move across my shoulders and settle there. It was Stipe.

"Thank you my friend," he said gently. He looked at me for a moment with a broad smile on his rugged face. "You did what you could, but I could not change my action, my original choice. I did what I had to do. I know the boy would be disappointed, but I tried. Up until the last moment I thought I could alter my action, and spare the rapist's life, but no, I could not. Two centuries I waited for that single moment, and then failed. I am not sorry Kristof. Some things are just meant to be. I am glad to be going home tonight. This time here has been good, but I am ready now to return to the quiet fields and groves of the happy place. I have made friends here and walked once again over the familiar hills of my beloved Croatia. The salt air of the sea has filled my lungs, and I have felt my strength. How I enjoyed that brawl in Makarska! Football. A fight over a child's game. But you know, I thought about it, and I came to realize that warriors are the athletes of their own day, just as your football players are the warriors of today. So it goes, my Kristof. So it goes."

"I am going to miss you Stipe," I said, looking at this broad hulk of a man standing before me. I was choked up and stifled a sob. I did not want him to think I was unmanly. But then I noticed large tears falling from his eyes and running down his cheeks in utter abandon. He turned away for a moment and wiped away his tears. Ante and Nikola were standing quietly beside him.

"Come and see us sometime," Ante said cheerfully, as if he were a relative about to return to a distant home. He stood near a teary-eyed Petar.

"Sometime, for sure, but don't wait up for me. I may be a while yet," I said.

"No problem, as they say here," Ante said with a twinkle in his eye. "We'll be waiting for you. But in the meantime, we'll keep an eye out for you as we did in Omiš. If you see a swallow in the skies, think of us."

"I will, to be sure." A tear ran down my cheek, but I still felt manly. A Croatian is OK with tears.

Nikola clapped me on the shoulder and then pulled me towards a group circling around one of the bonfires. "Time for kolo dancing before we leave. What do you say Kristof?"

"I say yes."

I noticed that groups of returned spirits and spirit guides were gathering around the other two bonfires as well. They were linking arms just as a dozen or more musicians were standing to one side and preparing to play. I looked around for Zora but could not find her. How I wished she were at my side. What a glorious night it was turning out to be. The sparks from the bonfires were still shooting high into the night sky.

Suddenly, it began. The music started and the kolo circles formed around each of the three bonfires. I held the hand of a person on my left, and another on my right. Slowly, we moved in rhythm in a clockwise direction. I had not met either of the women whose hands I held in mine, but the kolo circle was like a great wheel of life and we moved together as one. The dance steps were simple and easy to master. Gradually, we picked up speed and begin whirling around, moving with great deliberation and power. I felt the heat of the bonfire upon my face and I looked around at the charged exuberance of the flushed faces in the dance. Across from me I saw Ante and the other returned spirits with linked hands and joyful faces. Stipe let out a wild cry that carried over the field and into the dense darkness surrounding the bonfires and the rings of kolo dancers. We danced on and on as if we could go on forever within these circles of light and life. It felt as if we could. The music grew louder and the dance wheeled faster and faster until we had reached a limit, and then slowly, gradually, we began to move in a counter-clockwise direction, as if to catch our collective breath, and then abruptly, all three of the kolo dances stopped, and we regarded each other openly with love and fellowship. The dances ended but we continued to hold hands for a few moments longer, unwilling to have everything stop until we were finally ready.

And then the musicians begin to put away their instruments and a grand silence fell like a canopy over everything. I saw retuned spirits saying farewell in soft voices to spirit guides and then heading to the great white tent that had been cleared of the banquet things and readied for their departure. They went there to remove their modern clothing and thus leave it behind along with any other material objects from their sojourn here. Only their naked bodies would come out of the tent. Long moments passed and then I saw people moving towards the illuminated figure eight structure at the far end of the field close to dense woods. It was several feet off the ground. In front of the structure was a freestanding stairway made of karst stone, several steps high. And then, ever so slowly, the image turned to one side until it was entirely horizontal, like an infinity sign. It was quite remarkable. The left oval of the figure was fire-bright and burning with a soft intensity while the right side was as dark as the night with only the border outline clearly etched against the darkness. It was bizarre but real. I pulled out my iPhone to take a few pictures, but it was completely dead. I had charged it before I left Pula so I don't know what happened.

And then I saw naked bodies exiting the white tent and moving forward, towards the stairway leading to the infinity symbol. I know these were the returned spirits. I saw them ascending the karst stairway, one by one, only a few feet apart. They were magnificent in their glistening nakedness. On the last step, I saw each of them turn to the crowd below, and wave farewell. A touching wistfulness seemed to hover in the air for a moment. Finally, I beheld my own returned spirits, my friends, ascending the stairs, and then looking back, each in turn, naked, to wave goodbye. I saw them all. I saw Mia, Petar, Ante, Stipe, Nikola, Anka, Franja, Danica, and Marko, stopping at the top of the stairway, and waving to me, just before stepping into the infinity loop, and the far country they longed for. Stipe stopped, saw me, and then tossed something high into the air towards me. He shouted that I must be careful where I wear it. His hearty laughter filled the air. I caught the small bundle and unfolded it. It was a Dinamo Zagreb football jersey. My throat was choked with emotion as I waved to each of them, the spirits of the past who had become my dear friends. Suddenly, all grew quiet. The moment was long and still with the grand silence of the dead. They were gone, but not forgotten.

And then, just as I thought everything was over and finished, I beheld the strangest sight and sound. The infinity loop started twirling around like a large propeller, slowly at first, and then moving faster and faster until it became a brilliant disk of golden light. And as it did so, a miraculous humming sound began and seemed synchronized with it, with the circle of light. Together the broad golden circle and the rich, powerful sound seemed to mount to the heavens and hover above the entranced groups below.

The circle image held steady against the darkness of the night gradually changing shape once again. I stood and looked at it transfixed, watching the circle transform into a great golden double helix with the wonderful humming sound getting louder and louder. I felt the glory of the moment and wished with a forlorn hope that Zora were here to see it and hear it with me. Suddenly, the humming sound reached a crescendo that peaked momentarily and then, abruptly, fell into a profound quietude, just as the golden brilliance of the double helix particles reached its height and then dropped to the dark earth beneath, its ethereal light extinguished and gone.

The Temple of Augustus

It had been such a strange, triumphant evening. It was just after eleven in the evening. My friends were gone, but somehow I felt elated, happy that they had returned to their old home. Even if it were possible, not one of them wanted to stay here in the present. That intrigued me, as did their invitation for me to join them on the other side. Not yet, I thought, not yet.

I noticed, as I looked out from the deck of the ferry, towards the dark mass of the mainland, that there were fireworks going off that filled the sky with all of the colors of the spectrum. From that perspective, someone looking at Brijuni from the far shore would have thought that the brilliant double helix was just another fireworks display. Somehow I felt Mr. Šubić was behind it. On the ferry crossing back to the mainland there was an excited hubbub of voices around me talking about the events of the night on Brijuni. I felt glad to be one of the initiated. The cool night air felt good against my skin.

I decided then and there that I would try to see if I could find Zora. I would go directly to her apartment once the chartered bus had taken me from Fažana to Pula. I was so sorry she had missed witnessing the departure of the spirits. She would have loved the farewell ceremony that I was sure she had helped to organize. Something must have happened to keep her away. I had tried calling her cellphone several times but I could not get through. Perhaps she had not charged her mobitel as she called it. No sooner had I landed at the Fažana dock than a small, dark middle-aged man dressed in military fatigues approached me and asked my name. Then he asked to see my identification papers and when I showed him, he said he had some troubling news.

"What is it?" I asked. I felt a cold dread move through my body. Suddenly I was chilled to the marrow.

"Your friend, Zora Sekulić, has been abducted," he said. "I have been instructed to transport you to Pula. On the way there we will receive further directives from one of Mr. Šubić's aides. I am sorry, but that is all I know. Please follow me."

I followed him to a parking lot where he led me to a black SUV. He had a familiar military bearing like others I had seen around Mr. Šubić.

We quickly embarked and he hastened towards Pula. As I fastened my seatbelt, I realized I was wearing the canvas bag over my left shoulder. On top of that I was wearing a light jacket. I adjusted my jacket to accommodate the seatbelt. Within the bag were the Byzantine dagger and the silver armguard that Davor had given me. My mind was racing with all kinds of dark, negative thoughts. I feared for Zora's safety. I thought immediately of Malek and the vicious look on his face the last time I had seen him. Since then I knew he had been responsible for the deaths of many, and my throat felt dry all of a sudden.

Suddenly, the driver's cellphone rang, and he answered. He listened, nodding his head several times, and then spoke rapidly in a local dialect I couldn't understand. Then he placed his cellphone in the coffee holder between our seats, and was quiet for a moment.

He cleared his throat and glanced at me ominously before he spoke. "I am to take you to the Coliseum where we will meet with others for further instruction."

"But what has happened?" I asked, hearing a rising tone of panic in my own voice. "I need to know where she is. I need to know if she is safe."

"I am sorry sir. That is all I know." He gripped the steering wheel tightly and stared ahead into the darkness of the roadway. I could see that the knuckles on his hands as he grasped the wheel were white with tension. For the rest of the trip there was nothing but a grim silence festering in the dark cab of the vehicle. Although he was speeding, it felt like we were going at a snail's pace.

Once we'd parked outside the Coliseum he took me to a small office adjacent to a gift shop area near the entrance. He introduced me to a tall, thin man with rimless glasses and a great mane of thick blonde hair that fell to his shoulders. His jaw tightened as he spoke in a torrent of words that stunned me with their clinical matter-of-factness. I stared at him and listened intently.

"Here is what has happened. Zora Sekulić has been abducted. Earlier this evening as she was leaving her apartment, and as she was making her way to the Brijuni festivities, a white panel van stopped beside her. Two men, according to our eyewitness, came out of the vehicle, grabbed her forcibly, slid the side door open, and threw her into the van. The witness, who had heard her desperate cries for help, was unable to provide us with a license number, or a description of the abductors who wore white surgical masks. The van sped away in a westerly direction. That is all we know of the abduction.

An hour later, we received a call on the cellphone we have in our possession that belonged to one of Malek's agents, the cellphone containing the video of the death of two spirit guides. The caller stated that Malek wants to meet with you at half past two in the Temple of Augustus. If you do, the caller said that Ms. Sekulić will be released unharmed. Malek has become very emboldened despite our efforts, as you know. Several of the returned spirits have disappeared, and we believe Malek has killed them. We have come to a strange new juncture. Malek's Academy of Light initiatives and our own activities, those you have seen on Brijuni, are opposed. Both sides have taken pains to keep developments as secret as possible. Things are continuing to move at an alarming rate.

You have become very important to him. He wants to use you. We want to provide you with a body wire to monitor your conversation with him. As you speak with him, any clues regarding Ms. Sekulić's whereabouts will be acted upon immediately. She may already be dead of course I am sorry to say. But we want to use this opportunity to capture Malek if we can. If we have to kill him we will, but we need your help. There is also no guarantee that you will leave the Temple alive, but we know you are fully aware of that. We will also provide you with a device that will signal us to attack on your command. Our teams are already in place surrounding the Forum and the Temple, but our surveillance indicates that Malek's operatives, about five of them, are also entrenched in the buildings and cafes adjacent to the Temple. We had expected to encounter a much larger number. In that regard we are most lucky."

I nodded, stood stunned for a moment, and then allowed myself to be wired. I also took in hand the device that would signal them to attack and shoved it deep into my pocket. When I asked what I should do if I was subject to a body-search, they said that a non-negotiable condition of my meeting with Malek was that there would be no such search. Malek's caller had agreed saying it would be a breach of trust from both parties if that were to happen. I did not know what to make of that. It smelled a tad off as my mother used to say. I distrusted everything about Malek. I also remembered that Dr. Spehar had said that Malek thought himself invincible.

I had some time to think about things before they were to drive me to the Forum. I was offered a double espresso which I sipped as the meeting hour drew near. I needed to be alone. After I finished drinking the dregs of my coffee, I wandered out to the Coliseum, to the very center of the ancient killing place and stood looking straight up at the night sky. Everything was still and dark, with all of the lights off, and there was hardly a sound to be heard, just the light murmur of voices from the office I had just left on the perimeter of the Coliseum. The stars burned brightly in their far-off heavens and I felt like a tiny speck in an indifferent universe. My stomach felt hollow, but I would have walked into the jaws of hell itself to save Zora. Someone called my name and I walked towards the waiting car without looking back at the heavy darkness encircled by the great stonewalls of the Coliseum. It was time to move.

Neither of us spoke in the ride to the Forum. There were only the two of us, just the driver and myself, each caught up in his own thoughts. Once there, I nodded a farewell to him and he managed a crooked, wan smile, and waved. I walked across the stones of the Forum plaza and up the stairs fronting the Temple's portico. The door was open. Malek was standing there. He didn't offer his hand, nor did I. There were no pleasantries or small talk. He began speaking immediately.

"Everyone needs a second chance Christopher. I am giving you one here in the Temple of Augustus. Can you imagine what has taken place here? What strange rites have been performed within these stone walls- Emperor worship, blood sacrifice, strange nocturnal baptisms? I want you to join us."

"Where is Zora? What have you done to her? You said she would be freed if I came to you. Where is she?" I tried to sound calm and collected, but heard my voice rising slightly.

"Trust me. She is fine, for now. She is in a high place where lions attend her. Ah, yes. I didn't realize you had become so fond of her. Such a weakness it is. Some enlightened saint said that the best thing to come out of marriage was a virgin. At least the Christians got it right on that score. But I realize you are not married to Zora. It is a new relationship, yes? Perhaps it is just a passing fancy. Once you join me you can have any woman you wish and fortune beyond the dreams of kings and emperors. Fortunately, I am free of such sexual entanglements. Invariably they are dark and messy. The light has set me free of all that. Clear and free."

I glanced around at the surroundings. Three wall torches provided light, illuminating the small space within the Temple. I could see that on the far wall, above the stone torso of some Roman hero, there was a small baseball-shaped prism attached to the wall that caught the meager light from the torches within the Temple and refracted, not a spectrum of colors across the gray walls as you would expect from a prism, but white light that was directed beneath the prism to its attachment. Just below the prism I could just make out the shape of the attachment, a dark patch, a small black pocket or cloth sack of sorts, tied with a cord. It was about a foot square, and there appeared to be sporadic movements coming from the inside of the packet. The movements were very slow but steady, similar to the moving shapes I've seen in a retro lava lamp, but of course there was no light within the black pocket, only the suggestion of a sack and elastic lumps moving and writhing inside of it. I wondered what was within it. I knew it wasn't a living creature, but I could tell there was vital life in the movement, although it appeared somewhat agitated at times. Even the little I could see was mesmerizing. I remembered suddenly that when Gloria was pregnant with our son Peter, I had seen similar movements in her womb. It had felt so odd to touch the growing life within, the life that became my son Peter.

Malek took a few steps towards me and tried his best to smile without much success. As I looked into his face, it still struck me as peculiar that someone so handsome could be so evil.

"Christopher, join us now, or go the way of your people from the dead. The choice is yours, but only for a time. You have a few moments to decide, right here and now, whether you join the light or the darkness. There is however one small issue. I insist that you swear an oath of allegiance to me personally within these sacred walls. Here it is: 'I pledge to the leader,

Malek, as the supreme authority of the Academy of Light, obedience until death.' Simple but expedient. You can take a few moments, but I must hear it from your lips." He smiled wryly, giggled oddly, and then continued.

"I know now that your people are aware of my customized container at Rijeka. Your man Šubić is a cunning creature, cunning indeed, just what I'd expect from the last dregs of the defunct Croatian nobility.

The bit of light that the returned spirits brought with them from the afterlife is the very stuff of creation. I have smudged ten of these sorry creatures. I have captured their light essence, the life force that enabled them to cross the great divide from death to life. I saw you look at the prism behind me. That same prism was used to ignite the lighting systems within the containers, and once lit, the returned spirits were utterly destroyed, leaving only a dark smudge, a residue on the floor of the container. And the black patch that you see below the prism holds that precious cargo, the light that was saved when their physical presence was eliminated. It is a kind of tabernacle of spirits. It has taken a long time and countless efforts to close in on our goal. Now, with your help we can attain it. With your unique gifts you can help us. You can read retinas and distinguish lies from truth. We will have captured the light of the universe and the ability to move freely between life and death, at our will.

Your man Spehar expedited our work. He was a traitor to both your side and mine. He also provided us with the Tesla retina scanners. But he was a soft slug of a man and deserved his end. A talented genius whose greed got the better of him, and then he developed a conscience. Poor fool. Oh, I can see you didn't know that he has been dispatched. What a useful word: dispatched. Yes, just a few hours ago. Here, let me show you a picture. Being Christian you will recognize and appreciate the image. Please sit down."

He showed me a gruesome photo on his cellphone, holding it inches in front of my face. I didn't recognize the person. I couldn't make out the bloodied features of the poor soul. It was of a naked overweight man crucified by a roadside. There were stab wounds across the man's torso. On his head was a makeshift crown of razor wire. Malek continued to hold the cellphone before my eyes. I glanced up at him and saw a subtle smile spread across the pallor of his face. I could see he was inviting a response from me. He was enjoying the discomfort he was creating in me, feeding off it. I looked closely at the man's bloodied face and with a start suddenly recognized him. It was really Spehar.

"No, no, no," I cried out. "What have you done?"

Malek took a deep breath of satisfaction, and then pocketed his cell-phone. "A lesson from the Romans, my dear Christopher. How can you protect what is yours unless you are willing to take measures that punish disloyalty or threat or resistance? And perhaps you are aware of what happened to the little man, the diminutive Yankee, yes?"

"You're insane," I said. I groaned in horror at what he had done to Dr. Spehar and to Sam Stark, and countless others. The man was sick.

He walked over to the torso of the Roman officer behind him and pulled out a short sword from the scabbard and belt around the waist of the headless statue.

"Christopher, it is time for the oath. I need to hear it. What I hold in my hand is a Gladius Roman sword. It originated in Spain. This weapon is what really built the Roman Empire. You can thrust, cut, and slash with it. Here, I want you to feel the coolness of the blade." He drew the flat side of the sword across my cheek, very gently, the way you would a feather, and I could tell he was entranced by the motion. The blade felt cold against my skin. I trembled slightly, watching him. There was a bead of saliva on his lips that slowly ran down his chin. He was beginning to drool.

At that point I remembered Spehar's warning about the oath. I felt my hand reach beneath my jacket and slip into the canvas bag. I was enshrouded in darkness from the neck down. Malek could not see me withdraw the silver and iron armguard from the sack and insert my left hand and arm through it. I hesitated for a moment, watching him, and then slowly reached into the bag once again and carefully removed the Byzantine dagger from its scabbard, the same dagger that Anka had used to kill the cleric in ancient times, the dagger that Davor had given me. I could feel the intricate designs on the hilt of the dagger as I held it in an overhand grip. It felt so natural, like an extension of my arm and hand. I crouched slightly beneath Malek as he stood towering above me, the sword now positioned under my chin. I felt my head move back away from the point of the blade. Tense seconds passed.

"The oath, please," Malek commanded. "The oath or death. Once again, 'I pledge to the leader, Malek, as the supreme authority of the Academy of Light, obedience until death.' The choice is yours. Make it now!"

"No," I said, as the word escaped my mouth, unbidden. In the same instant I sprang away from the chair, knocking it over in my haste to be out of his reach. I leapt towards the dark corner to my left, upsetting a rack of tourist postcards on a metal stand. He shouted something at me and then moved with lightning speed, raising his sword with both hands and striking down at me. I felt my arm raise itself high in a sudden protective gesture, and in the same second I felt the cutting edge of his sword descend and bite into the armguard, holding it there for a brief blink of eternity as I instinctively summoned a response. The blade of the sword had not penetrated to my skin. The Byzantine dagger was firmly cradled within my hand.

He raised the sword again and slashed away at me, from left to right and then back again, with startling speed, but I darted backwards escaping the blows and suddenly felt the hard stone of the temple wall pressed against my back. I crouched down, beneath him, my knees bent and ready to spring up. He raised his arms high above his head, preparing to come down with the sword in a shattering fatal blow. He hesitated for an instant, taking aim and relishing what he was about to do, gloating over it, when my dagger soared upwards and cut through the darkness, extending itself backwards behind me with its hilt almost touching the wall, before it came down in a fell motion that struck Malek dead. His flesh seemed startled at first, and then relaxed completely, quivering around the blade in submission to it. His heart was pierced to the quick and he was dead as he stood. I drove the blade down and swung across his chest, and then pulled it out, its work finished. His body fell inert and heavy, face-first, to the stone floor. The so-called light of the heavens was extinguished and none to soon. Malek was dead.

I stood breathless for a moment, strangely savoring what I had done. Then I wiped the blood from the dagger's blade across the back of Malek's finely tailored jacket and placed the weapon in its sheath, and then into the canvas bag beneath my jacket. I went over to the wall and, taking the chair with me, placed it against the wall beneath the prism and its sack attachment. Then I stood up onto the chair to remove both the prism and sack. I first of all disconnected the cloth sack from the prism attachment and then carefully placed it into my canvas bag. I felt a strange elation as I deposited it into my bag. Men and spirits had died because of it and I knew Mr. Šubić would know what to do with the precious bag. But instinctively, I knew there was something else that I had to do.

Still standing on the metal chair, I ripped the prism completely from its hook on the wall and smashed it down onto the floor with both hands, making sure I kept my balance on the chair as I did so. It shattered into a thousand tiny pieces of brilliant color, all the colors of the spectrum. I looked and saw red, orange, yellow, green, blue, indigo, and violet, shades of every color. It was magnificent. There was no white light whatsoever, as I had seen earlier when it was attached to the sack. I sat for a moment on the chair, looking at Malek's body, his face pressed against the stone floor. All of his efforts had come to nothing, nothing except for the pain and suffering he had caused. But he had been stopped, and I had stopped him. There was a grim satisfaction in that.

◆ ◆ ◆

I walked out of the Temple and simply stood there, leaning against one of the pillars of the portico. The fingers of my right hand were covered in blood and sticky. I was surprised at how sticky it was, binding my fingers together. On the periphery of my vision I saw three of the people from the Coliseum run behind me and into the Temple with weapons drawn.

He was dead and I was glad of it. He fancied himself a creature of light, but was nothing but a murderous thug. I had stopped him. When I thought about Sam and the little migrant girl, I was sorry he could only die once. I remembered Stipe and what he had gone through. Some things must be avenged for evil to stop. Davor was avenged.

The night air felt good against my skin, and it felt great to be alive. Soon, I thought, it would be the dawn again, and that thought made me ineffably sad. Then I caught sight of a flurry of movement below me.

From where I stood on the portico I saw five bodies on the flagstones of the Forum. They were being carried away by men and women I had seen at the Coliseum. One of them was the tall, lean man with the thick head of hair, the man who looked like a lion. He smiled and put his arm around my shoulders for a moment.

"It's over," he said. "There were only five of them after all. We cut the light and power to this area, and with night vision goggles, it was like picking low hanging fruit. They didn't have a chance. We lost no one, not one." He was smiling broadly and shaking his head in disbelief at our good fortune. "He must have thought himself invincible. He needed a reality check. Such stupid pride and folly."

From behind him someone pushed forward towards me, his face bright and ecstatic.

"Good news," he said. It was the driver who had met me at the Fažana docks and taken me to Pula and then afterwards to the Forum. He spoke in spurts of words, pausing for breath in the middle of his sentences. "Our intelligence people had listened carefully to Malek from the wire you wore. He said, 'The high place where lions attend her.' They thought about that and our teams raced to nearby churches. One, in particular caught our interest. The Church of St. Euphemia. Two lions. One of our men, from Rovinj, told us that in the church there, there is a mural in the sarcophagus room showing Euphemia being bothered by two lions. She was found in the Campanile there, trussed up but unharmed, tied between two huge stuffed lions, the kind children play with, but life-sized. The only injuries were to two of our security people who fell through some rickety stairs in the Campanile. She is safe. She is alive."

♦ ♦ ♦

Seeing Zora again was a blessed relief to me. After all of my fears and dark, wild imaginings she was standing there before me in her Pula apartment, alive but numb from her experience and still somewhat in shock. She had thought Malek's people would kill her. She had prepared herself to die she said to me. When I told her about Dr. Spehar, she nodded sadly with moist tears of compassion in her eyes.

"Antun Spehar was a good man, brilliant and intellectual, but flawed like the rest of us. In the end the fortune he thought he wanted was contrary to his heartfelt values. The money meant nothing to him after he had seen the deaths he had caused through his betrayal. He warned you and paid with his life." She walked to her kitchen then, opened the cupboard door beneath the sink, and pulled out a bottle of unopened brandy. She poured us each a tumbler full and carried it to the living room where we sat quietly for a moment, she on the couch and I on her rocking chair, sipping our drinks.

She put her glass down on the coffee table and looked at me with wonder in her eyes, and something new that I hadn't seen before, something starkly appreciative.

"Kristof, you killed him. You killed Malek. You have saved countless lives with your action. My Canadian-Croatian man. What are you feeling?"

"Relief, immense relief. That's all. I'm so glad it's over. It's been so strange."

"Will you return to Canada? Perhaps you miss your life there, yes?"

I twirled the glass in my hand releasing the heady scent, and then took a slow sip of the brandy, savouring its smoky taste as I pondered the question. "My life is here now, with you, if that's OK with you." When I said that she started laughing, as if I had just told a wonderful joke.

"What about Gloria?"

"Sic transit, Gloria mundi."

"I don't know Latin, Kristof."

"It's over. My life with Gloria is over and gone. But one day though, I'd like you to meet my son Peter and see my wonderful Canada. We have two countries now."

Zora began laughing again then and patted the cushion on the couch beside her, inviting me to join her there.

Nin

The world had become strange but familiar. Zora and I were together in the back seat of a small black SUV making our way to Nin. It was late in the afternoon. The driver was quiet, allowing Zora and I to converse easily without having to make third party conversation. We were part of a small motorcade heading northeast from Zadar, about 14 km from Nin. The evening before we had arrived in Zadar, and met with Mr. Šubić, who greeted us graciously and with great personal warmth. He said he wanted us to share in this special occasion, a small but significant occasion, like Brijuni he said but only on a smaller scale. He was glowing with pleasure and the anticipation of the next day's celebration. It was a private event and one that signaled closure for the returned spirits. Mr. Šubić had arranged that the small village be evacuated for our celebration. Zora informed me that the villagers were richly compensated for their trouble.

A week earlier I had given one of Mr. Šubić's aides the black rectangular sack that I had taken from The Temple of Augustus after I had killed Malek. Within that sack was the light essence of ten returned spirits who had been smudged by Malek within his customized shipping container. The special event at Nin was to release the ten returned spirits to the afterlife as we had done with the other seventy returned spirits at Brijuni. I felt very special to be a part of this celebratory group, especially with Zora at my side, as we made our way to Nin, which was once, she told me, a major settlement of the Liburnians, an Illyrian people, hundreds of years before the Romans came.

The cavalcade stopped near a church built atop a hillock in the middle of a field. I thought we had reached our destination, but Zora informed me that it was St. Nicholas's Church, a remarkable 12th century architectural form that looked intriguingly like a cake ornament. We stayed in the car as I watched one of Mr. Šubić's aides run up to the structure and fill a small silver container with soil from near the front of the church doors. He raced back down, holding the small box to his chest, and went back inside the lead car.

Very soon, we were there, at the Church of the Holy Cross, an 8th-century structure no bigger than a small house. Nin was connected to the mainland by two small bridges. We walked to it by way of the pedestrian lower bridge. Zora was excited as we looked about the ancient building. It was a simple white-washed, mini cathedral with three naves, a solid cylindrical top, and a few high Romanesque windows. I noticed too the remarkable doorway with plaitwork on top that looked Celtic. I could feel there was something very special about the church, and the spirit of the place surrounding it. There were the ruins of other foundations that could be seen around the church as well. Perhaps Illyrian, I thought, or Roman, or maybe even long, long before that. There was no end to my speculation about the people who came before. Some people, I thought, without a feeling for the spirit of place, might think of the tiny church as merely quaint, but that would show a total absence of awareness of what informs such a place as this, one that engenders the birth of a nation.

Small groups of people were walking around. I noticed a few familiar faces, spirit guides that I recognized from Brijuni, though I didn't know their names. We smiled at each other enjoying the ambience of the place.

In a small field nearby there was a good-sized circular mound of firewood that had been prepared for a bonfire. Three old women dressed completely in black with kerchiefs tied about their heads were walking around the mound placing kindling in spots where they could be ignited easily. Off to one side I saw a freestanding staircase made of oak. It was about ten feet high and there were carvings upon it, but I could not see it clearly from where I was standing. It reminded me of the karst staircase I had seen at Brijuni. I glanced behind me and saw the old women begin lighting the mound of kindling and firewood.

It was nearing dusk when I saw Mr. Šubić speaking to two huge men, men as big as Stipe had been. Although I was too far away to hear what was being said, I saw him point to the church and give instructions of some sort. A few minutes later I saw the men carry a stone basin and bring it into the church. They were struggling with its weight but they held it carefully in their arms. Zora walked up to me from where she was standing by the open church doors, and whispered to me in a quiet voice filled with reverence and awe. Her face was flushed with emotion.

"We are fortunate. What you see being carried in is the baptistery font of ancient Croatian royalty. Carved into the stone is the name of Prince Višeslav. Mr. Šubić must have arranged for the font to be brought from the museum where it is kept. This is indeed an honor for us to be here."

I watched intrigued as Mr. Šubić led a small procession to the front of the church, and then sprinkled some earth on the threshold from the same silver container I had seen one of his aides with earlier. Then to my surprise he sought me out by name and within a minute one of his aides escorted me to the front entrance where Mr. Šubić stood by in an elegant uniform that I had never seen him wear before. It was blue-gray with red and gold piping on his chest. On his shoulders were elegant gold epaulettes. He wore high leather boots polished black to a high sheen, and the sides of his blue-gray trousers had a thin gold stripe running from below his jacket to the top of his boots. He was wearing a large black cravat that was knotted elegantly at his throat.

I looked to Zora behind me and she was smiling from ear to ear, happy for my recognition. I could see her eyes were moist even from where I stood. Two of his aides brought a small table and set it beside Mr. Šubić. Still another aide carried a small bundle and placed it very carefully on the tabletop.

"Now Kristof, because of you we can release the final returned spirits. After their brief spell of confinement, they will have the freedom of the universe once again. Only because of you is Malek vanquished and gone. You will be the only person allowed entry into the church. You will place the black cloth upon the baptistery of our Višeslav that sits before the altar, and then pull the gold cord before you leave."

His face was bright with excitement and energy. He nodded for me to take the bundle into the church. I took it and felt subtle movement from within the black cloth covering. The door closed behind me, and I was completely alone. I walked a few short steps into the small, dimly lit church and carefully placed the bundle into Višeslav's baptistery font. I stood for a moment fully aware of the significance of the event. My head bowed slightly and I pulled the gold cord and then slowly turned and walked away. I opened the church door and closed it behind me, with reverence in my heart.

Outside, the bonfire was blazing away. Off to one side of the fire, a group of musicians, perhaps twenty of them, were playing on their stringed instruments. All of them, men and women both, were dressed completely in white with black, tasseled caps on their heads and vary large black cravats knotted at their throats. One of two bass players had the name *Zvonimir* printed on his instrument. There was a small open-sided tent and a large table with cold meat platters and appetizers upon it. A few people were standing and eating from paper plates, as there were no chairs.

All of a sudden I heard the assembled crowd let out a collective gasp and the music stopped as intense, brilliant light broke from the narrow windows. The church door flung open and light spilled out everywhere around the church, and it seemed for a splendid, miraculous moment as if it were noon on a sunny day. The moment of light held briefly, defying any sense of reality. And then the light fell back upon itself and into the church once again, leaving darkness in its wake. It was night again, and human figures began emerging from the lighted entrance of the church.

What I saw then was remarkable, and I could tell from the sighs and muted, awestruck sounds of the people standing that they too were experiencing the same wonder that my eyes beheld.

They came out one by one from the entrance of the church. They wore no clothes. They walked easily as you would expect from people in their early to mid-twenties. Their bodies were vibrant and robust, glistening with health and vitality. They were magnificent. Slowly, they moved towards the bonfire, and as they did so, they gently took the hands of those nearby. Some of those whose hands they joined with their own were spirit guides, others were members of Mr. Šubić's staff, still others were the old women who had tended the bonfire. No one was excluded. Everyone was welcome and belonged. Gradually, they formed into a traditional kolo dancing circle and began the ancient movements, keeping time to the music that had begun earlier. Around and around the dancers went, and when some left the dance, others took their place and joined in. Zora and I took our turn and moved with the circle and its rhythms, happy and joyous to be in this time and place. I looked at her beaming face and the faces of those around me, flushed from the heat of the bonfire, and the exertions of the dance. I thought I saw Mr. Šubić join in, but I couldn't be sure. I noticed that the image of a figure eight was forming nearby, illuminating the darkness at one end of a small field. It was smaller than the one I had seen on Brijuni, but the light delineating it burned just as intensely.

After a time, I saw the returned spirits somewhat reluctantly move from the kolo dance to where the oak stairwell was situated. And each of the ten returned spirits, in their turn, walked up the stairs, hesitated a moment to look back and wave, and then stepped off the top of the stairs to the glowing figure eight structure, a mere step away.

Three women, proceeding one by one, were the first to step into the bottom part of the brightly glowing figure eight, each in turn. They were not rushed. They were not hurried. Their motions were as insouciant as if they were walking across a green field on a summer's day. They were followed by six men who walked singly into the darkness and the abyss as easily as if they were going to rest in the bed of their childhood home. Finally, there was only one returned spirit left, a woman. Something about her was familiar. I looked closely for I felt I knew her. And then I recognized her with a start. She was Marija, the returned spirit I had met briefly in Zagreb but had not worked with. She ascended the stairs effortlessly, and then, with a gracious wave of her pink arm, she stepped off into the rich darkness contained within the bottom of the figure eight. A flush of rose into the infinite looping darkness, and she was gone, gone away from Nin and this earth to fuse with the timeless mystery of her destination and her destiny.

Within a moment, the figure eight leaned to one side and became a kind of propeller that moved faster and faster becoming a golden disk that lit up the night skies around Nin. As it glowed sharply against the rich darkness of the night a humming sound could be heard that grew louder and louder, synchronized with the brilliant light in the heavens. At last, the brilliant disk gave way to a change that saw a double helix form above the small church at Nin. It shot high into the heavens, held there for a long moment, and then descended in particles of broken, radiant light to the welcoming dark earth below.

Epilogue

A FORTNIGHT EARLIER I HAD BEEN in Pula where Mr. Šubić had politely reminded me that weeks before I had agreed to free some foreign spirits along the Makarska Riviera. I remembered and immediately set about complying with his request. He always made sure I was well paid, but I would have done it for him regardless of the compensation.

Two weeks to the day after the conversation with Mr. Šubić, and after arriving in the town and checking into my apartment at the Rare Pink Bird apartment complex, I had followed Mr. Šubić's directions to the letter. I had purchased two large buckets and filled them with stones from the beach beside an upscale restaurant, the very same beach where Malek's thugs had tried to capture and kill me. Then I had rented a speedboat with a skipper and loaded it with the filled buckets of stone. I had him take the boat out to about a mile from the shore, and that's where I began to seed the stones. Actually, that was Mr. Šubić's phrase, that I must "seed the sea with stones." I had the puzzled skipper, a tall, lean local man with enormous moustaches, steer the boat parallel to the shoreline at speed, and then I dropped the stones into the water, one at a time, as the boat sped on. It felt as if I was seeding a field rather than a turquoise sea. The skipper appeared confused and incredulous but said nothing. I was paying him extremely well, so his consternation was short-lived.

That evening I found myself sitting in an outdoor café on the Makarska Promenade, one of the ones favored by Stipe and Nikola. The first pint of Ožujsko went down well as I sat beneath a huge towering palm with rough, hard bark. It was at least fifty or sixty meters high and was like a huge phallus before me. Neon lights danced along up and down its trunk. The splendid palm had the diameter of about a meter. I was alone but I felt empowered and content and not a little joyful. I was in this incredibly lovely town once again. Just a few nights before the returned spirits had gone home, and it seemed to me that all was well, especially with Malek gone. How I wished Zora were with me. I enjoyed a few pints more before deciding to call it a night.

It was nearing dusk, and streetlights were turning on as I made my way from the Promenade to the Square by the church and then across the street to the narrow lane that led to my apartment. Two cars were descending the lane and I had to press myself against the wall of a building to avoid contact. Once in the apartment, I sat content in my living room for several moments and then decided to go to bed. I was tired from travel and drowsy from the pints of beer that I had consumed.

I rose very early the next morning, just before daybreak. From my third floor balcony, where I took my first cup of coffee, I could barely see beyond the promontory to Brač and far to the left, the island of Hvar. I sat in the patio chair and sipped at my coffee. I was in the same apartment the three Croatian-Canadian brothers and their wives had stayed in weeks earlier. I didn't need such a large apartment but it was the only one available. It felt comfortable, and I liked the fact that they had stayed there. I remembered them with affection.

My eyes have never been the best, but I coud see well enough to distinguish distant shapes and movement even as the light had not yet broken through the curtain of darkness. But what I thought I was seeing in the far distance was preposterous. I blinked, rubbed my eyes and looked again. There, there on the horizon, on the line between darkness and light there was massive movement on the sea. The sky was brightening above. It looked like a huge wave was building in the far distance. Heavy rainclouds were moving in to shore. I felt a cool breeze with tiny droplets of water coming in.

I went inside, found my binoculars, and raced back to the balcony. I manipulated the lens controls, adjusting them to the far distance. I looked, put the binoculars down for a moment, and then looked again. I couldn't believe what I was seeing.

It was as if an unbroken line of human figures was advancing across the wine-purple sea towards landfall. Interspersed across the advancing line were the faded colors of lost flags, lost empires. Below the colors, the spume and spray of the sea marked the line as it moved slowly towards land and towards me. Even in the early morning it was magnificent. Closer and closer it came befuddling me with its improbability. Such things don't happen. Such things couldn't happen. My old world was gone, utterly gone.

I adjusted the binoculars once again. And there, in the middle of the approaching wave, or what looked like a wave, was the half figure of a man holding a banner with a lion's image upon it. From the waist down he was part of the churning waters, but the other half was the upper body of a man with a face that was bloodied but resolute. On either side of him there were tiered ranks of mariners and soldiers clearly discernible from the waist up but part of the waters from the waist down. They were coming nearer to the promontory of St. Peter's in a steady, stately sweep of movement that seemed inexorable and fated. The music of Ravel's Bolero came to my ears from the depths of my memory, and I stood transfixed with the sight before me, and the haunting, hypnotic music in my head.

I lost sight of them for a few moments as light rain spattered down upon me as I stood on my balcony. I swung the strap of the binoculars over my shoulder and hastened down hill from my apartment to the sheltered bay on the near side of the peninsula, near the church atop a hill. I was curious and not sure what to expect but I needed to get closer to what was happening.

I ran down to the marina skirting the promontory and hastened to gain the heights by the ancient stone church to see what I could of the impending wave. It was obvious that the few locals I had passed by were not seeing what I plainly saw. They shouted at me to get inside from the storm. But they were seeing a tidal wave. I was seeing the dead seeking landfall and peace.

The improbability of what was happening quickened my steps. It was excitement I felt, not dread. The dead spirits were seeking release I thought. They were finally quitting the tiresome limbo of their days deep within the sea. Somehow I knew that I had been instrumental in making this happen by seeding the sea with stones the day before. I had helped to pardon these wayward lost spirits and facilitate the peace they sought. It began with the recognition that the dead are with us until they or we dissolve that tenuous bond and allow them their rest and transformation. Just that. That is what death is, I thought. A belated final change and the bond with life is severed, but not forgotten.

And I sensed there was a joy in the sea air, in the early morning that was around me as I scrambled for purchase on the stonewall by the church atop the promontory. I leaned against the wall looking seaward, and behind me in the untended graveyard were the forgotten unkempt graves of the ancient plague dead from centuries before. I could see clearly despite the thin gray light that fell in upon me from the heavens above that were burdened with heavy rain clouds. I felt no fear or trepidation. It felt more like a benediction than anything else.

I levelled my binoculars at the horizon. The line of the dead was fast approaching. The sound of Ravel's haunting music, ever increasing in volume and power, was playing in my consciousness. The bottom half of the line before me was a churning, undulating wave of water and above it the torsos and faces of so many long lost soldiers and warriors. There were women among them with fierce visages that showed no fear. The clothing and armour they wore was richly coloured as if newly made, many having banners behind them that I did not recognize. I did recognize from old drawings the figure in the center of the line, the one with the banner of St. Mark's behind him, the lion of St. Mark's. It was the lost Doge of Venice, Pietro Candiano. To his right and to the east were the Ottomans with curved scimitars and golden robes and crimson cloaks. And to the left of the Doge an assortment of Franks and Goths and others that I knew not of. The space between where I stood and the line moving towards me was smaller and smaller. They would soon be upon me, and I was utterly fascinated. I dropped the binoculars and waited. In the space of a few moments the glorious wave crashed against the rocky shore below me, below the solid stone church, and now the full figures of the advancing line could be seen. They were magnificent.

I was mesmerized by curious expectation. What would happen next? I was wishing Davor was with me here, right here, in this spot by the low wall close to St. Peter's Church. A few dozen meters below me were the churning waters of the Adriatic. And then to my surprise, the advancing line of bodies divided, a large group moving to the east and another to the west with only the Doge and his retinue holding to the middle. They were ascending the cliff face below and were almost upon me when I crouched low and pressed my left shoulder against the stonewall and held my breath.

There was a whisper in the air above my head. It was Davor's voice that I heard. "Everything lives." Great winds were blowing in from the sea, the sea that held so many secrets and lost lives. "Everything lives," the haunting voice exclaimed. I stood up and looked about me.

The binoculars dropped from my hand. And I was stunned at what I beheld. I turned to my left and saw scimitars flash as ancient Ottoman warriors transitioned and sought welcome and final refuge in the hard ground beneath the standing statue of St. Peter. A last flourish and a flash and they were gone, gone and at one with the earth at last, after a long sojourn beneath the sea.

The figure of the Venetian Doge rose from the sea and ascended up the precipice and stopped suspended for a fleeting moment just above the low wall where I stood. He looked at me and smiled and then soared above me and beyond me to the heights of Biokovo. My incredulous eyes followed him, fixing on the crimson cape that he wore. I picked up the binoculars and followed his flight. The splendid colours he wore faded as he disappeared into the grey stone of Biokovo. He became one with it, with the denuded stone that flanked the town of Makarska. It was brilliant, and I could see it all. Ravel's music stopped suddenly at the same instant, loudly, and with finality. The Doge was inseparable from the stone.

I wondered over the strange transformations that were happening all along this enchanted coast. But then I remembered the returned spirits I had worked with. I remembered their choices and final redemption. I remembered Mia, Petar, Ante, Stipe, Nikola, Anka, Franja, Danica, and Marko. Transformation and change happens everywhere I thought, and it was good to be a part of that, especially in my ancestral homeland, my beloved Croatia.

◆ ◆ ◆

The next morning I wandered through the town feeling like a native. I walked through the ancient streets stopping by the bronze statue of a famous Croatian poet, Tin Ujević, who was in a sitting pose in the small square, writing a poem. I touched his hand for luck. How I wished he were alive to write a poem or two of the birth and death of empires and fallen Doges.

From there I strolled to the waterfront, and that's when I saw it. Although I had been to Makarska so many times before, I had missed it. It was sand coloured and circular. Not big. Not small. A smooth stone fountain, just off the Promenade, where you could refresh yourself with cool, clean fresh water. There were a few spigots handy and I opened one, turning the faucet counter clockwise until it poured forth in a steady stream. I heard someone over my shoulder saying the water was piped in for some distance and was very old and very special. When I finished drinking with cupped hands and then splashed myself with the precious water, I wiped my face with my sleeve and smiled at the old man behind me who was obviously enjoying seeing my pleasure in taking the water. He laughed heartily and then bid me good-bye with a wave of his hand that seemed more a blessing than a farewell. I held my face to the sun for a moment and then continued on my way in the direction of Tučepi.

◆ ◆ ◆

It was early afternoon, and I was feeling on top of the world after my hike, as I walked up the hill to my apartment. I had seen things that my old self could never have seen. Soon the metal gate clanged behind me in the apartment yard and I was just about to ascend the stairs to my third floor apartment when my landlady waved me over with a huge welcoming smile. She stood triumphantly, with her yellow hose in hand, watering her small, well-tended patch of a garden, waiting for me. She was a large florid woman, middle-aged, with sharp eyes that measured the value of everything she looked upon.

"Oh, Mr. Christopher, I have good news for you," she said, with an air of breathless excitement and merry anticipation. Small, white butterflies were darting about in the sunshine.

"Yes Marta, what is it?"

"You have a guest," she said happily. "Of course, I let her into your apartment when she told me she was your wife. Very beautiful."

In a split second my world fell into a heap at my feet. Gloria, here, of all places to be, after what I had just experienced. I remembered her e-mail saying she might surprise me by coming to Croatia. My face must have betrayed my bitter disappointment at the news for suddenly there was a searching look of grave concern on my landlady's face. I saw her expression and recovered quickly.

"Oh, I didn't expect her yet. Thank you," I said.

I could see that she felt somewhat awkward. I smiled at her and doubled my steps up the concrete stairs. The apartment door was slightly ajar. She wasn't in the living room or in the adjoining kitchen. A blue piece of luggage sat on the floor beside the couch. The bedroom door was closed. I hesitated for the briefest moment and then opened the door. The shock of seeing her standing there left me breathless.

"Zora!" I exclaimed. "Zora, it's you."

"Yes. Surprise!" she said. "To keep things simple, I told your landlady I was your wife. I hope that was all right. I was tired from the journey and wanted to get into the apartment and nap."

"Of course," I said, feeling utterly relieved and ecstatic.

"Why don't you join me?" she said with a trace of glorious mischief in her voice.

"Just a minute," I replied. I smiled like it was an early Christmas and retraced my steps, closing and locking the front door, and then drawing the curtains in one majestic sweep. As I did so, I noticed Marta, the landlady, smiling up at me from the garden below, and then looking away quickly, as she watered a ripening tomato plant.

Acknowlegements

Special thanks are owed to Laurie and David Buchar who provided editing and valued suggestions on the text. Likewise, my daughter and son, Lara and Marco Buchar, proved extremely helpful. Thanks are also given to Connor Shipman who supplied a key idea in the storyline.

www.ingramcontent.com/pod-product-compliance
Lightning Source LLC
Chambersburg PA
CBHW021313190726
48288CB00003B/832